Human
By
Design

A novel by

Carter Richards

Copyright © 2019 by Russell Carter
Published in The United States.

ISBN 978-1-070-40164-5

Book design by Russell Carter
Jacket design and illustration by Russell Carter

To Katie

Human
by
Design

PROLOGUE

AFRICAN CONTINENT

100,000 YEARS AGO

Two figures sat at the front of a cave, watching the end of a fire. They were brothers of the Homo erectus family and had hunted together that day and done well. Rare was the occasion to bring home such large game, and as the tribe feasted, they shared their encounter with the dangerous bison. While they described their near death experiences, they had enjoyed making the women gasp and seeing the children look up at them in awe. But now, they were alone, savoring the waning moments of their precious ritual, and as the tribe slept over the pounding of the ocean waves on the rocks below, they relaxed.

The younger brother finally succumbed to exhaustion, collapsed on his side to the soft sand and fell fast asleep. His older brother looked on, smiling, and as the leader of the tribe felt it fitting he was the last to turn in. He wasn't finished reliving the moment though, picking up the beast's massive thigh bone and stoking the fire with it. He had been eyeing it all night, thinking it would make a fine club.

He let it linger in the flames, watching it dry, taking it out to scrape flesh off it with a rock. He held it up, admired it, feeling the weight of it and noticed something peculiar off in the distance moving on the water. He didn't understand what the moon and stars were but knew that their reflection on the ocean's surface should not be moving. He laid the bone across his lap and looked up into the night, locating the moon he knew so well. It was where it should be, appearing motionless at the far edge of the sky while the smaller moon was moving, zipping here and there and playfully darting about. He reached for his brother and shook him but could only get him to stir. He shook him harder, calling out to him, waiting for him to open his eyes when suddenly the light of day came into the cave.

Turning back, he saw the little moon had arrived, filling the cave's opening, and a wave of drowsiness came over him. He struggled to stay awake, looking through heavy eyes as a small pale person stepped out of it into his cave. Something came into his eyes and he had to blink very hard, rubbing them. When he opened them he was on his back looking up into a white face with large black eyes. He was tired and confused and had to close them again, barely noticing the odd tugging on his body. When he opened his eyes again, he was on his side, facing the fire. He couldn't lift his head but squirmed and somehow managed to look toward the little moon. Two of the strange creatures, one taller than the other, were standing at an opening in its bright surface, staring at him, and somehow he knew they were talking about him. Something burned in his eyes; they were dry and he rolled them under his eyelids, soothing them. He felt cold and looked at the fire and saw it was dead and had been out for a long while. Puzzled and weary, he fought through sleepiness, forcing himself to look around. It was quiet now, nothing was moving and at the mouth of the cave he saw the little moon had left, and he drifted off to sleep.

Chapter 1

Present Day

Fry cook David Cooper took a spatula, scooped up two hamburger patties and set them on toasted buns nestled next to piles of crispy fries. He plucked parsley from a bowl, garnished the plates and slid them under the hot lamps. As he whacked the pickup bell, he took a moment to look out at his diner and the ambiance he had missed so much. It was good to be home.

He saw it was a typical Friday night, about half full, mostly locals with a few strangers, probably tourists passing through. Two of his regulars, Big Red and Wesley, were having dinner at the counter in their usual spots. The way Red was waving his hand around, it appeared they were in another one of their dramatic conversations, one he would most likely be asked to weigh in on later.

He scanned the front of the restaurant, noticing a white-bearded old timer sitting by himself off in the corner booth. At first, he thought it was another one of the UFO nuts frequenting the Roswell museum, but he took another look. Maybe not; this stranger looked a bit rough around the edges.

"Large onions with sauce!" the waitress's husky voice cracked while she swept the burgers off the shelf.

"Got it!" David fired back, and as he dropped a bundle of frozen onion rings in the deep fryer, the back door opened and a young man stepped into the kitchen. David glanced over, acknowledging his cook, "Hey, Roberto, take over for me, will you? I need to give Pam a hand out in front."

"You got it, Boss," Roberto said over his shoulder while washing up.

David stepped into the diner, picked up a pot of coffee and began a job he had enjoyed ever since he was a kid helping his mom run the diner. He headed for the counter and when Red saw him approaching broke out into one of his jolly smiles.

"Here comes the orphan," Wesley blurted through a mouth full of food.

Red backhanded him on the shoulder, "Shuuut up. What the hell's wrong with you?"

Wesley answered with a snarky look, keeping his head low over his meal and went back to eating.

"Hey, Red, Wesley…how you guys doing?" David asked, ignoring Wesley's wisecrack as he'd done ever since their grade school days.

"Doing just fine, David…you?" Red said, shifting his eyes to the steaming liquid pouring into his cup.

"I'm good," David replied, but sensing tension in the air, set the coffee down and looked at his old friend, "What's up?"

Big Red squinted over rosy cheeks and grew a slight smile, "Wes and I were just speculating on what you might be thinking of doing. You know, with the diner and all…I mean, nobody would blame ya for selling the family homestead and moving on."

The family homestead. The words seemed to vibrate in his head as his eyes swept over the little diner his grandparents opened up in the early '40s. The notion of selling had crossed his mind a number of times in the last six months but something kept bothering him, getting in the way and he would have to stop thinking about it.

"Sell it to me." Wesley interjected, "This thing's a gold mine."

"No, thanks." Red quipped, "I've had your coffee."

"Oh, yeah? I've noticed you like any coffee as long as it's free."

"I've got to be able to drink it…not eat it."

David smiled at his friends' usual bantering and looked back over the diner that was so dear to his mom. At her insistence, he left for college, graduated, and even though he was working in LA, building a career in business and engaged to a beautiful woman, he was miserable. He should have considered himself spot on; they were a handsome couple and he just turned thirty, a good age to start a family, but instead he felt off his path and trapped. But the monumental troubles he was facing became trivial when he got the call, his mom had passed. Since he had no brothers or sisters and never knew his father, it was all up to him now and unfortunately he was starting to feel like he jumped from one frying pan into another.

David glanced at Red who was sipping and watching him over his coffee cup. "Red, when you put it that way it sounds like I'd be ending some legacy or something."

"Well…in a way you would be," Red elaborated, "everybody in town has their own story about this place, with you and your mom running it. Hell there's a lot of folks here that remember your grandparents."

"Yeah…you mean, like *you*?" David said, smiling.

Red nodded and studied David for a moment. "You know…I'm sure your mom thought of selling the place after losing them. You gotta hand it to her, as a young woman taking over the restaurant, keeping it afloat."

David looked at his mom's best friend, recalling many stories he heard of how much Red helped her in those early years, and was about to remind him but got cut off. "And then you came along. The whole town loved watching you grow up," Red chuckled.

"Yeah, yeah, yeah…" David droned, picked up the coffee and poured for Wesley.

"Why'd they name this place *Apache* if they were foreigners?" Wesley asked.

"My grandparents were from Chicago, Wesley." David said flatly, topping his cup off.

"Chicago! *Sheeeit*…might as well been foreigners," Wesley muttered and reached for the sugar.

"You of all people should know that the ranch your folks own…in fact all this land used to be Apache territory, so I'm sure it was named for the location," David reasoned.

"And it's a perfect location, just far enough out of town to get way from all the craziness," Red chuckled and noticed David drift off into a vacant look. "What about your job in LA?"

"Quit…not going back." David sighed and looked like he wanted to change the subject. Red paused, studied him then added, "And that cute fiancée of yours?"

"Didn't work out…we both decided to call it off," David said, trying to sound nonchalant but obviously was still feeling it.

"You're crazy, man, she was gorgeous…playgirl material!" Wesley declared.

David frowned, suddenly feeling as though they were back on the playground in elementary school.

"Look," Red said warmly, "you're bound to need time to process stuff. Everybody's different, so don't worry about it. You'll figure it out…and don't pay any mind to dufus here."

He looked at the big guy looming in front of him as so much more than just a family friend, and secretly, had always considered him a father figure. "Thanks, Red, I appreciate it," David said.

Red chuckled, "Well, you know you can always count on me being here for you."

"Yeah…" Wesley chimed in, "as long as you keep that thing over there full of pie." He pointed at the glass carousel on the counter.

Red flashed a stink eye at Wesley but cut it short and smiled unoffended at his skinny companion's inability to appreciate one of the great pleasures of life. Besides, it just meant more pie for him. "Nobody in the world makes pie like your mom's, except you, and you have no idea how much that means to me," Red confessed.

David put his hand on Red's shoulder. "Actually I do, Red. Let me get you guys a piece on the house, for old time's sake."

Red frowned and glanced at an empty plate in front of him. "Dang, already had one." he said.

"That never stopped you before." Wesley countered.

"What, did you have one before dinner?" David asked.

Red shifted a little on the bar stool. "I like to change it up now and then, you know."

"Sure, why not? Before *and* after a meal!" Wesley mocked.

David chuckled as his friends stared each other down and looked past them to the front of the diner. The bearded old man sitting in the corner booth had his coffee cup up but Pam hadn't noticed and was walking back toward the kitchen. David picked up the pot of coffee. "I'll catch you guys next time," he said, patting Red's shoulder and heading for the corner booth.

***

All he could see was the top of the stranger's well-weathered hat as he hunched over his meal, beard hanging down, shaking from some serious chewing. "Another shot of coffee?" David gestured with the pot.

"Bout time," the old man grumbled while cutting into the last of his steak.

"Sorry about that. We're a little short-handed right now," David said, pouring slowly to give him time to check out his new customer. He looked past the beat up old hat to the cracked and worn leather jacket and could hear his mom now. "Vagrant," she would say whenever the homeless came in. There weren't many in the New Mexico desert, but when one did come in, he would do just like she did and his grandparents before her and give them a free meal.

David's eyes wandered over the sun-bleached shirt that revealed a tuft of gray chest hair spouting out at the neckline and spotted a slide rule peeking out of his breast pocket. No, this wasn't a guy down on his luck; more like a geologist or archeologist that was probably out in the field a lot.

"What brings you around these parts?" David asked in friendly conversation, "You hunting for rocks or fossils maybe?"

The ornery old man ignored him, sticking his fork into the last bite of his steak and stuffing it into his overgrown beard. It was the kind that makes you wonder how he didn't eat hair along with anything he shoved into it. The old man set his fork down on the empty plate but kept his head down, chewing quietly, staring at nothing. David finished filling his cup and assumed he wanted to be left alone.

"I'll take that for you," David said, reaching for the empty plate, preparing to politely back away. The frayed rim of the old hat suddenly flipped up and a pair of ice blue, steely eyes were staring at him. "Uhh, is there anything else I can get for you?" David asked, tentatively picking up the plate. The old man gestured for him to sit down while continuing to chew the last of his meal. David obliged and while patiently waiting, noticed something about him.

"You know, you kind of look familiar…Have you been in here before?" David asked.

The old man swallowed, grabbed his napkin and looked David over while wiping his beard. "Never seen you before, but heard you grilled a good steak," he gruffly said and abruptly threw the napkin down on the table.

"You bet!" David broke into his spiel, "Local grown…grass fed…

The old man waved him off. "It was okay," he said and reached inside his jacket, "I really came here for another reason." His liver-spotted hand shook as he pulled out a small black box about the size of a deck of cards and set it on the table.

"I have something here I'm hoping you can help me with," the old man grumbled, sliding the top of the mysterious box open. He delicately reached in and pulled out a string with a key dangling at the end of it. "You see, I collect antiques, and came across this wedged in the back of an old chest I've had for years."

David stared hypnotically at the long brass key bouncing around in front of him. There was a tag attached to it with some handwriting on it. *Apache Diner.* "What the…" David muttered and grabbed for the key.

The old man saw David do a double take at the unique tooth pattern. "See something familiar?" the old man said, leaning forward.

"What kind of a chest was this key from?" David asked, but never got an answer. A sudden crashing sound filled the diner and he leaped from his seat. He saw Pam wrestling with her boyfriend at the counter. He appeared to be drunk, his plate on the floor and his arms flailing dangerously close to the glass carousel of desserts. David raced toward them, seeing Pam grab an arm, but her boyfriend violently yanked it away, smacking his elbow against the glass display.

Time morphed into slow motion as David reached for the carousel that was sliding away from him, down the counter like a shuffleboard puck. It teetered at the counter's edge and David realized he had another chance to save it. But before he could reach for it, it fell, bounced on a stool and tumbled to the floor with an explosion of glass and the splattering of desserts. An eerie hush settled over the diner and David groaned as if he had just witnessed the death of a family pet.

"Ohh jeez!!! Damn it, Roy!!!" Pam cried out and slugged her boyfriend on the shoulder. He jiggled, his head bobbing over the breakage as he numbly watched David bend down to pick up a shard of glass. David held it out in front of him, studying what was now a remnant of one of the first things his grandparents bought for the diner. Now here's the end of a legacy he thought.

Roberto dragged a trash can as he rolled up with a mop in a bucket of water and started scraping up the debris with a dust pan.

David swung the fragment around letting it bleed cherry topping into the can, then solemnly dropped it with a sense of finality.

"Sorry, Mr. Cooper," Roy slurred pitifully as Pam attempted to drag him away from the scene.

David ignored him, pointing to the front of the diner. "Pam, take him over there and call a cab," he said, glancing toward the corner booth where the old man had been sitting and saw it empty.

He looked around at his customers, seeing they were looking on uncomfortably. "Sorry folks…we'll get this cleaned up in a moment," he said, relieved to see Roberto making quick work of it. "At least nobody got hurt," he added in an attempt to be upbeat.

"That's a matter of opinion," Big Red boomed.

"Maybe I spoke too soon," David said making light of it but saw Red was serious and nodded understandingly at him. He grabbed a towel, moved behind the counter, and while wiping his hands actually had a strange sense of relief. "I don't know…maybe this is a good thing," he mumbled to himself, but Red overheard him.

Red turned to him, dismayed. "Talk me off the ledge here Davey…how's this a good thing?"

David saw Red was upset and thought fast. "Oh, I was just thinking that the display wasn't big enough," he said, resting his hand on Red's shoulder. "We'll get another…the Apache has to have a decent sized place for desserts."

Red watched David walk off into the kitchen then glanced down at the carnage, shaking his head. "A crying shame…" he muttered.

***

David let the last few customers out and locked the door behind them while Pam and Roberto cleaned up. Pam was wiping down a table nearby and glanced at him, watching him flip the open sign over. "David, I'm really sorry about that, it's because we broke up…I'll make him pay for it, I swear," she said.

He glanced at her knowing he'd never see a dime of it. "Oh, don't worry about it. We all have our problems. Besides, the diner is due for a new display anyway. Sorry to hear about your break up," he said turning away.

"Thanks," she responded then added, "sorry to hear about your break up, too." David didn't notice her subtle come-on and shrugged as he headed for the register.

The ding of the cash drawer sent him into a hypnotic daze, jogging an old memory when he was standing on his tiptoes, watching his mom methodically inserting the bills into the register's old wooden slots. She then diligently made change and arranged it in a neat pile in his hand with the change on top. *Be sure to tell them thank you, sweetie,"* she'd say, looking proudly at him and sending him back to the customers. He learned so much about people from her. She just loved everyone, and it was still a mystery to him as to why.

Pans banging in the kitchen brought him back and he slowly looked around at the empty diner. It seemed so lifeless now as he slowly closed the register drawer.

***

Pam sat in the chair in front of David's desk nervously bouncing her knee while sucking on a cigarette. Roberto sat on top of a side desk, calmly swinging his legs, watching her.

David sat down and held an ashtray out to Pam without even looking at her and she reluctantly grabbed it. She snuffed her cigarette out, glanced at Roberto then to David while he studied their time cards. "Uhhhh, David?" she said, "Roberto and I were wondering what your plans are…" Her words hung in the air while she nibbled on her lip.

David looked up at them as he pulled out his checkbook and slowly set it down in front of him. "Oh, I'm sorry, you guys, I should be keeping you more in the loop with my Mom's affairs, I mean concerning the restaurant."

Roberto chimed in, "We're not rushing you or anything, Boss…we just thought we probably should know if we're supposed to be doing something…making plans or something."

David nodded. "Sure, I understand and believe me, I haven't got anything in the works for selling the place or anything like that…really." He opened his checkbook and continued talking while he wrote. "I'll tell you what. If something comes up that's going to change things around here, we'll have a meeting and you guys will be the first to know, OK?" He ripped their checks out and held them up.

"Awesome! Thanks, Boss!" Roberto said, jumped off the table with a festive spin and grabbed his check. He breezed past Pam while she slowly got up, her eyes locked on David. She began coyly slinking to the front of his desk making sure he had time to check out her seductive presentation. She did have an ample rack, and he certainly would have been better persuaded if it hadn't been for the stains and food spots on her apron. She beamed with confidence, bending toward him, gently taking hold of her check and shifting her weight to her hand planted in the middle of his desk.

A moment passed as they both held onto the check, staring at each other, when David became aware of her open blouse. When she saw him look, she purred seductively, "You know David, you're only eight years older than me and I don't care if you don't care." Then on perfect cue, her hair fell forward and seemed to reach for him, pulling him into her. Pheromone intoxication caused a momentary loss of words as his ex-fiancée came to mind and their traditional lazy Sunday mornings in bed till noon.

He finally pulled his eyes up and smiled at her. "You know, Pam, smokers just don't turn me on."

"Damn!" She smacked the table, snatched her check out of his hand and almost collided with Roberto as she wheeled around.

"Hey, Boss...I almost forgot, I found this while cleaning up," he said dropping the item on David's checkbook. It was the key. Roberto turned and hurried to catch up with Pam as she opened the back door, evoking the familiar twang from its stretching spring.

"See you tomorrow, Boss!" Roberto shouted as the door banged shut behind them.

In the midst of running restaurant equipment and under the buzzing lights, David looked down at his desk and stared at the old brass key.

CHAPTER 2

David picked up the key and examined it under the lamp. He paused to stare at the unusual configuration of the teeth and again, wondered where he had seen it before. He tapped it in his open hand while trying to recall and his eyes drifted up to the clock.

"Holy shit!" he said aloud, tossing the key on the desk. He liked to be upstairs by now relaxing, having a beer. He glanced at the cash and tickets on his desk. "I'll count this tomorrow," he muttered and pulled a bank bag out of the bottom drawer.

He rolled his chair backwards to the floor safe, set its metal cover aside with a loud clank on the concrete floor and gazed at the old relic. There were a few iconic stories in the diner's history that gave him a glimpse of what his grandparents were like, and the safe was one of them. It was out of place, overqualified for a little restaurant and more suited to a large cash flow business, but he liked it and apparently so did his grandfather.

According to his mom, his grandfather was a bargain hunter and got a deal on it he couldn't pass up. Maybe it was the way the bolts solidly retracted into the lid or the quality of the lock when spun through the numbers that made it easy to overlook its one flaw. It had an unusable compartment at the bottom, an extra security measure for an employer to have if workers were accessing the safe. The door was stuck closed though, the lock broken. When asked, his grandfather had said he'd fix it when he got around to it—but he never did.

David knew his grandparents had died unexpectedly in a car crash but the accident was hard to wrap his head around, especially since his mom wouldn't talk about it. She would only repeat the same story he had been told when he was growing up, but if he pried for details, she would clam up. Even the people in town were reluctant to tell him anything and he had better luck with his school friends that had overheard them talking about it.

From what he had gathered, thirty plus years ago, his mom was kidnapped by the cook who apparently had a crush on her. She was in her twenties and he was a lot older, like twice her age. One night while she was locking up the diner the cook grabbed her and forced her into his car. His grandparents just happened to be returning to the restaurant for something they had forgotten and spotted them racing out of the parking lot. A chase ensued that rapidly got out of hand and soon they were speeding through the desert to that tragic ending.

The cook was convicted of double manslaughter and would have been out of jail by now if he hadn't been so combative. Word was that not long after he arrived he killed an inmate that got him a longtime residency. Thing was, it was baffling to David how he sensed such negativity about the cook from everyone except his mom. She would always keep her feelings private, but once he recalled catching her off guard when he asked some random question about the incident. In her hesitation she seemed to be reflecting on something, something he felt wasn't all bad. Unfortunately he was resolved never to know her secret now that she had taken it to her grave.

He bent over, spun the dial back and forth through the combination and twisted the lever. The bolts clunked into the lid and as he opened it like a submarine hatch, wondered if his grandfather would have opened it the same way.

He dangled the bag over the opening, about to let go but stopped cold in his tracks with his eyes fixated on the compartment door at the bottom with its peculiar keyhole.

"No," he muttered in disbelief, glancing back to his desk and seeing the brass key under the light, glistening in beckoning gold. "It does have the diner's name on it" he muttered, picking the key up and holding the tag under the light. He eyed the teeth all the way back to the safe and got on his knees. With a quick glance at the compartment door, he plunged his arm toward it and slid the key into the lockset. "It fits!" he said aloud and gave it a twist. The compartment door unlocked with a smooth click like a fine-oiled machine and David pulled it open, expecting it to be empty.

"What the…?" he said, looking at a carefully placed, brown book tucked away nice and neat. He grasped it, noticing a folded up piece of paper next to it and carefully pulled them both out. He cradled them in his hands, ambled to his desk and set the book down. Unfolding the paper, he immediately recognized the famous front page of the *Roswell Daily Record* dated July 8, 1947.

RAAF CAPTURES FLYING SAUCER ON RANCH IN ROSWELL REGION!

He almost crumpled it up as everyone in the country had seen it at one time or another but hesitated, looking closer. Maybe this was an original front page. He set it aside and picked up the book, clamped his thumb on the front cover and fanned through the musty pages. A puff of stale air made him gag and he coughed, exhaling hard. Someone had done a lot of writing in the book, he noticed.

He looked at the leather cover's frayed edges and thought of his grandfather. His heart began to pound. "Could this be his?" he hoped, as he opened and read the first page.

Don Reynolds

May 12th, 1947

"My grandfather!" he said aloud, falling into his chair. He scooted closer to the light and under its warmth, began to read.

***

Some things have happened that I can't tell anyone about, so I have decided to write them down for the record. I want all of the truth to be known, so I am going to start from the beginning. I am going to start with the first time I met Rishi, the Indian, and I don't

---

16

mean Indian like Apache. He was from India or at least, I thought so at the time.

It was early April, 1946. My wife Casey and I were working the diner when I looked out from the kitchen and saw an oddly dressed customer sitting at a booth holding Casey's hand. She looked uncomfortable as if he had grabbed it abruptly and surprised her. I was about to come out of the kitchen but he let go and she seemed all right so I went back to work. I asked her about it later and she said he was new in this country and suspected that where he was from, men just treated women differently.

He became a regular and during that time, I noticed him displaying more and more of his customary touching not only toward her but all women. It seemed creepy to me but the girls said they liked it. I think Rishi knew I disapproved of his antics because he kept his encounters with me brief.

I really didn't think much of it until the night I woke up and saw him standing at the foot of my bed.

***

A sudden noise outside made David look up at the bag of money sitting next to the open safe. He knew it was the trash bin doors banging in the breeze like they do sometimes but decided it was better to read his grandfather's book uninterrupted upstairs in the comfort of his home. He grabbed the bank bag, dropped it in the safe, spun the dial and threw his jacket on.

He looked intrigued at the worn edges of the book as he walked out of his office, not noticing the bright light shining under the back door. He stuffed the journal into his inside pocket, gave his kitchen a final glance, turned off the lights and swung the back door open.

"FREEZE, MOTHERFUCKER! DON'T MOVE!" a voice yelled. It was coming from a dark figure whose silhouette was distorted by a car's blazing headlights behind him. David froze, squinting past the barrel of a pistol and flashlight pointed at him to the man with a familiar twang, "Josh? Is that you?" he said.

"Oh, hey, Cooper. Jeeze, you kinda surprised me there. We were on our way out here when we heard you had a 211 in progress," he said, thrusting his barrel chest out while holstering his weapon, "You know that means, you were being robbed."

David smiled at him and noticed his ego hadn't changed a bit since they grew up together. They were acquaintances but not close friends. "Oh, no, everything's OK, but, you know, I think it's better to be robbed than shot coming out of my own restaurant."

Josh's quick glare turned into a mischievous smile, "Yeah? Well, it would've been a waste of bullets anyways," he countered while rearranging his jacket.

David chuckled, looking past him, searching the vacant parking lot, "So, what do you mean, *we*?"

Josh's face contorted painfully as he did a quick glance to the side and lowered his voice. "Oh my god, she's a freaking bitch— some kind of special agent crap."

David smiled and nodded, mostly to appear sympathetic, but he knew what a chauvinistic pig Josh was.

"Officer Bowman!" a woman's voice rang out from the far corner of the parking lot, "Are we clear?"

"Clear, Special Agent!" Josh yelled back, hinting with sarcasm, then solemnly turned to David and whispered, "Kill me, please, take my pistol and kill me."

David laughed and looked back at the slim figure approaching in a quick step, her dark wavy hair bouncing as she held her weapon down at her side. Then, in a seamless sweep, she swung it around and tucked it behind her back without breaking stride. David's eyebrows went up. This was not just an ordinary field officer. She walked with a definite air of confidence and vitality with every sure-footed step.

"Special Agent Kim Nichols, Mr. Cooper." She extended her hand and David felt strong fingers wrap around his palm. "How are you this evening?" she asked.

"Uhh, fine, I guess…What's going on?"

She noted his good looks, broad shoulders, and shifted her attention to the building behind him. "Do you mind if I ask you a few questions?" She was standing with confidence, hands on hips, flaring her jacket back and revealing the badge on her belt. Peaked eyebrows framed her dark brown eyes as she trained them on him waiting for an answer.

"Oh, uhh…yeah, sure…you want to come inside?" he offered, backing into the restaurant and turning the lights back on.

She motioned to Josh that they were accepting the invitation but stopped short when David held the door open for her and said politely, "After you."

Chapter 3

Josh and Special Agent Nichols took their time following David to his office for different reasons. The small town cop had a reputation for being consistently lethargic whereas the agent was actively making her observations and noting her surroundings.

David sat down at his desk, spotted the old newspaper clipping of the alien crash and without giving it another thought, crumpled it up and threw it in the trash can. When he looked up, he saw Agent Nichols watching. She stared at him as if taking note, then calmly sat down and crossed her legs without a word.

Josh pulled a chair over, dragging it on the floor the whole way and flopped into it. He looked around like a bored kid only to end up clasping his fingers over his big belly and fidgeting with them while staring at David.

"What's going on?" David inquired, watching Agent Nichols reach for something in her jacket.

Josh had moved on to studying his finger nails and announced, "Special Agent Nichols here is on an official—UGH!"

A blurring thump to the chest stopped Josh cold as Agent Nichol's hand grabbed his shirt and some chest hair along with it. "I got this, Sergeant. Thank you, though," she said pleasantly and let go of his shirt. She then calmly opened up her notebook, "Mr. Cooper…first let's start with what you can tell me about this building." She thumb-clicked her pen and made a few notes.

At the look on Josh's face, David had to cover his mouth and forcibly hold down a grin; seeing him struggling to tuck his shirt back in over his ballooned belly only made it worse. Josh noticed him looking and mouthed the words, *fucking bitch* and David had to look away or lose his composure. Agent Nichols was watching and waiting, so he cleared his throat and gave her his best serious look. "As I understand it, this building was originally an old warehouse my grandparents bought in the '40s to convert into a restaurant with living quarters upstairs. It's been in the family ever since," he said with a shrug.

Agent Nichols nodded, made a few notes and pulled a photo from her notebook. She set it on the desk in front of him. "Do you recognize this man?" she said, watching him closely.

David looked at the picture and recognized the old man who had brought the key into the diner. "Yeah…the antique collector, he was here tonight."

"Antiques, huh," she said sarcastically, "What else did he tell you?"

David knew she was fishing and it suddenly occurred to him it would lead to the key. "Not much really. He told me he came by to try my steak dinner. I asked him if he was looking for fossils. What's going on here, is he in trouble with you guys?"

Agent Nichols tilted her head a little while she listened. "I thought you said he was an antique collector…" she said, her tone of questioning shifting and sounding more like an interrogation.

"He said that he was a collector, but when I saw his clothes, dirt and all, I thought he was an archeologist. I actually thought he was a bum at first glance," David said and then caught himself. He suddenly felt like he was volunteering too much information. He turned his attention to relaxing and vowed to be vague from then on because there was no way in the world he was giving up his grandfather's book.

Agent Nichol's pressed on, "What made him start talking about collecting antiques?"

"Like I said, I asked if he was a rock hunter or something like that, and he told me he was into collecting antiques…that's it…simple as that," David answered, unwilling to be intimidated.

She stared at him for a moment then made a few notes and tried another angle. "Did he happen to mention that his name is Carl?" She paused, looked for a reaction and seeing none, adding, "and that he used to work here?" The look on David's face told her what she wanted to know before he even answered.

"What…" David stammered, "*That* old man is the kidnapper?"

She appeared insensitive but she had to do it, she had to find it. She'd been after it for so many years and she knew she was close.

"I thought I was supposed to get some kind of warning when he was getting out!" David lashed out and glanced over at Josh who was looking at him with a twisted weird smile. David shot a WTF look at him and then turned it on her, too.

Agent Nichol's was frowning. "You're right," she acknowledged "you should have been notified about his parole, but don't worry about it…we're keeping an eye on him."

David looked down at the picture of the scruffy, bearded man in the orange jumpsuit and tried to recall all of their conversation. If he didn't want him to know who he was then he must have been hoping for a certain answer. The key was obviously his grandfather's and the old man must have taken it and probably didn't know what it went to. Maybe he didn't know the combination and needed him to get the book out. There must be something in the book he needs to know…or maybe there is something he doesn't want anyone to know. Anyway, it didn't matter anymore because the book was his now.

He picked up the picture and held it out to her. "So, that's it…you guys came all the way out here to tell me you are keeping an eye on him?" he asked.

She got up and studied him while slipping the picture back into her notebook. "Look," she said, "I can tell you he stole government property but I can't tell you what it is because it's classified. However, I can tell you that when he tries to retrieve it, we will be there." She then held her card out, "Here's my number. Call me anytime if anything comes to mind."

David looked at it, and like any single guy looking at an attractive girl's business card, entertained the notion of calling her on a more unofficial matter. But on second thought, he wasn't sure if he wanted to tangle with this one. Nevertheless, he tentatively took her card.

She bent down and picked the crumpled paper out of the trash, "You believe in this stuff?" she asked unfolding it and setting it back on his desk in front of him.

"Maybe. You noticed I threw it away, right?" he replied, looking up at her then curiously asked, "What do you know about it?"

She just smiled at him for a moment. "Good night, Mr. Cooper," she said and headed for the back door. "Sergeant?" she snapped as she went by Josh.

Josh twitched out of his drowsiness and slowly pried himself out of the chair. "See ya, Coop," he muttered and lumbered along behind her.

David watched them walk out the back door more baffled than ever. It seemed the closer he got to the truth about his grandfather he ended up with more questions than answers.

Chapter 4

David retraced his steps, closed up the restaurant and once outside was too distracted to appreciate the moonlit landscape. He was thinking of his grandparents, eager to learn more about them and skipped steps as he ran up the stairs to his apartment. He locked the front door and walked into the family room to a round pine table his grandfather had made and set the book under the low hanging pendant light.

He tossed his jacket over a chair and headed to the kitchen for a glass of water, eyeing the book the whole way. At the kitchen island he used as a bar, he grabbed a glass but paused with it under the faucet and decided he was going to relax and enjoy this. He wanted to get to know his grandfather as if they were sitting man to man having a drink together. He set the glass down, pulled out a bottle of Irish whisky and poured himself a couple of fingers.

Back at the table, he gave the whisky at the bottom of the glass a swirl, took a sip and set it down next to him. He thumbed through the pages of the old book to the place where he had left off—the strange Indian man standing at the foot of his grandfather's bed.

***

I saw Rishi and jolted angrily out of bed, ready to fight but felt so stupid, standing there naked, alone because he was gone. I glanced at Casey but she hadn't woken up. I checked the house for signs of any intruder and finding none, decided I must have dreamt it.

I kept the dream to myself and the next-day when Rishi came in, I watched him but nothing had changed so I forgot about it.

About a month after the dream Casey got sick. She thought it was the stomach flu since she couldn't keep anything down and finally I took her to see Doc. I'll never forget listening to him telling us she was pregnant. He was so embarrassed since he had told us a year earlier it could never happen because Casey was barren.

We didn't care why, we were just so happy making plans; a baby room, a crib, and she even started watching what she ate. We shared the news with all our customers. Then one day I looked out the kitchen and saw Rishi patting Casey's stomach. It was creepy and rubbed me the wrong way and even when he shook my hand, congratulating me, I couldn't get past the awkward feeling.

Then our Julie was born. She was a healthy baby and we were on our way to building our new family. I worked the diner while Casey brought her downstairs to visit with friends and customers. It was a wonderful time in our lives.

The reason I am writing in this book is because of what happened next. It began with a dream. I was in bed and couldn't open my eyes or move my body. I could hear strange shuffling sounds in the bedroom. I heard Julie make a noise and then I realized it wasn't a dream.

It was hard but somehow I managed to get one eye partway open and saw Rishi standing by Julie's crib. I could've killed him, but I could only turn my head enough to look over Casey to the top of Julie's crib. I thought I saw her blanket come out of the crib but it was too low to see. I tried to raise my head but could only hear her fussing. I looked at Rishi and he was looking down, turning as he watched something take my daughter toward the bedroom door. I could only see the top of the door open and heard Julie's cries as she was carried from the room. Rishi walked to the door and stopped to look at me. I know he saw me awake but he didn't seem to care and instead coldly stared at me for a moment then walked out.

I was raging inside and somehow slowly managed to get out of bed. It seemed to take forever, but I finally threw some clothes on and raced to the front door. There was a full moon so I could see Rishi out in the desert walking toward the rocky knoll accompanied by some tiny figures dressed in matching silver jumpsuits.

I frantically ran, following them as they made their way to a cluster of rocks. When I finally got there, turning into the opening I almost ran my head into a metal edge sticking out at me. I had heard of them before but had never seen one in real life. But there it was, sitting in front of me under the moonlight, a flying saucer.

I couldn't believe my eyes, but then didn't care because all I could think about was my baby daughter, and when I saw the boarding ramp still down, I ran over to it.

I surprised myself by not even caring who or what I was about to encounter. I snuck into the ship just as it closed up. The ceiling was so low I almost had to get on all fours while I hid behind some odd equipment. Three of the aliens were sitting with their backs to me, oblivious to my presence and busy at the controls. Another alien was walking toward them and away from what looked like an open drawer sticking out of the wall with a sheet of blue light covering it.

There was no sign of Rishi but I didn't care when I saw Julie's arm come out of the drawer, through the blue light and wave around. Her little hand grabbed my finger and I could tell she was scared as I gently picked her up and hugged her. She let out a murmuring fuss which, unfortunately, the aliens heard.

I could feel them in my head and seeing a couple of them coming at me, I backed away. I bumped into something, felt it break and heard a broken piece hit the floor behind me as the ship started to wobble. I didn't even know we were airborne and the aliens suddenly didn't care about me or Julie. They were running around, flipping levers and pushing buttons. The wobbling got worse and it felt like the ship was out of control. I wedged us into a corner and all I could think about was protecting Julie.

I don't remember the crash, and when I came to, we had been thrown clear of the wreckage and ended up in a huge clump of buffalo grass. Julie was crying but somehow we were both unhurt. While getting up and holding her close I heard a sound and saw an injured alien crawling in the wreckage. I had to get us away as fast as possible. I saw a triangular object on the ground next to us. It was from the ship and without thinking I picked it up. I don't know why I did, maybe as a souvenir or proof of this experience but I took it.

I walked for hours, glad that Julie slept most of the way except for an occasional sigh, then back to sleep. When we got to the road, I saw we were a couple of miles from the diner and got us home before sunrise without seeing a single car. The upstairs front door was wide open, Casey was still asleep and I managed to put Julie back in her crib without waking her. I couldn't sleep so I sat at the table and studied the alien triangle until I heard Casey wake up. I knew she would freak out if she knew what happened to Julie, so I hid the object and decided to keep the whole incident to myself.

The next day I came out of the kitchen and saw three of my customers in a serious huddle talking in hushed tones and had a feeling it was about the crash. They didn't mind when I joined them and even let me see the piece of debris the ranch foreman had brought. I recognized the markings on it, they were the same as what I had seen in the alien ship, but I kept quiet. The other two were telling the foreman he should go into the next town and tell the sheriff since they believed it was a government project gone bad. The foreman was upset because his sheep wouldn't cross the long debris field to graze, and he wanted to know who was going to clean it up. Finally, the foreman took off to go see the sheriff and we all thought that was going to be the end of it. But when the government later announced it was an alien ship that crashed, I almost came forward.

Government agents showed up acting like they were on a fact finding mission and talking to everybody, but something told me not to trust them. Turned out I was right because a few days later, anyone that said they saw or knew anything about the crash was taken away. The foreman disappeared and we didn't see him for over a week and when we finally did, he had a strange, detached look on his face, telling a different story, something about a "weather balloon."

Then the agents began terrorizing the town, threatening to arrest anybody who discussed the aliens saying they would be charged with trying to create "mass hysteria." It reminded me of Nazi Germany, and I was glad I hadn't told Casey. God love her, but she can't keep a secret.

Later I heard they were searching homes and decided it was time to hide my secret somewhere no one would ever find it. There are times I think of taking it from its hiding place to prove that the aliens really do exist and the crash really happened but then I always ask myself why? To what end?

Anyway, this is why I decided to write about my secret in this book and be satisfied with just looking at the concrete patch on the wall in my office and know that my secret is safely hidden away until the time is right.

***

David choked. Whiskey he had just sipped got caught in his throat but he didn't care. He stood up coughing while reading the last part over and over again. He knew exactly where the wall was and the patch his grandfather was talking about. Many times while sitting at the office desk, on the phone or just thinking things over, he had studied the same trowel marks on the wall. He also knew it happened to be currently covered by a chalkboard that his mom had hung up while he was at college. He threw his jacket back on, stuffed the journal into the inside pocket and bolted out the front door.

Chapter 5

David slid to a stop at the back door with his hand digging deep into his pocket. He groped and yanked at his keys, fumbling with them all the way to the ground. *Calm down!* he told himself and purposely slowed his reach, carefully picking them up and then methodically picked out the back door key.

Holding the key up to the door about to insert it, he suddenly got an eerie feeling and turned around to a dark figure standing behind him. "Jeez," he gasped, "I'm sorry...we're...we're closed," he said, squinting, trying to see who it was under the moonlit hat.

"Shut up and get inside," the figure growled, gesturing with something in his hand. David looked and saw it was a gun.

"Okay...okay, this is a small diner, I don't have much here, but you can have it all," David complied unlocking the door and a prompt shove from behind, sent him sprawling to the floor.

"Where ya going in such a hurry, Cooper?" the figure demanded, closing the door behind him.

The lights came on and David saw it was Carl. "What the hell do you think you are doing?" David yelled angrily as he got up. Carl looked stronger, younger, and David realized he had been pushing the old man routine a bit.

"What did you do with my key, David?"

"Don't you mean my grandfather's key?" David countered.

Carl's eyes narrowed, "What did you find?"

"I know who you are!" David declared, hoping to change the subject.

"I doubt it," Carl scoffed.

"I know you just got out of jail. Why didn't you tell me you used to work here?"

"Oh God!" Carl said, lowering his pistol in disgust. "Let me guess...I suppose you've been talking to that cute little brunette number."

"She told me everything and why they let you out. You know they're watching you."

Carl shook his head. "They're idiots. They think I don't know what they're up to. They have no idea who I am...and neither do you. Your grandfather took something...something I need."

"Isn't it enough you killed him, you son of a bitch. It's because of you I never knew my grandparents."

Carl stared at him with indifference and stepped closer. "Well now, let's see. If you know it was your grandfather's key, then you must have found what it went to. But it wasn't what I'm looking for now was it?" He stared through David, distant in thought. "So, why would you be running down here in such a hurry?" he pondered as he looked around. "It's down here isn't it?" he exclaimed, excited and shoved the gun in David's face. "*Isn't it?*"

David jerked his hands up, stumbling backward, his mind racing and Carl noticed him taking a quick glance in the direction of the office. A fiendish smile began to grow under his beard as he stared at David. "Of course, the safe," he muttered then motioned with his gun, "Let's go...open it up."

David begrudgingly led the way into his office, apparently too slow for Carl and earned a quick jab with the pistol for it. "Move it!" Carl snapped.

David silently cussed himself out for giving away the safe and didn't dare peek toward the chalkboard. He opened the safe and stepped to the side putting Carl's back to the patched up wall. The maneuver caught Carl's attention, seemingly a tad too deliberate, and he glared at David. But after a moment, he lost interest, anxious to get into the safe. "Let's go…empty it," he demanded, waving the pistol.

David reluctantly bent down, and when he pulled the money bag out, Carl saw the key, "Ahh…now we are getting somewhere," he said at the sight of it neatly placed on top of the compartment door, "so that's what it goes to—open it!"

David opened it and backed away. Carl leaned in and stood over it, staring into the empty compartment. "What was in it?" he pried.

"Nothing, some old papers." David said pointing to the trash can. "You want me to show you?"

"Really—" Carl said doubtfully, not believing a word of it. He shoved the pistol into David's ribs. "I know there's a connection between that key and what I'm looking for…you might as well tell me…" Carl's voice trailed off with his expression going blank.

David realized the gun barrel was pressing against the journal through his jacket and Carl was poking it and feeling around with the end of the pistol. David's mind scrambled for something to say but Carl beat him to it, relaxed now with a slight smile.

"You know…" Carl began, bringing his free hand up, straightening the lapel on David's jacket, "one time I remember seeing the old man writing in a small brown book, and when he realized I was watching him, he got really weird," Carl said, reaching into David's jacket and pulling out the journal. "Well, what'd ya know…"

Chapter 6

Carl stepped back keeping the pistol pointed at David and began leafing through the book with his other hand. David watched for a moment then cautiously took his first glance at the chalkboard. He could just make out the bottom of the patch peeking out from under it. He desperately looked around and for a brief insane moment, thought about doing something crazy. He took a couple of deep breaths and braced while looking for an opening to jump Carl.

Carl abruptly stopped fumbling with one hand, frustrated and angrily waved his pistol toward the desk. "Sit!" he ordered. David reluctantly sat down, seeing his chance slipping away, realizing it was going to be a lot harder to leap out of a chair, especially one with wheels on it.

Carl clamped the pistol under his arm and began quickly flipping through the book's pages, scanning as he went, while David dared another look at the patch.

"I knew it!" Carl yelled, slamming the book shut. He held the book against his chest while studying the walls of the office. "That's why you were in such a hurry to get down here," he muttered. He turned back to David and growled, "I don't have time for a treasure hunt. No more games – where is it?"

David dared not look toward the chalkboard and when Carl shoved the pistol in his face he took a scared glance at the other wall, hoping for a diversion. Carl took the bait, whipping around, staring at the wall where David looked and walked over to it. He began knocking with his knuckles, listening for hollowness and David realized it was futile, he had bought maybe a minute or two.

He held his breath, watching Carl methodically rapping his way toward the patch and his heart sank when Carl stopped and bent over to look under the chalkboard. He was looking closely under the eraser tray and running his fingers over the rough surface.

David was desperate and was about to burst from his chair and attack when a peculiar sound caught his attention. It was so subtle that only one who had spent years in this kitchen, surrounded by these appliances would have noticed it. The backdoor would always rattle, ever so slightly when opened from its sticky threshold. He glanced over and saw Kim and Josh creeping in and taking cover behind some rolling cabinets. Kim caught his eye and did a circling hand signal which he assumed was for him to distract Carl in some way. Carl was still pointing the pistol in his direction while studying the wall.

"Hey! Do you have to point that thing at me?" David yelled, loud enough for Kim to know Carl was armed. "At least take your finger off the trigger for Christ's sake!"

Carl whipped around and the look on his face told David he was about to get more than he bargained for. Especially when he saw Carl pull the hammer back on the revolver and a bullet rotate behind the barrel. "I think we're about done here," Carl hissed.

"Whoa, whoa! I know where it is!" David yelled, waving his hands.

Carl smiled, "Of course you do. I knew you did all along," he grumbled and flicked the gun's barrel toward the chalkboard. "Tell me it's not in there." The look on David's face told him he had found it. "Like I said, we're done." He brought the pistol up, but saw David's attention had shifted to something behind him.

David's eyes were locked on the back wall of the kitchen where a broom leaning against it was moving. It was behind Josh who didn't realize he was nudging it with his foot.

"Oh, please—I'm not falling for that." Carl scoffed, waving the pistol in David's line of sight. "Look at me…I want you to see it coming." But David's eyes got huge and Carl couldn't know the broom was now sliding along the wall on its way to the floor.

"What are you looking at?" Carl demanded, whipping around just as the handle loudly clacked on the concrete. He flinched and accidently fired his gun.

David sat in shock and disbelief, his ears ringing numbly, thinking he had seen it all until Josh popped up like a prairie dog and began blasting away with his eyes closed.

Carl crouched, returning fire while David dove for cover and hit the ground as bits of glass rained down on top of him. He crawled toward his desk, looking over at Kim and saw her yelling at Josh to stop firing, but he looked determined to empty his gun.

David managed to snake his way through a debris field of food stuffs, puddling oils and syrups and balled up under his desk just as the lights went out. He heard footsteps running away, distant yelling and then silence. In the quiet he began to check for wounds, starting at his feet. He wiggled his toes, and then flexed the muscles in his legs, so far so good, his thighs and then his stomach and chest. Somehow, it appeared he had escaped without being shot.

The lights came back on and he peeked out from under the desk and saw Kim's hand. "You Okay?" she asked.

"Uh, yeah…I think so." he said crawling out, grabbing her hand and was surprised by her strength. She holstered her weapon and stood squarely in front of him with her hands on his shoulders.

"Are you sure?" she persisted, not waiting for an answer, and slowly ran her hands down his arms with momentary squeezes along the way. "Sometimes people don't realize they've been injured in all the excitement," she explained.

He wasn't really listening but was rather enjoying her attentiveness and how attractive she was while doing it. The way she was jostling him about, it seemed so familiar that without giving it a second thought, he steadied himself by putting his hands on her waist.

Startled, Kim stopped and looked at him with such a sultry look that any normal guy would've expected to be smacked.

"Uh…thanks for caring," he expressed tentatively, about to remove his hands but noticed her eyes turn soft and bounce back and forth on his a couple of times. He smiled, wondering what she was searching for in his eyes and at the same time, they both realized her hands were still on his arms. She pushed him off, turned away and took a few steps to peer into the open safe. "Was he robbing you?" she asked.

"No, didn't touch the money. He just wanted to look in it for some reason," David muttered.

She thought out loud, "It doesn't make sense…It's too big to fit in there. Why would he want to look in there?"

"What's too big to fit in there? What is this thing everyone's looking for?" he grumbled.

She turned to him. "It's the classified device we are after and I heard you say you knew where it was."

"You did see the pistol pointed at my head…right? I would have told him anything."

She kept watching him and slyly smiled, "You didn't answer my question."

"I didn't hear a question," he countered with raised eyebrows.

"Alright then, just answer the question…do you have it?"

"No…I…don't," he declared with a clear conscience because technically he didn't yet. But if she had asked him if he knew where it was, he would have had to outright lie and he was glad he didn't have to.

Her eyes narrowed, sensing something had slipped past her but Josh burst in, interrupting them. "They spotted him!" he yelled and promptly bent over, struggling to talk between gasps, "heading...towards town...they want us...to assist pursuit." Josh's physical condition was painful to watch as his stomach muscles strained to tighten over his enormous belly.

Kim turned away and faced David. "Look, if you come across it, please be careful. Call me if you do and by all means don't touch it," she said, then lowered her voice and added, "I wish I could tell you more, but what I can tell you is that it is extremely powerful, dangerously powerful." She emphasized the last part then paused, briefly studying him before turning away.

David abruptly reached out and grabbed her. "Wait! Dangerous like a bomb?"

She smiled, pleased to see he was genuinely concerned, patted his hand and headed for the door.

David watched Kim rush out with Josh, her words still ringing in his ears, and took a cautious glance at the wall. He thought of his grandfather and found it hard to believe he would hide something so dangerous in his restaurant and wondered if they were talking about the same thing. He wondered why Carl would be after something his grandfather had taken from the aliens and how did he even know about it in the first place? And then there was the government, how did they get involved?

He headed to close the back door, hearing Josh's patrol car speeding out of the parking lot, gravel rattling in its fender wells. He secured the door, leaned against it and surveyed the damage to his kitchen, amazed nobody had been killed. "What a mess." he sighed and opened a nearby closet where the mop was. He reached for it but his hand went past it, plunging deep into a dark corner and after some fishing around, pulled out a ten-pound sledge.

He juggled the weight of the heavy head in his free hand, stared past the debris toward his office and muttered, "I guess a little more of a mess won't matter at this point."

Chapter 7

Having removed the chalkboard, David stared at the patched-up wall for a moment then choked up on the hammer. He tapped the heavy head against the concrete. It was hollow. He stepped back, swung the hammer behind him and let it fly. The head broke through, knocking chucks of concrete loose and he heard them falling inside the wall. It took some wrestling to get the hammer free, and then he took a look into the fist-sized hole. All he could see was darkness. He started opening it up, gently hitting the edges with the sledge in one hand and grabbing the broken pieces with the other. A huge chunk finally broke loose and peeking in, he saw something at the bottom, wrapped in a gunny sack, covered with dust.

He plunged his arm deep into the wall, his cheek pressed hard against the cement blocks, stretching and groping until he felt his fingertips graze the bunched up fabric. He steadied his hand, found and grasped it and then gently pulled up. Something was wrong! The material must have a hole in it because the sack felt empty. But when he brought his arm out of the wall, he was surprised to see it wasn't.

He held the sack at arm's length watching it spin, slowly unwinding its twisted bindings. He frowned as he laid it down on a stainless steel table. This couldn't be what everyone was after and certainly couldn't be dangerous. What did she say? *Dangerously powerful?* He scoffed at Kim's warning while crunching through debris to his desk for a pair of scissors.

He snipped the air a couple of times while eyeing the dirty sack on his way back and hesitated briefly at the leather string. He pictured his grandfather tying it up and after a moment, abruptly cut it off. After a few more snips the sack was cut down the center and while setting the scissors aside, he caught a glimpse of silver.

"What the…" he muttered, thinking any metallic material would have to be paper thin, aluminum foil maybe and hollow or over foam. He held the fabric apart and stared, mesmerized, letting it drop to the sides and experienced what every treasure hunter experienced in the moment of a dream find.

It was triangle-shaped with three arms each about ten inches long, extending from a round body, all glistening in brushed silver. In the middle were seven clear stones in a row, aligned with one of the arms. At the end of each arm was a similar stone. He counted ten stones in all and wondered if they might possibly be diamonds.

They were smooth on the surface but the pattern cuts underneath made them sparkle with hints of color, something you just don't get from glass. He wanted to believe it, picking a fingernail at one of them but it was too smooth. The craftsmanship was excellent. Running a finger over it, he couldn't feel any transition between it and the metal.

Made by aliens...he mumbled skeptically, holding it out in front of him and noticing the surface was changing. He looked closely and saw faint, etched images, subtly appearing and disappearing depending on the angle of the reflecting light. It was definitely unique.

He pushed the old fabric off the table and spread out a clean white towel and set the silver object on it. With little tugs on the towel, he could slowly turn it and observed the reflections carefully. He saw figures, some very similar to Egyptian hieroglyphics. He thought he saw a human holding something and tugged on the towel to see it better but, oddly, it wouldn't move.

Weird, he thought. Stainless steel tables have nothing to snag on and he reached for it to turn it by hand. Suddenly the table groaned as if something extremely heavy had just been placed on it. He froze and saw the towel under the object was visibly pushing into the table. He stepped back, scratching his head when it slowly began rising back up. Somehow it was changing its weight.

Is that possible? he wondered and reached for it again. Immediately the table sank, deeply indenting the metal. He jerked his hands back. "Holy shit!" he exclaimed and watched in disbelief as the towel came back up and the metal table popped flat again.

"What the hell…is it aware of me?" he said loudly, reaching for it again and this time keeping an eye on the towel.

It happened so fast, in the corner of his eye, a sudden red flash! He jerked his hand back, staring at the clear stone at the end of the row, the one he thought it came from. He waited as moments passed and nothing happened. He began to wonder if he had imagined it. He looked around. Could it have been a reflection from something in the room? He looked up. He knew the smoke detector had a red light on it but it wasn't even on and it wouldn't have been bright enough anyway. Baffled, he looked down in front of him and a chill to the bone ran through him. The glass stone on the end was flashing a bright red.

He stared, petrified as he realized the flashing was getting faster. A voice in his head screamed, countdown! He couldn't move his legs and the horrible thought that maybe Agent Nichols was right. He had to run! It was about to explode! Suddenly it jerked across the table towards him. He recoiled backwards, slipping and falling to the floor. He frantically thrashed about to get back on his feet and froze…it was gone. He spun away from the table, stopping in a paralyzing jolt as it was hovering inches behind him, motionless without a sound. The glass stones had come alive now, randomly flashing in vibrant colors. Red on the bottom, orange, yellow, green in the middle then blue above it to purple with violet at the top.

He froze in place and watched it slowly drift away and was relieved to see it turn its attention to the table. That is until the glass stones at the end of its arms began to glow a yellow gold and rotate, spinning faster and faster. They disappeared into a blur, a golden circle around its body with the row of blinking stones staying vertical.

The thought of leaving at this point seemed like a good idea with running being the best way. He braced to leave but, surprisingly, felt unthreatened and in fact was a bit more intrigued than anything. Out of curiosity he watched, almost mesmerized and wondered, was he hypnotized?

There was so much action without a sound, not even a whoosh. Streaks of light streamed from the circle to a focal point on the center of the table.

David thought the spinning object was trying to burn a hole in the table as the beams flickered in a fizzling cloud of gas.

Then in the haze, something began to develop. It was creating something. The laser thin lines continued to leap from the circle, randomly zapping over the form as it grew larger and larger and David began to see a shape…a shape of a person.

Chapter 8

He sat like a Buddhist monk in meditation, eyes closed, legs folded, his index fingers circled to thumbs with his forearms resting on his knees, all while breathing deeply. He was shirtless, barefooted, with only a white cloth draped around his waist and looking like a scene right out of a Tibetan monastery.

David's peripheral vision caught something moving, and he looked just in time to see the hovering triangle disappear. He stared in disbelief at the space where it had been, wondering how any of this was possible.

He turned back, startled to see the man's eyes open now looking at him and wished he wasn't standing so close to the table. But it did enable him to see the realistic, saggy skin, moles, cracks and texture. There were even wild hairs sprouting off his shoulders and if he hadn't seen it with his own eyes he wouldn't have questioned it being a real human. It had the appearance of a living organism of solid mass and it even displayed emotional expressions on its face. David actually saw it showing curiosity and then it seemed to be pondering. It was fantastic!

The way it kept looking at him led him to believe there might be something going on inside and it might be possible to communicate with it. "Can you speak?" David asked being careful of his pronunciation just in case there was a translation program in place.

The man's eyes suddenly sparkled alive, then he blinked and started to chuckle, shaking his head. "You don't buy this either, huh?" he said looking down at his half naked body and then waving a hand in the air. The triangle quickly re-materialized with its lights on and arms spinning and began creating clothes on the man. "They thought it would be a good idea if you saw it happen. Can't blame them really…in their infinite world, first time experiences are always exceptional," he said, unfolding his legs and sliding off the table. He did a light stretch as the triangle finished clothing him, dressing him in a light blue, open-collar dress shirt with casual tan pants and penny loafers.

"Who are you?" David stammered, taking a tentative step back.

The man looked at him with strong, gripping yet wise eyes and answered, "I am Rishi."

The name gave David a chill. "You…" David said, taking more steps backward. "You're the one my grandfather spoke of."

Rishi didn't respond, appearing indifferent and just staring at David.

"You were in my grandparents' bedroom…you took my mom when she was a baby." David said, raising his voice.

Rishi relaxed and began looking around. "Well now, that's not entirely accurate. Yes, I was there but as an observer only," he said.

"An observer…what's the difference if you were standing there watching or grabbing the victim…you're still a kidnapper," David said, irritated. "What were you planning to do to my mother?"

"I wasn't planning to do anything but observe."

"Is that what the aliens made you for, just to watch them do stuff? Are you some kind of documenting program?" David asked.

Rishi chuckled with contempt, "The aliens didn't make me."

"I saw the spinning triangle thing make you and my grandfather took it from the aliens, so tell me how that doesn't make you made by aliens."

Rishi nodded, thought for a moment then said, "I see your logic. Your grandfather couldn't have known that the *spinning triangle,* as you call it, was actually a passenger on the ship like he was and, like him, the aliens didn't know it was there. And by the way it's called a Fabricator and it saved the lives of your grandfather and mother in the crash."

"My grandfather said they landed in grass," David said.

"The Fabricator put them there or they would have both perished."

David crinkled up his forehead, "So, if the aliens didn't make the *Fabricator,* then who did?" As soon as he asked, he realized it was a silly question and the look on Rishi's face confirmed it.

"It's a long story but look at it this way," Rishi explained. "The Fabricator is like a machine that can create a vehicle for you to navigate in a landscape that is different from your world…it's just a tool."

"Okay…" David ventured, "so, if you're not with the aliens, are you from a different planet than the aliens?"

"More like a different dimension."

David watched him walking around, surveying the damaged kitchen and said, "So, when my grandfather conveniently happened upon the Fabricator, it wasn't by accident…was it?"

Rishi was looking closely at a salt shaker he had picked up off the floor and said, "Nope, it was meant to be taken by him."

"*Why?*"

Rishi set the shaker down on a table and turned to him. "For this moment David…for this very moment."

"What…what's going to happen?" David said almost in a whisper.

"What if I told you that you already know the answers to all these questions and you just need to remember," Rishi said, rolling the office chair toward him, "and in order for you to remember, you must first forget…" He rotated the chair toward David, "Have a seat."

"Forget what?" David said, tentatively sitting down.

Rishi began walking around him, pushing debris away with his shoes. "Taking possession of a body in the beginning of its life cycle is a wonderful and powerful experience but it has its drawbacks," he said, leaning against a table and folding his arms. "When I take possession of a body in adult form I can easily differentiate between the being I am and the life experiences I have in it. You need to forget who you think you are, David…and remember who you really are."

David caught a glimpse of something in his peripheral vision. The room was swirling. He started to panic. He looked at Rishi and was strangely quelled by the way the wise man was watching over him. He actually felt protected, even as he left his body.

Chapter 9

He felt good, the warmth of the sun shining on him, a breeze of fresh air in his face. He was standing in a meadow with many people, people he knew very well, and felt the union of their camaraderie. They were crowded around a table with a clear dome on it with images moving inside it. He looked closer and saw a young boy with his mother growing up in life from a baby to a toddler, to a rambunctious youngster and then past his teenage years leaving home for college, graduating, working, and then coming home when his mother dies and discovering his true purpose. He watched with the group quietly standing and observing, all aware of the question. Who among them would be the one to accept this path? The group weighed this energy as a whole and it seemed to flow to him. It felt right that it was for him.

The group turned to him in recognition and he looked into the dome and recognized himself as David growing up in the little desert town.

A special person next to him touched him and they embraced, promising to look for each other during the lifetime ahead and knew it wouldn't be easy…it never was.

Chapter 10

Special Agent Nichols took in the sunrise through her windshield while waiting outside the chain link gates. On the tall fencing was a crooked and badly weathered sign that read "Dept. of Agriculture Restricted Area." She glanced inside at the large two-story greenhouse that was nearly as long as a football field. Aside from a few dust-covered cars parked in front, it looked abandoned, like something one might expect to see in the middle of the desert.

There was a small house off to the side with a rickety porch and a green front door. A soldier emerged, casually walking up to the gate and waving. Her tires unintentionally broke loose in the gravel, kicking up swirls of dust while the guard held the gate open and, this time, his waving was not at her.

She pulled into an open space and got a sudden bad feeling while stepping out of her car. She glanced around, biting her lip, frowning. She hated it when her gut instincts were going off and not knowing why. Coffee…she silently declared as the antidote, heading to the guard shack and the pot he always had brewing.

"Hey, Willis…how's it shakin'?" she said, not surprised he was resuming his duties with his head buried in the newspaper.

"Same ol…same ol…You here all day?" he said without looking.

"No, just a debriefing," she said while pouring coffee. She blew into her cup and tentatively sipped, thinking of the incident at the Apache Diner the night before. Was that it, why she felt this way? Shots were fired, that might be it, she thought. She had some explaining to do, especially since the local police were involved. They had their own protocol which was in the public eye, unlike her department. She quickly dismissed it, having had to deal with much messier situations.

She sipped some more, recalling the stand down order from Roberts while on her way to the chase scene. Seemed unusual now but at the time she figured it was to keep the bungling individual sitting next to her out of a possible witness situation.

She glanced toward the guard then looked out the window at the desert scenery. "Say, Willis...Do you notice something different today? Did somebody cut down a cactus or something?"

"Ha ha, funny..." he said, fake laughing and scrunched his paper down to look at her. It took a moment before he realized, she didn't know. "You haven't heard? I was wondering why you were so laid back this morning," he said thrilled that he knew something important before an agent did, especially one of her caliber.

Kim whipped around so suddenly and with such intensity that it took him by surprise. "What happened?" she demanded. She hated surprises, especially in this business, because the ones who found out last were the ones most vulnerable and she hated feeling vulnerable.

"Uhhhh..." Willis squirmed. "There've been a lot of people through here in the last twenty-four..." His voice suddenly clamped up, his throat growing tighter with every step she took toward him. He couldn't breathe, recalling rumors of her ability to thrust her foot above her head, kicking a groping guard unconscious once. She was close now, standing in front of him.

"Spit it the fuck out, Willis!" she demanded, but Willis could only mumble incoherently. She couldn't wait for his answer and rushed to a nearby door, flinging it open. It slammed hard against the wall and she stepped into what looked like a small storage room.

"You're not supposed to go that way!" Willis finally managed.

She ignored him like she always did and reached for a hidden lever. The wall opened up and she stepped through it as she heard him yell after her, "They got it going! It turned on!"

The door closed and within seconds she was in a service elevator, descending into the depths of the desert. With his words ringing in her ears, she wondered how many calls she must have missed on her phone. She couldn't know since it went missing sometime during the skirmish at the restaurant.

The elevator stopped and didn't open fast enough for her, as she forced her way through the doors. A couple of soldiers at a desk in the receiving room looked her way. "Hey, Nichols," one of them said and a tech leaning against a wall nearby looked up.

"Kim!" he yelled, tucking his tablet under his arm, "Where have you been? We've been trying to reach you." He pulled on her, "Come on! The Colonel ordered me to get you to the conference room as soon as possible."

They raced down the hallway "What's going on?" she managed while dodging techs and soldiers along the way.

"The ship works! It was just for a few seconds but, man…it was awesome!" he exclaimed, stopping outside the conference room

"What finally worked?"

"Don't know for sure" he explained, grabbing the door and opening it for her, "but there's been a rumor going around that it was not what they expected."

Chapter 11

David woke up looking through his patio doors at the morning sun slowly working its way down the jagged knoll off in the distance. The sun's leading edge seemed warmer than usual, a golden orange, and was a strong contrast against the cool shaded area below it. He took it all in without moving his head off the pillow, studying the colorful layers. Even though he was familiar with the scene, everything seemed more vibrant than ever before. He also noticed how exceptionally good he felt.

He kicked the covers off, swung his legs out of bed and with a profound sense of well being, broke into a long stretch. He got up to get dressed, pausing to stare at his clothes neatly folded on a chair and not recalling folding them before going to bed. He took his pants and while stepping into them, images of a meadow full of people around him drifted in and out of his mind. "Crazy dream," he mumbled, buckling his pants, and the image of Kim drifted in front of him. A surge of excitement engulfed him, thinking of her as he pulled his head through his shirt and he suddenly remembered and groaned, "Oh, god…the kitchen."

David looked at the chair again and now realized he didn't remember getting into bed at all. In, fact he didn't remember anything after his encounter in the kitchen. Pleasant thoughts of Kim vanished and were replaced with Rishi and the Fabricator. He nervously looked around while slipping his shoes on and glanced at the clock. Roberto and Pam will be showing up for work soon. He stopped and tried to think, did he lock up? God, he couldn't remember anything. He had to get downstairs to the diner.

He raced to the bedroom door, grabbed the knob but hesitated and slowly, quietly cracked the door open. He ventured a peek and after seeing nothing unusual, swung it wide open. Out of sheer habit, he walked straight to the coffee maker but stopped with his hand on the empty pot. No, no…he would go downstairs to make it and he could start the clean up.

He cautiously glanced around, still weirded out by the thought that Rishi must have brought him up here and…did he undress him? He shuddered at the bizarre thought, pushing away images of him being tucked in bed and Rishi folding his clothes while he slept. The phone next to him suddenly rang and he jumped. "Damn it," he growled and let it ring a couple of times before picking up the receiver.

"Boss! Madre de Dios…" Roberto shouted.

"Roberto stop, wait a minute," David said. "It's ok, everything's ok, just…just start cleaning up," he instructed and then paused. He had said what he needed and was now letting Roberto complain a bit. "I know…I…," David chimed in while glancing at the coffee, now thinking he might just walk down with a cup. He wedged the phone against his shoulder and reached for the kettle but something outside on the patio caught his eye.

From the kitchen he could see out the sliding glass doors where potted plants along the railing threw their shadows across the terracotta tiles in the morning sun. The shadow of a tall shrub just around the corner seemed to be moving oddly in the desert breeze.

He assumed it was probably a large bird until an arm came out and grabbed the railing.

He flinched, the phone fell from his shoulder and he stared, realizing somebody was out there.

He kept his eyes on the shadow, moving sideways across the back of the room until he could see who it was and stopped to chuckle, "There must be a mistake," he said, staring at the pudgy lady in a bright yellow dress.

She looked to be middle aged with a matching yellow hat and purse, all with large flower prints of daisies on them. She was leaning against the railing, looking out at the desert as if on vacation. He walked straight to the doors and slid them open. "Excuse me, can I help you?" he said.

The lady didn't answer and kept looking out at the desert. He wondered if she might be hard of hearing and stepped out onto the patio next to her and said loudly, "Excuse me, this is a private res – "

"I love this time in the morning," she exclaimed, cutting him off but keeping her gaze on the horizon. She took a deep breath and exhaled slowly. "Smell the fresh air…Everything is waking up, coming to life for a new day." She then rolled on the railing to face him. "And how are *you* feeling this morning, David?"

Perplexed, David's eyes darted over her face. "Have we met before?" he asked.

"Oh, yes…" she said, keeping a curious eye on him. "So? How do you feel?"

David politely but firmly answered, "Fine, but you need to tell me who you are and what you're doing here."

She smiled a little mischievously with a sparkle in her eye and said, "David, do you truly believe you are talking to a little old lady?"

Stunned, he took a step back "No, not another one…"

"Bingo," she said gleefully and walked over to one of the lounge chairs. "I love that word," she added while sitting down, then gestured for him to join her.

"What happened to the bald guy…Rishi?" David asked.

"Oh, you'll see him again," she said, reaching into her purse and pulling out a tube of lipstick. "You had a lot on your mind last night." She said while eyeing the rotating red tip popping up.

He grimaced and rubbed his face. "Rishi showed me something…he told me I had to remember something," he said, looking out at the desert and straining with brain fog.

"And, do you?" she asked while peering into a compact and circling her lips.

David shook his head. "Bits and pieces," he muttered. He looked back at her and was struck by the way she was doing her lips, pursed, head tilted back slightly while gazing into the mirror…all exactly the way his Aunt Margie used to do.

He had lost his Aunt Margie when he was a kid but never forgot the summers he spent visiting her. She lived in a quaint San Diego bay beach-front cottage. He had made lots of friends in the neighborhood, and they all looked forward to playing together on those long summer days, sometimes in the water, sometimes until dark, but always tons of fun.

One summer in particular turned out to be very important and special to him. It was a time of awkwardness, his body and mind struggling to agree on how to handle the different dynamics going on inside him, hormonal mostly. He woke up every morning to more muscles, growing hair in new places, embarrassing pimples and an unrelenting impulse, pulling his attention to his groin area.

Somehow Aunt Margie knew, and through casual but very interesting conversations, she offered valuable guidance for him. She would bring up random species in the animal kingdom or facts about early humans breeding habits; even plants and insects weren't excluded from her parables. They would have interesting, mostly one-sided conversations where he could ask anything he wanted, and she would present it in such a way that he could privately apply it to his life.

With her help, he realized he was normal with perfectly normal urges. She made him feel safe and comfortable. He cherished their brief encounters at breakfast or sitting out on the deck, sharing her wisdom of the world. He didn't realize until long after she was gone just how smart she really was and how much she really cared for him, in a way his mother had trouble showing.

It had been such a long time since he had seen her. He looked at this person on his patio, amazed at how remarkably similar she was. Even the way she closed the lipstick dispenser, dropped it in her purse along with the compact and snapped the whole works shut. It was unnerving.

The lady in yellow looked up from her purse with the familiar glint in her eye and the smile that always accompanied it and said, "There's my Davy."

Chapter 12

Kim looked into the packed conference room and saw Roberts standing at the podium. He was reviewing his notes while soldiers, techs and suits were milling around, getting settled for the meeting. She spotted a few agents from her department in the back row and headed for them.

Roberts looked up occasionally, scouring the crowd very much like a predator and noticed Kim making her way through the noisy room. He watched her all the way until she took a seat, and when she looked up, their eyes met. For reasons unknown, she has always been immune to his intimidating tactics and kept her attention on him, unblinking, unwavering until he looked away.

"Mother fuck! Did you see the look Roberts was giving you?" the agent next to her said and then turned to the other agent next to him. "Did you see that?"

"Yeah…holy shit." the other agent said out the side of his mouth.

"You gonna be OK, Nichols?" the agent next to her asked with a chuckle.

"He always does that," she droned, "but he does seem edgier than usual today."

"*Oh*, that's right, I heard your partner got a little trigger happy last night," the agent snickered.

Kim turned to him, "I wish someone would explain to me the logic for teaming us up with the local yokels. He almost got me killed."

"Been there," one agent said, laughing, and the other added, "At least your contact survived, unlike mine last year." Both agents chuckled now while Kim glanced around, then the agent next to her sneered again, "So did you get yours to talk without kicking the shit out of him?"

"No…" she said hesitantly but added, "Doesn't mean I won't later."

The other two agents glanced at each other and laughed. She knew they were acknowledging her reputation. She was one of the agency's top assets who frequently and consistently used her abilities to get results. She had considered Cooper as just another assignment, but her emotions kept taking her by surprise and she realized she was stewing.

No, Cooper wasn't just another assignment. Something else was going on and she was having trouble putting her finger on it. While wondering why she didn't smack him when he put his hands on her she felt it again. It wasn't what he did but how he did it that threw her. There were feelings that came along with it that needed to be understood. She looked around the conference room and she had to stop thinking about him, it was distracting and taking her off her game.

Roberts abruptly looked up from his notes, "OK, gentlemen…Let's get started," he said pausing, giving the crowd a chance to quiet down. "As you all know, we had an incident last night that has changed the dynamics of our program." He paused again, until the stragglers wrapped up their conversations. "For over ten years we have been prodding and probing for answers and finally we got some. We now have a mountain of data that needs to be deciphered to give this department the best comprehensive interpretation and that is why you are here. You have all been selected for your abilities to contribute to this program and you newcomers will be expected to fill in areas lacking. It is of the utmost importance that we function as a group and communicate accordingly," he said. He paused to check out the room, wanting to look everyone in the eye. He then held up a folder. "On the cover of your briefing folder there is a room number informing you where your assigned group will meet. There you will find your team leader who will guide your efforts." He paused again to let the group absorb this.

"Gentlemen, we are only interested in results for the benefit of this program and do not have time for dramas or egos…those who insist on expelling energy on either will be gone."

"Colonel?" a voice rang out from a group of men mostly wearing lab coats. It was an older man with wild, unkempt white hair, flipping through his briefing papers. "Can you elaborate on the data you have here?" he said skeptically "…antigravity?"

Roberts glanced to the front row. "Professor?"

There was a stirring in the front and Professor Cathcart stood up and began making his way to the podium. "Professor Cathcart will now answer any of your technical questions," Roberts said as he stepped back.

Cathcart stepped behind the podium, glanced at the colleague who had spoken out and they exchanged nods. "Good morning, gentlemen…and ladies," he said acknowledging the half dozen or so women scattered in the group.

"Yesterday morning at this time, if you had said to me that we had on this base an anti-gravity machine, I would have had you escorted out of here," Cathcart elaborated as he looked to his colleague again. "Larry, you know as well as I do that for me to explain anti-gravity, I need to be able to explain gravity first and no one has been able to do that yet. Well, let me rephrase that. No one except the individuals who created the craft in our possession." A slight smile grew on his face. "And what's really amazing about this is…they were doing it over a million years ago."

"Excuse me, Professor," a crusty military man gruffly interrupted, "for breaking into your intimate moment of science appreciation, but I would like to get back to brass tacks, if you don't mind."

"Certainly," Cathcart said, squinting to see the officer's rank. "What would you like to know, General?"

"What's the curb weight on this thing?"

"Ten tons, give or take," Cathcart answered dryly.

"Give or take?" the officer replied irritated. "Don't you know how much it weighs? What kind of— "

"—it fluctuates." Cathcart stopped him with a hand up.

The officer looked surprised, "What do you mean it fluctuates?"

"Since last night's incident, its "curb" weight, as you put it, has not been consistent by as much as 300 lbs.

A notable wave of murmuring made its way through the group while the officer shook his head. "Well, I have to see this for myself. When are you showing the footage?"

Cathcart glanced at his notes for a second then said, "Maybe it's best to run the video now and then discuss it later. Does anyone have any comments or questions before we do?" A silent pause followed and he gave a nod toward the back of the room. The lights went out and a large screen lit up behind him, displaying an image that brought a few gasps around the room.

It wasn't the fact that there weren't any fins or wings or even an exhaust port. It was the light-absorbing blackness of it. Closely resembling the body of a stealth fighter, it was relatively flat on the bottom, but the rounded top section was covered with geometrically angled protrusions. It was so effective at not reflecting light that it better resembled a black hole in the screen with only its silhouette being visible.

Cathcart glanced up from his notes to the screen and leaned into the microphone, "Show the interior feed first."

The screen blipped and the image on the wall changed to a lab tech reading from a tablet while another tech entered information on a digital display. They were recording the time, date and take number with a title of the procedure about to be done. One of the techs then reached to a dark gray surface, relatively flat with a slight tilt toward him on what appeared to be a control panel. It was embedded with an assortment of different-sized, brushed silver spheres with approximately the top third of them exposed and randomly placed. The camera followed his hand as he reached for one of them and paused. A laser counter came on with a digital readout that began a count as he slowly moved it to a predetermined position. "Check," the tech noted when done.

Cathcart again leaned into the microphone and stated, "It will happen during the third sequence."

The group hushed while they watched. The stillness became unnerving as life in the room seemed to stop. All eyes were on the tech's hand, slowly turning the sphere in the third sequence when the video image began to move erratically.

"Earthquake!" someone yelled in the video as it became impossible to follow, slashing side-to-side. There was a sudden radical jerk and then the picture stabilized. A tech's face popped onto the screen, excitedly yelling, pointing to the control panel, and the camera swung over to the instruments seemingly alive and lit up with a stunning display of lights.

"Pause it," Cathcart ordered.

Arms came up, pointing fingers with excited murmuring amongst the members of the group.

The still image had captured blue illuminated holograms floating over the spheres with integrated patterns of unfamiliar shapes and symbols. No one said it, and no one had to, that whoever created and piloted this craft was light years ahead of humans.

"OK, run the outside feed now," Cathcart directed. The illuminated image flickered away and the ship's exterior image blipped up on the screen. "On the lower right, gentlemen, it will happen at 22:46, 38 sec," he stated.

The room came alive briefly, the group exchanging theories, and quickly hushed in anticipation as the clock counted down.

Within seconds of the target time, there was a slight shaking but it was minimal since the exterior camera was securely mounted at a distance. But the rumbling could clearly be heard and the techs working under it could be seen struggling not to fall, some grabbing hold of nearby equipment. Then the ship began to rise and the restraining cables became taught, the shortest one first, throwing the craft into a wobble. But the ship stabilized and levitated inches above the manmade supports. For a moment, ominously still on the screen, the ship hovered then slowly settled to a soft landing.

The lights came back on and Roberts again took his place at the podium. "As you can see, gentlemen, we have more questions than answers and time is of the essence," he said, studying the faces of the racing minds deep in thought. "You will now report to your group locations for your selective briefings…that is all."

Kim heard her name called over the rustling and looked toward Roberts. "My office," he said with a piercing look.

"Oooh shit, man…I don't envy you," one agent said.

"What, are you kidding?" she replied to both agents grinning at her, "The pressure's off, *man*. My job was to help get this thing started and now I bet I'm getting some time off…I'm thinking the Bahamas," she speculated, rolling her eyes.

Both agents lost their smartass smiles and the one closest to her sheepishly replied with lifted eyebrows, "Want some company?" his words hanging in the air.

She gave him a smile and a look that said "in your dreams" and turned away.

Chapter 13

On her way to Roberts's office, Kim wondered if it was something she had for breakfast that wasn't agreeing with her. She still couldn't shake the jittery feeling that something was not right; it just didn't make sense and she should be feeling great.

Roberts was sitting at his desk poring over a file. "Shut the door and have a seat," he said without looking. She sat down with perfect posture, crossed her legs and waited patiently. He was scrutinizing something in the file and she wondered why he wasn't in a better mood. Then again, in all the years she had known him, she had never seen him smile…ever. Some people are just like that, she reminded herself, and speculated that his next move would be to figure out how to weaponize the ship. He's probably doing that right now, she thought, and was glad that it wasn't in her field of expertise. She was an investigator and interrogator and could smell a lie a mile away, but science and mechanics baffled her. She watched him flip through a couple of pages and thought it funny that she worked for a guy that, of all the people she had ever met, was one of the hardest to read.

"What do you have for me, Nichols?" he abruptly said, looking up from his paperwork.

She was ready for him and began her report. "Sir, I assessed Cooper not to be an active threat against national security and presently without cause for any future concern. He basically is clueless to the asset we are seeking and why he has been a person of interest."

"Not anymore, he isn't," Roberts said, slapping the file closed. "Turns out he found what we're looking for and has already secured it in another location."

"What?" Kim said, aghast, "I…I know he didn't have it when I interviewed him," she said frowning, noticing the nagging feeling getting stronger in her gut. She thought for a moment then asked, "How do you know he has it?"

"Once I knew of the device's location in the restaurant, I sent a recon team in and found evidence that Cooper had removed it."

"You've already searched his home?"

"A quick sweep, while he slept. He doesn't know we've been there but now that the ship has become active I'm going to take him into custody and tear that place apart to find it."

She tried to hide her uneasiness, knowing the department wasn't exactly on the grid for any kind of human rights regulations.

Roberts's sharp eye caught her subtle show of emotion, and studying her, he got an idea. "Nichols, I need you to focus on finding the device and this is how you are going to do it. I want you to go to Cooper's house and see if you can get him to give it up voluntarily. You'll be wired and we will be in your perimeter." He then surprised her with a slight smile. It was forced and awkward and she didn't trust it for a second. "You see, Nichols, once I have what I want, I won't have any use for Cooper anymore," he said, his smile growing.

Kim already knew he was lying, but her mind was elsewhere. Something was wrong, none of this made sense. "But, sir…uhh…what's the big deal now that you got the ship working? You did it without the device, so Carl was wrong. Why all the drama?"

Roberts dropped the smile, stared at her for a hard moment and finally said, "This doesn't leave this room."

She was taken aback and had never heard him talk this way before, "Okay…yes, sir," she said tentatively.

His voice became low and grim, "We didn't start up the ship," he admitted.

"But I saw…"

"It was done remotely by the device and I believe it was Cooper. We traced the signal to his house."

She turned numb inside, reeling at just how serious the situation was. There were a number of questionable items on the ship that were still unexplained and could possibly be weapons. Now, if it could be controlled from a distance…she shuddered at how they could all be vulnerable.

Roberts watched her for a moment and said, "Nichols, I like it when somebody keeps one in the chamber." He looked up and yelled, "Jackson!"

The door flew open and his assistant, a muscular six-foot-five soldier, came in and snapped to attention. "Sir!"

"It's time...let's roll."

Chapter 14

"How? I went to your funeral…you're dead," David said.

"Dead?" she said, frowning, "It sounds so final when you say it that way."

"Well, people usually don't come back," he said, warily looking her over, "Wait a minute…how do I know that thing…the *Fabricator*, didn't just read my mind and make you from my memories?"

"You don't," she giggled, seemingly enjoying their conversation. "Look, you understand enough now to know that I'm from another world and trying to define me in earthly terms is going to be difficult. I suggest an open-minded approach." She paused, giving him time to think it over, just like she used to do when he was a kid.

He looked at her a little miffed. "So, my Aunt Margie wasn't real?"

"I assure you, I was and am as human as you are," she said.

"I find that hard to believe," he said skeptically and stared at her for a moment. "Rishi said he was from another dimension and his body was made for him so he could exist here. I assume it's the same for you?"

"That's right," she said, and set her purse down on the floor next to her, adjusting her seat and crossing her ankles.

David stayed standing. He wasn't ready to get comfortable just yet. "So, what are you then…when not in *this* dimension? Are you like an entity or something?"

"That's a perfect word for it," she said, tapping her finger on the chair's arm "This sort of thing doesn't exist where I come from."

"You don't have lounge chairs?"

She smiled endearingly at him. "Matter, David...stuff...things are done differently there."

"Differently where—where *is* this place?"

She thought for a moment. "Words...it's hard to describe something so abstract, but probably the most familiar name to you that best describes it would be Aether...*the Aether*."

"Ether...a gas?"

She chuckled, "Sounds the same, but it's a place where matter cannot exist, not even gas."

"So its matter you're here to study."

"At first we were, we tried to bring matter into our world, but it became too unstable there and we realized it was better to study it in its own setting. The only catch was we needed to figure out how to get into a body to explore this dimension, and that happened around a million of your Earth years ago."

David's expression turned to disbelief. "You've been visiting Earth for a million years."

"In the flesh, yes."

"How long does it take to study matter?"

Aunt Margie chuckled at his sarcasm. "There are a lot more differences in our worlds than the absence of matter, for instance the need for a lifespan."

David scoffed, "Oh, now you're saying you live forever?"

"You are thinking in Earthly terms, David. Consider the differences between our worlds. Evolution in my world is achieved through the growth of consciousness, but on Earth evolution is a process of the planet's species, constantly adjusting to a changing environment through evolving generations."

"Your world hasn't changed…at all…for a million years," he said.

She watched him for a moment then asked, "Have you ever noticed that everything you relate to is influenced by the fact that you have a lifespan? Thirty, fifty, eighty years ago…a lifetime ago seems like such a long time to you, but in all actuality, it's but a minuscule blip in your evolution."

He nodded along, droning, "Yeah, heard it before, *we're but a grain of sand on the beach of life.*"

"My world hasn't changed for billions of your Earth years…yet it doesn't seem like such a long time to me."

He thought for a moment, "Why come as my aunt then, if you're here to explore matter?"

"If I had taken the form of, say, a Kodiak bear, would you want to be having a conversation with me? Of course not, we wouldn't be getting anywhere now, would we? It's always been a juggling act between the necessity to fit in and being effective," she said, raising her eyebrows. "Don't you see?"

"So, you're not here just to learn about matter, you're doing something with humans, too," he said.

"Matter and all of Earth's creatures were understood quickly, except for humans, something happened…something we needed to understand. It happened the first time we set foot on this planet *as* a human."

"Why, did one of your clones malfunction?" He chuckled.

"Not as a human clone, as a human *born*."

"How does that happen?" he asked. His demeanor turning serious, "You take over a body in the womb?"

"Who said anything about taking over a body?"

"What about the poor soul that was supposed to live that life?

"No, David, there isn't any replacing of a person with an Entity."

"How else do you get involved when two humans are mating?"

She looked at him, head leaning a little to the side and her eyes sparkling, "Easy when one of the partners is a clone. Then it's just a matter of good old fashion mating."

"Your clones had sex with Earthlings?"

She looked surprised at him, "Why should we be denied such a pleasant experience?"

David stared at her speechless while she waved him off. "We had been having sex for hundreds of years before we decided to conceive. Anyway, where was I?"

"Something happened," David muttered, still groping for a level perspective.

"Right, an unexpected result came when merging the world of the Aether and the human ancestral lineage."

David glanced at her, "I'll bet that was weird."

"To say the least. Turns out we are stripped of all cognitive knowledge and essentially reborn as a human infant with human ancestral instincts, but also with intuitive links to the Aether at the same time."

"So you don't know you are an Entity when you do this? What was that like, growing up a million years ago, in a tribe as a hominid?"

"Luckily, not much is expected from a new-born and actually the same applied to the cloned individuals we had in place to help guide the whole works."

"In place? How did you manage that?"

"When they showed up with game and a knack for building shelters, they were eagerly welcomed into the tribe and especially by the target female who was drawn to the individual specially cloned for her."

"I still don't get it, what's in it for you?"

"It's the journey of self discovery we had never experienced before. When a life cycle was completed and we returned to the Aether we discovered it was a new way to grow, it was a new type of consciousness. Our beings were enriched."

He glanced at her pudgy figure, poised so comfortably in the lounge chair. "Then why come as clones anymore?"

"There are times, lots of them actually, when we need to appear to offer guidance to Entities struggling and help them stay on their path. We don't always appear as people; sometimes we appear as animals, you know, pets, that sort of thing."

David slowly sat down and thought for a moment. "What if you appeared as a bear…a clone of a Kodiak bear, would you think as you are now and be in a bear's body talking with me or think like a real bear and just want to eat me?"

She chuckled briefly at the thought, then soberly said, "We never forget who we are when we take over a *cloned* body, no matter what the species or its stage of growth. You see, all things created are done so for a purpose. Now, if my purpose was to appear here and eat you, then a bear would have been a good choice and even though a talking bear is possible, it really doesn't make much sense, now does it?"

David glanced at his lap and shook his head, "I guess I could have phrased that better," he said and looked at her with a question he had to ask: "Are you the same *entity* that was my Aunt Margie when I was a kid?"

"Yes, of course, David…it's me."

"Then, if you can come here and do all this stuff, anyway you want…why did you leave?"

She affectionately looked at him and said, "So you could grow, David, take what I gave you and claim it as yours."

He felt a rush of emotion as he remembered so many things he wanted to tell her after she was gone. "You know, you did some really special things for me while I was growing up and it means more than anything to me…you changed my life."

"You've always been a very special person to me, David, and it's important that while you are here, you get your chance to have the experiences you are meant to have."

A quiet moment followed while they sat in the lounge chairs, the morning sun warming them in the pleasant desert breeze. David curiously looked at her and said, "Is that why you've come back?"

"Oh, yes. You are going to need some help…a lot sooner than you think."

Puzzled, he stared at her for a moment as someone knocked on the front door.

Chapter15

Kim was waiting with her hands clasped behind her back. "Morning, David…can we talk?" she asked, brushing past him without waiting for an answer.

"Well, now's not really a good time…" he said.

Kim stopped in her tracks when she saw Aunt Margie coming in from the patio. "Oh, I'm sorry, you have company?"

"Uh, Kim, this is my Aunt Margie."

"Well, hello there, Kim." Aunt Margie took her hand and gently shook it. "I'm so glad to finally meet you. David has spoken so highly of you," she said, smiling.

Kim's eyes narrowed. "So, what side of the family are you on?" she inquired, holding still to give the camera on her lapel the best viewing angle.

Aunt Margie grinned. "Right…David said you are an excellent investigator." She patted her hand and let go, talking as she walked to the sofa, "I'm Julie's sister, and I'm here checking up on my nephew," she said and sat down.

"Oh, I see, and where are you from?" Kim asked as cordially as she could but baffled as they had not come across any of David's living relatives.

"England, I'm from England dear, ever been?"

In an unmarked van not far from the diner, Roberts looked over the shoulder of a soldier peering at a computer with Aunt Margie's information popping up under her picture.

He stopped reading the unremarkable mounds of data verifying a life that never existed and spoke into Kim's earpiece, "Nichols, forget her and focus on getting the device."

Kim smiled at the lady and said, "No, I haven't and I'm very sorry for your loss, but, would you mind if I have a word with David alone?"

"Certainly not, my dear," she said, getting up, "and might I suggest having your visit out on the patio where it is a *beautiful* day." She smiled, "Would you like some tea?" she added while heading toward the kitchen.

"No, thank you," Kim replied, watching her until she was at the sink running water. She lost her smile and turned to David. "Why didn't you tell me you knew where it was?" she growled.

David's eyebrows went up. "Whoa, now wait a minute," he said, stepping back.

"You're a liar! That's what you are!" she snapped.

"Look, first of all, I don't know what you are talking about."

"You come on as a nice guy, but you're just like all the rest; selfish, manipulative, a rat bastard!"

He glanced toward Aunt Margie who still had her back to them and reached for Kim's arm. "Maybe we should take this outside," he whispered.

Kim wheeled her arm free and shoved him. "Just answer me, where is it?!" she demanded.

David stared at her in disbelief and then said through gritted teeth, "If you want to talk, I'll be out on the patio."

In the surveillance van, Roberts and his soldiers were captivated, staring at their monitors as if watching an episode of their favorite soap opera. "Nichols, what the hell are you doing?" Roberts finally said into her earpiece.

Kim reached up and promptly pulled it out of her ear and stuffed it into her pocket, wondering the same thing.

David was waiting for her. "How did you know I have it?" he demanded, folding his arms.

She stared at him, her mouth dropping, "So, you *do* have it!" she fumed.

He cringed. That was not the reaction he was expecting. He leaned against the railing and exhaled, "Did...I *did* have it, but not anymore." He then calmly walked to a lounge chair and sat down.

"What do you mean?" she said, following him and sitting down in the chair next to him "David, we don't have much time. The Agency knows you have it."

David scoffed, brushing at his wrinkled pants. "Agency? And what agency is this again?"

"You don't know these guys. They don't play by any rules. This can get ugly, fast."

"Oh, god, a secret agency, really?" he groaned.

Kim couldn't be more serious. "David, people have disappeared and have never been seen again."

David glanced at her. "They can't do that, it's illegal!" he said with contempt, then became indifferent, leaning back in his chair. "It doesn't matter anyway, once it came on and started flying around. Well, I can tell you this...there is no controlling it," he declared.

"What do you mean it came on...it actually turned on?" Kim stammered.

"Oh, yeah," David laughed lightly. "You could say that," he joked, pausing when he saw her frantically looking around the patio. "What's the matter, what is it?" he asked. She was too upset to talk. "Look," he said, trying to calm her, "it's here on a peaceful mission, it's totally nonviolent!"

"What?!" she gasped, her huge eyes locked on him, "You communicated with it?"

"Will you calm down and let me explain?"

"Are you crazy? You have no idea what you are dealing with here. Where is it now?" she demanded.

"Relax. There's nothing to worry about." David fanned his palms at her. She was being ridiculous. "Look, I was afraid of it, too…especially when I saw it could disappear. Now, that was a surprise I never expected, but—"

Kim bolted to her feet, standing on top of the chair, weapon drawn and began circling, frantically.

"Whoa, whoa, whoa!" David yelled, ducking every time her gun swung past him. "What the hell are you doing?"

A thunderous blast suddenly vibrated the walls of the house, spinning Kim around before she fell on the ground at David's feet. They froze in disbelief, staring into the darkness of the living room at a swarm of green lasers, bristling in all directions. Tactical soldiers in black gear poured out onto the patio, screaming profanities and pointing their assault weapons at David.

"Don't move," Kim said, getting up.

"Wouldn't think of it," David said, looking at the cluster of green dots on his chest while slowly raising his hands.

"Make a hole!" Roberts' voice boomed inside.

Hushed and parting like the Red Sea for Moses, Roberts paraded through his men onto the patio like an ego-twisted dictator.

Kim began to say, "Sir, it can cloak—"

"—I heard!" Roberts cut her off and motioned to a couple of soldiers next to David. "Get him up."

"All right, all right, take it easy. I'm getting up," David said, but was abruptly yanked to his feet anyway and dragged to Roberts.

Roberts eyeballed him all the way over and stared hard at him for a moment, then bellowed, "Well, anything?"

"Negative, Sir." A soldier nearby sounded off, his eyes glued to a handheld scanner.

Roberts scowled. "Scan the whole place!" and a handful of soldiers, all with scanners, quickly set out in different directions.

Roberts turned to David. "Do you like your restaurant and home here, Cooper?"

David didn't respond and Roberts didn't care. "Because if I don't get what I want, I will tear this place apart until I do."

"You don't have to do that, I'll tell you exactly what I told her, I don't have it, alright? I don't have it!" David declared.

A commotion at the doorway drew everyone's attention and there was ornery Aunt Margie resisting the soldiers' awkward attempts to get her to come out to the patio. David flattened his eyebrows at her while Roberts briefly looked her up and down with indifference.

"Last chance, Cooper," Roberts sneered. "What did you do with it? And don't tell me it just disappeared."

David stared blankly back at Roberts, paralyzed by the words taken right out of his mouth.

"Take him!" Roberts snapped, his patience gone. He headed for the door and saw Aunt Margie standing there, looking on. "Her, too!" he ordered loudly, then hollered over his shoulder on his way out, "Find it gentlemen!"

David was being led away by the two soldiers when he stopped at the pile of food on his kitchen floor. "Oh, come on you guys," he yelled at the soldiers digging in his pantry. "You're not going to find anything in there!"

"Let's go!" the soldier behind him growled with a shove, "I'll cuff you if I have to."

David glanced over his shoulder as the soldiers led him away and saw Kim coming up behind him.

"I'll take him from here," she said and the soldiers let go. David wouldn't look at her as they walked quietly to the door, but she glanced at him a number of times. "Look, I'm really sorry about all this," she said, as they started down the stairs. "Hopefully this won't take long, and don't worry about Roberts. He's just mad because, well…he's always mad."

David kept quiet all the way to the car where they stopped and she stepped in front of him. "David, you said it can camouflage itself, but do you have any idea where it might have gone?"

He was looking off to the side, wondering why he was playing this stupid game of guilt. He wanted her to be interested in him but this wasn't the way to do it.

"David, look at me," she snapped.

He faced her, looking tired and irritated. "Look, it's like I said, it can fly and disappear but what I didn't tell you…" He paused, glancing past her to Aunt Margie pleasantly chatting with a couple of soldiers. He couldn't think of one reason to give her up and decided to keep her secret for now. "What I didn't tell you is that it can fly without a sound and could be floating right here next to us…right now."

Her expression kept changing back and forth between disbelief and fear while looking around, wondering if it was possible.

"In you go," a soldier barked, opening the door for David, and a perplexed Kim watched him slowly get in. She circled around to the other side of the car, and when she slid in, he caught a glimpse of her legs, very much like a dancer's, he thought.

She sat closer than she needed to but her mind seemed elsewhere as he let his eyes wander over her, welcoming the distraction. He gazed past her, out her window to Aunt Margie sitting in the back seat of the car next to them, talking away. She had all the soldiers smiling, explaining something, and he heard them all laugh loudly.

Kim looked over, too, and groaned, "David, I'm really sorry about getting your aunt involved with all this, too. I don't think she should have been taken along."

He chuckled, glancing at her, "Oh, don't worry about my aunt. She can take care of herself and, believe me, those guys have no idea who they are dealing with."

"Oh, god!" Kim whispered and he felt her hand squeeze his knee as the passenger door opened.

Professor Cathcart got in but David couldn't care less. He was more concerned about the hold Kim's hand had on his leg. Out of context, of course, he began entertaining tinges of lust for her, but she pulled her hand away as the professor spun around.

Throwing his elbow over the seat, the professor fumbled with his recorder and quickly became irritated that it wasn't cooperating. "David, tell me everything you can about the device and start from the beginning," he said, still fighting with the recorder and finally pushing the right button.

"And you are…?" David said with as much snarkiness as he could muster.

Cathcart abruptly looked up, surprised, then incensed, turned the recorder off.

Kim quickly jumped in to defuse the pending confrontation. "David, this is Professor Cathcart. He's head of the scientific division of our agency."

"Oh, right, the highly classified *secret* agency," David said sarcastically.

Kim stared at him, slightly shaking her head as if to say, *don't, this is not a person to screw with.*

"Listen, mister, the moment you decided to dabble with highly classified property of the United States government, you made a huge mistake!" the professor berated.

David stared back, concerned, then turned to Kim. "Did he just call me mister? Because it's about time I got some respect around here."

Kim turned away, looked down, letting her hair cover her face.

"I'm going to get what I want, one way or another," Cathcart hissed, "so you might as well cooperate."

They stared at each other in silence as the driver's door opened up, and a soldier got in and started the car. They were jostling through the dirt parking lot when the professor finally said, "Ok Cooper, have it your way. I can see right now, I'm going to have a ball taking you apart, piece by piece."

David grimaced, and then interjected, "You know, your head was bobbling around a lot when you said that, so it's really kind of hard to take you seriously."

The professor smiled as he turned away and David looked at Kim for approval, but she was looking out her window. He didn't care what anybody thought because this whole thing sucked. Who the hell do these people think they are? Just because they have convinced themselves they have some imperative agenda going on, they think they are justified to impose their crap on other people's lives? It's a bunch of bull shit, he thought, clenching his teeth.

They drove through the desert in silence while David scanned the dry plains, trying to guess where they were taking him. It was obviously somewhere out in the desert, but where? They were headed for some low-rolling hills where he and his buddies used to ride their dirt bikes. One time he recalled getting kicked out of a fenced-in area, a government agricultural project of some sort. They were about fourteen and they had stopped their bikes at the fence and looked at the giant greenhouse. There was a rumor going around school that huge pot plants were being grown inside. They didn't see anybody as they looked around and even the caretaker's house seemed abandoned. They decided to investigate. They steeled themselves, opened the fence and snuck in.

After wiping the dust off the first window, they saw ordinary plants and a worker tending them in the distance. "Hey! You kids get outta here!!" the man in overalls yelled at them from the porch. It scared them and they ran like hell to their dirt bikes. He remembered looking over his shoulder and seeing the man laughing. They saw exactly what everyone in town had been saying for years. It was a perfect example of our tax dollars being wasted and, of course, they kept the story alive.

They rode quietly as the car jostled along and he wondered why they would be growing plants way out in the middle of the desert. He looked at the back of Cathcart's head and the thought of torture crossed his mind. He felt a chill. Maybe he'd been handling this all wrong.

Chapter 16

The greenhouse looked the same, covered with years of dust, sun bleached and weather beaten along with everything else around it. They raced through the open gate, held open by soldiers, and David stared at the assault weapons slung over their shoulders. Now that was new. The lead jeep veered off toward the guard shack while the convoy swiftly accelerated, past the greenhouse, throwing dust and rocks along the way.

They careened deep into the restricted area, passing a line of quonset huts surrounded by more trucks and jeeps. A large building with a helicopter sitting in front of it appeared to be their destination. Its huge doors, large enough for an airplane to get through, opened and the caravan entered without slowing.

Tires screeched on concrete as they raced through the spacious building and descended down a ramp. Tail lights shone brightly in front of them as they leaned to the side, corkscrewing into the ground. They ended up in a huge underground parking area and drove past more trucks and military vehicles, including a jeep with a submachine gun mounted in the back. David glanced around at the huge facility wondering how nobody in town knew about any of this. They must have been working in the middle of the night for years.

Aunt Margie and her escorts were out of the lead vehicle and walking to a set of steel doors where Roberts' assistant, Jackson, was standing, half a head higher than the rest of the soldiers. David's car pulled into a parking space as he watched Aunt Margie reaching out to shake Jackson's hand.

Suddenly his door opened. "Out you go," the soldier ordered.

David got out, gawking at the ceiling that was at least twenty feet high. "What is this place? It's *huge*," he said.

"The less you know the better, really," Kim said, gesturing for him to follow Cathcart. She put her hand on the small of his back, not pushy but friendly. He looked at her and saw her smile. It was guarded and brief but better than nothing. At this point he was grateful for any allies he could get…he had decided to cooperate.

They came up as Jackson stood in the middle of the soldiers, all listening intently to Aunt Margie while she waved her hands, animating a story. "So, you see, the locals ran up to the plane just as the propellers were stopping and began celebrating their rescue, expecting to see their hero come out of the cockpit and greet them. But instead, the pilot had to pee so badly that he didn't even notice them as he stood on the edge of the wing relieving himself."

The eruption of laughter filled the underground parking lot like an echoing cavern.

"Ten – Hut!" a voice rang out.

The laughter stopped and the clomping of boots echoed in the underground as Roberts stood in the midst of his men. "Sounds to me like there's a party going on and I haven't been invited!" he bellowed.

"Sir! No sir!" the soldiers yelled in unison.

David looked on disgusted by the ego shit show and glanced at Kim. She didn't appear to be impressed either.

Roberts took a moment to savor the discipline he had over his men, then barked, "Get them to their rooms! Cathcart, Nichols, my office!" Roberts observed the scuttling activity, then beckoned to Jackson.

"Sir!" Jackson stiffly retorted.

"At ease, Sergeant."

Jackson widened his stance, hands clasped behind his back and stood looking straight ahead. "What's the story on the aunt?" Roberts asked.

"Not much, Sir. She's oblivious to anything concerning the device. It appears she is here to help Cooper get his ass in gear and enjoy some time in the States while she's at it." He ended his remarks with a slight smile recalling something she said but caught Roberts's look and wiped it off.

Roberts thoughtfully looked away, rubbing his chin then said, "Watch her. We'll do the kid first – dismissed."

"Yes, Sir!" Jackson snapped a salute and left.

Roberts stood alone, watching the steel doors close behind Jackson and thought again how all he needed was one last thing to make it all complete. Everything he had worked for was inside those doors. Once he had control of the ship, there would be nothing to prevent him from imposing his will throughout the world.

Chapter 17

Kim crossed her legs while fondling the transmitter in her hand. She was baffled by her actions at David's house and noticed the bad feeling in her gut had returned. *What the hell is going on?* It was frustrating not being able to shake this unsettling feeling. She looked around Roberts's office and saw Cathcart had repositioned his chair, distancing himself from her. She didn't take it personally since she knew it was his way, *to keep his writings private,* he would always say, but she also knew he was socially inept. She studied him, wondering what horrific things he might have planned for David.

Suddenly the thought of David being tortured crossed her mind and simultaneously the knot in her belly intensified. She thought for a moment and realized she had been letting these feelings linger, playing in the background, expecting them to fizzle out like they had with other men she had been attracted to. Sure, he was handsome, but she found his presumptuousness irritating. Still, here she sat, waiting for Roberts, stuck with this knot of butterflies in her stomach. She had to decide whether to acknowledge her feelings and see where they led or turn her back on them and go her own way.

Roberts came in, and since neither of them was military, they remained seated. It was something he never got used to. It was one of the bitter pills he had to put up with when working with civilians.

"Nichols, let's start with you," he said, getting right to it as he sat down.

"Well, sir, Cooper told me he was in the device's presence when it became activated, apparently on its own, and it displayed acts of intelligence. Some sort of flashing lights in patterns. He said it somehow communicated with him before showing its ability to camouflage and become invisible. Unfortunately, I was unable to pursue any further questioning after that."

Roberts studied her for a moment while listening intently, "What was that I heard about being harmless and on a peaceful mission?"

"Cooper claimed it communicated this to him but, again, Sir, I was unable to continue interviewing after the interjection."

"Do you believe him?" Roberts questioned skeptically.

"Seems farfetched, but I believe *he* believes what he is saying."

Roberts listened with a few calculated nods, keeping his eyes locked on her. "One more thing, Nichols. Why'd you pull the earpiece?"

This question she had anticipated and was ready for. "I had to avoid being diverted, sir. I felt I had him reeling and ready to talk." It was a lie and she had to concentrate on her breathing to appear calm and believable. She wasn't really sure why she had pulled it, but things were starting to make sense. She had a hunch that deep down there was something going on that she needed to understand before anyone else, especially Roberts.

Roberts stared at her for a moment and then glanced at Cathcart who appeared to be amused. He leaned back in his chair and clasped his fingers behind his head. "Your thoughts, Cathcart?"

Cathcart folded his hands on his clipboard and exhaled hard. "I think it's time to abandon these lower level processes regarding Cooper and take seriously the technical challenges presenting themselves as we speak."

"So, what are you saying? This has been a total waste of time?" Roberts countered.

"All of the analytical explanations we have come up with so far have fallen short. It's imperative that we establish a credible position as to his ability to possess the device in the first place."

"So, what do you suggest?" Roberts said, leaning forward.

"Show it to him. Once inside, monitor him for any candid reactions to see if he verifies the shape of the device in the docking station."

Roberts thought it over for a moment, then slowly nodded. "Ok, so what if he recognizes the outline of the device, then what?"

"Well, if he substantiates he had possession of it, then I can eliminate any concerns for concocted facts and won't be wasting *my* time."

Roberts stared at the professor for a moment, chuckled and said, "Ok, professor, go ahead…set it up."

Kim took a deep breath and relaxed at this decision. Now if she could just figure out what was causing this pesky knot in her gut.

Chapter 18

David sat on the floor with his back to the wall, sizing up his situation. It didn't look good. He was in what looked like an operating room with two agitated soldiers guarding the door, glaring at him as if waiting for any reason to shoot him.

"You sure you guys got me in the right room?" he yelled across to them, not expecting an answer and getting none. His attention kept going to the center of the room where a solid base table was positioned under a cluster of high intensity lamps with restraining straps hanging down all around it. All it needed was blood dripping from it to complete this nightmare.

The door opened and Jackson came over, wringing his hands. "Let's go, Cooper…on the table. Doc is going to give you a little *checkup*."

"Really? Come on. You guys don't have to do this!" David said as the soldiers lifted him up to his feet. "What do you want to know? I'll tell you everything!"

"You're damn straight you will," Jackson retorted.

"Great, where do we start?" David said while his feet were dragged to the table, his hands out, catching the table's edge.

Jackson grabbed him and threw him up on the table like a toy and strapped him down in seconds.

"I said I'd cooperate," David said, now pinned on his back.

"You had your chance, Cooper! Now we're going to do it our way." Jackson said pulling something out of his cargo pants.

"You can't be serious! How am I going to talk with that thing on?" David said at the red ball attached to the leather straps dangling in front of him.

"Maybe we aren't interested in anything you gotta say," Jackson said grinning, then glanced to the side and nodded to someone out of view. In the corner of his eye, David saw a huge hypodermic moving toward him dripping a clear liquid. He squirmed in horror, yelling as it pressed against his skin, dimpling, then puncturing.

"Hold up!" A voice rang out in the room and everyone froze. Cathcart came up next to David and gestured for the injection to be withdrawn. He then glanced at Jackson's hands, still holding the leather gag and frowned.

"Just having a little fun," Jackson said, swinging the gag strap behind him.

Cathcart turned back to David and looked him over indifferently. "Undo those straps and let's get him up," he ordered.

"I tried to tell them I was cooperating," David said.

Cathcart ignored him and said blandly, "Ok, bring him along."

"Wait a minute…have I been arrested?" David demanded.

One of the soldiers chuckled as Cathcart turned back, studying David for a long, uncomfortable moment as if he were an idiot.

***

David was surrounded by soldiers as they followed Cathcart down a hallway. It had a slight curve to it and he realized they were walking in a giant underground circle. They came up to a well-guarded set of double doors held open for Cathcart by one of the soldiers.

David's escorts nudged him to follow and, stepping into the underground auditorium, was awestruck at the size of it. It was massive, at least eighty yards in diameter and probably five stories high. Highlighted in the center of the vastness surrounded by theatrical seating was a black geometrically shaped object that appeared better suited to streaking through the universe on a celestial mission than sitting motionless on manmade supports. It was elevated approximately ten feet in the air by four concrete pillars with a handful of technicians working around it.

"Keep moving," a soldier ordered with a shove. David stumbled after Cathcart who was heading toward a set of stairs. The professor stopped at the top, on a platform that stretched all the way to an opening at the side of the ship and waited for him. "See anything that looks familiar?" Cathcart asked.

David looked at him perplexed. "What, are you kidding? When would I have ever seen anything like this?"

"Just answer the question." Cathcart said, watching him closely.

"No," David answered emphatically.

"Alright, I want you to see something else. Come with me," Cathcart briskly walked toward the ship where techs were inside working under portable lights.

David had been on a few airplanes and had seen lots of pictures of the Apollo ships the U.S. used for space exploration. There was a big difference in the object he was walking into now; not really something more but rather something lacking. There were no rivets, seams, or compartment doors or openings. There were no windows. It was as if it was a solid one-piece cast object.

David followed Cathcart into the ship, looking side-to-side, and paused at what he assumed was an instrument panel. In earthly terms it seemed incomplete, lacking dials, switches or sliding levers. It only had silver spheres of different sizes randomly embedded in it. His eyes wandered over it with an intriguing sense of familiarity and then he saw it. Cathcart and the cameras were waiting, catching his reaction. "What is it, David?" Cathcart asked with bated breath.

"That—" David pointed at the recessed area in the dash, recognizing the silhouette. "The Fabricator could fit perfectly in there," he said, looking around inside. "This must be its ship."

Cathcart appeared puzzled and demanded, "Why do you call it that?"

David seemed to ignore him but was reeling at the revelation of being in the entities' vehicle.

"Answer me!" Cathcart yelled with an impatient poke for David's attention.

Startled, David took a clumsy step back. "Oh, that's right, you guys don't know about that yet," he chuckled, reaching out to steady himself and accidentally touching the control panel.

The console came to life. Holograms sprouted up above the spheres with colorful lights, some blinking, illuminating the entire surface of the panel. They stood stunned, staring at the heads-up displays of illuminated, unearthly gauges and dials in strange symbols. A deep, low shuddering began to vibrate in the ship. It grew stronger and stronger as if it were a huge bass speaker thundering and encompassing the atmosphere around them – being felt more than heard.

Someone was yelling outside. The ship moved, briefly rising up a few feet while Cathcart frantically scanned the control panel trying to understand what was happening. Suddenly the ship settled back down onto the supports and turned off.

Cathcart pushed David back, away from the control panel. "What did you touch?" he demanded.

"Ahhh, this…I think it was this," he said, pointing to one of the spheres.

Cathcart touched it. Nothing happened. "Are you sure, absolutely sure?"

"Yes…that's the one," David assured.

***

Roberts darted out of the control room as Kim turned to the tech recording the incident. "Back up the feed on Cooper," she said, and they both watched in slow motion, David backing away from Cathcart, his arm swinging down to his side. "There! Stop!" she said. "Back it up a little more. Ok, now, slowly." The monitor showed David's hand in slow motion moving over the panel with a tiny blue spark jumping up to it. His hand continued to the sphere, touching it, and a bright surge of blue energy flowed back into the panel.

***

"What happened?" Roberts yelled, bursting into the ship.

"Cooper touched it," Cathcart replied, staring at the controls in a thoughtful daze.

"Where, what'd you touch?" Roberts demanded.

David pointed.

Roberts touched it—nothing happened.

"Didn't work for me either," Cathcart said.

"Do it again!" Roberts ordered David.

David sighed. "Alright, but I have no idea what I am doing here," he said and tentatively reached out and touched it. The ship immediately shuddered, lights came back on the same as before, but this time it was brief and the ship quickly turned off.

"Whoa…that was amazing," David said, staring at his hand, mesmerized.

"Do it again!" Roberts demanded "This time keep your hand on it."

90

David touched the sphere again, keeping his hand on it as Roberts directed, but this time nothing worked. He tried touching it quickly, slowly, with a variety of motions. He even tried rubbing it, but all further attempts were fruitless.

"Hold it." Roberts finally said, stopping him and turning to Cathcart. "Well, Professor, any ideas?"

Cathcart was scratching his head and mumbled, "I'll have to look at the data."

Roberts waved a couple of soldiers over. "Put him in with his aunt," he ordered, but as they started to lead David away, Cathcart grabbed his arm. He looked closely at the palm of David's hand and then to each fingertip before letting go and turning away.

Roberts jerked his head at the soldiers to take David and waited until they were out of the ship. "What are you thinking, Cathcart?" he asked.

"Well, there is one thing that is unique about him from everyone else. When he touched the device maybe it left some kind of energy signature on him, something that it recognizes."

Roberts took a breath, fighting impatience, and glared at his professor. "We need to find out what he just did, and I don't give a shit if we have to take him apart piece by piece. I want to be able to turn my ship on without him. You think that's something you can handle?"

Cathcart took a big breath and looked up thoughtfully. "I'll need to review all the data. I'll see what I can come up with."

"How much time do you need?" Roberts asked.

"Umm, give me three hours."

"You've got two," Roberts said and turned to leave, but hesitated at the control panel. He felt it again, an excitement he had been anticipating for a long time. He went outside and paused, looked at the ship with new eyes and for the first time, allowed himself to covet it. He was so close to the power he had only dreamed of before and now it was within reach, a power he deserved.

Chapter 19

Aunt Margie appeared to be reading, slowly turning the pages of a gossip magazine but actually was listening more than anything. She was doing this solely for the benefit of the two soldiers in the adjacent room who were keeping a watchful eye on her while she communicated with the Fabricator. Having the ability to dematerialize and reappear in different rooms and cloaked to boot had its perks, and one of them was roaming throughout the base undetected. Aunt Margie sat back, relaxed, allowing the soldiers in charge of her to do the same all the while getting updates on the status of her mission.

The soldiers alternated their attention on her between the large two-way mirror in the common wall and their monitors, one to a camera inside and one out in the hallway where they noticed David being escorted to her room. The lead soldier rapped on her door a few times and they saw her look up and say something, but the audio was out.

"That's the second time that's done that. What the hell is wrong with that thing?" one of the soldiers questioned.

The other soldier shook his head and picked up the phone. "I'll call the techs."

"Excuse us, Ma'am," the soldier said to Aunt Margie and swung the door open for David.

"Well, hello, Dearie, come join me," she said patting the chair next to her.

David walked to her and sat down, but didn't return her smile.

"How are you, David?" she asked.

He turned away to watch the last soldier leave and when he closed the door behind him turned to her. "Let's cut the crap, shall we?"

"You'll have to be more specific, David, and don't forget we are not alone," she said, playfully rolling her eyes toward the large two-way mirror. "I took care of the microphone but left their visual imaging alone."

He glanced at the mirror and lowered his voice. "They can't hear us then?"

"Nope, but they can see us."

He nodded and turned toward her, "They showed me a ship, an alien ship, I think it belongs to you and your world."

"Yes, I was hoping they would," she said grinning.

"It started up when I touched the controls – why?"

She chuckled, "Why do you think?"

"Can't you just tell me?"

"I wouldn't be doing you any good if I did your thinking for you, now would I?" she responded.

"Just give me a hint."

She thought for a moment then smiled, "okay, did it start up for them?"

"No."

"So, it won't start up for them but it will for you…and me."

Chapter 20

Roberts looked determined, stepping lively with his heels pounding and echoing down the empty corridor. Without breaking stride, he turned and pushed through a door next to a sign that said STOCKADE, catching the soldiers inside off guard.

They jolted to attention with an officer standing up behind his desk, saluting. "At ease," Roberts said eager to get to the matter at hand. "Is he ready?"

"Yes, sir," the officer replied and handed him a file.

Roberts opened it up, muttering, "All right, what's the F.B.I. got on this guy." He flipped up Carl's mug shot with his thumb and scanned down the page to personal history and saw there was no birth record, nothing before his twenties. He turned to the next earmarked page with C.I.A. letterhead and found even fewer results. "Is this it?" Roberts asked in disbelief to the officer.

"Yes, sir, that's it, from all agencies."

Roberts scanned the folder again a little baffled but also intrigued at the interview he was about to have. This was one of the most extreme examples of a hidden identity that he had ever seen. Well past the name changes, plastic surgeries and deliberate shifting of behavior patterns, this individual had successfully avoided a genetic footprint all the way from birth. He had heard of a few cases of reclusive people living in the back country, born and raised without any history of the doctor visits where most DNA samples were attained. He flipped the page to their DNA results and found the one match they had discovered and wondered if the old man knew about it.

He closed the file, nodded to the sergeant, and the thick glass security door was unlocked. Two soldiers, armed with stun sticks, followed him down the hallway lined with detention doors to the last door, the only one being guarded.

Roberts stopped to peer through the door's observation window and saw his prisoner, head buried in his arms, shackled to a bolted-down table in the middle of the interrogation room. He stepped back as the heavy steel door swung open and Carl looked up, sneering. Parading into the room with indifference, Roberts adjusted the chair to his liking, taking his time and sitting down at his convenience. The two soldiers kept walking and Carl stared at their stun sticks as they circled behind him.

"I see you've brought some toys," Carl hissed. "What game are we playing today?"

Roberts leaned back in his chair, staring at his prisoner while clasping his hands over his stomach. "Refresh my memory, Carl…why were you let out of jail?"

"I can't get it if I'm locked up, now can I."

"Get *what,* Carl?"

Carl exhaled with contempt and looked away, mumbling something inaudible.

"I didn't catch that, Carl," Roberts said, flatly. "You know, Carl, I'd be more apt to believe your story if you called it by its real name."

Carl looked back surprised, eyes narrowed. "Well now, you found something, but you still don't have it, or you wouldn't be here," he grumbled.

Roberts got up, walked over to a side table and poured coffee. He turned and held it up, blew on it while eyeing Carl, in no rush, letting it cool a bit before taking a tentative sip. Carl watched him walk back to the table, seemingly amused.

Roberts sat down and set his coffee aside to pick up a file. He flipped through it and stopped at an earmarked page. "Says here you described the object to the F.B.I. as if you had seen it," Roberts said.

"Of course, I did. I'd say anything to get out of that place," Carl said with a big grin, and leaning back in his chair, began chuckling loudly. "Man, are you in for a big surprise," he blurted and broke out into a roaring laugh.

Roberts glared at him in disbelief, picked up his coffee as if he was going to take a sip but instead, gave one of the guards a quick nod. Eighteen million volts charged through Carl's left kidney and his jubilance abruptly shifted to a horrific bellow. The guards outside glanced at each other and smiled.

Carl collapsed, groaning, his head falling to the table and his back arching in the aftermath of convulsing waves. After a few agonizing moments, Carl twisted around to the soldier smiling tauntingly back at him. "I am going to *fuck* you up," Carl growled through gritted teeth at the red-haired soldier's boyish face.

Roberts looked on amused, glanced at the cup in his hand and took a long sip.

"Why the fuck did you do that?" Carl snapped at Roberts. Then suddenly he grimaced, his head fell forward, and he groaned from another convulsing wave.

"You need to bring it down a notch, Carl," Roberts said while glancing back into the file. "Let's try this again and I'll rephrase my question. When was the first time you saw this device?"

"You have no idea what you're fucking with," Carl said, bringing his eyes up to a piercing level.

"Just answer the question," Roberts persisted.

"You can fuck off," Carl fumed.

Roberts patiently waited, seeing Carl needed a little more time. "You know, Carl, when I first heard your story I thought it was a load of crap but I decided to go along with it. I really had nothing to lose anyway, even when the Feds agreed to let you go with an ankle tracker—unbelievable," he said shaking his head. "But when the ship came on, everything changed. You see, I figured we had finally cracked this nut and I didn't have any use for you or that thing anymore. That is, until I found out somebody else was controlling my ship and that's something I just can't have. So, let's start from the beginning. Tell me about the first time you saw this…what's it called?"

Carl cleared his throat and stared at the table. "Fabricator, it's called a Fabricator and when I was working at the diner I came into the kitchen after hours for, I can't remember what, but I saw the old man standing over it at one of the prep tables." Carl paused and groaned at another convulsing wave.

"And what happened then?" Roberts asked.

"He freaked, told me to get out and stepped in front of it, trying to hide it, but I got a good look."

"Keep going, tell me how you got hooked up with the F.B.I."

"When I was in prison, I heard this guy talking about an archeological dig he was on years ago, some spaceship buried in the Antarctic over a million years ago. Nobody believed him but me, and when he mentioned the device missing from the ship, I told him I knew where it was. He didn't believe me at first, saying no way. He claimed the archeologists knew it was in the ice around the ship somewhere. But when I described it in perfect detail, it blew his fucking mind."

Roberts was listening intently and it sounded feasible. "How could you describe it in such great detail from a quick glance in the kitchen?"

"I have great eyes and an awesome memory," Carl said defiantly.

Roberts stared warily at him for a moment, then shook his head and said, "So, let's sum it up. A young man comes out of nowhere without a trace and takes a job at a diner and stays there for what…twenty plus years? And then suddenly turns perv, kidnapping their daughter, raping her and then sits in prison for thirty years. Sounds like a pretty fucked up life to me."

"So, what's your point?" Carl scowled.

"My point is that you are holding out on me, Carl. Even when I caught you with Cooper's stupid book I didn't think much of it until he walked into my ship and started it up with the touch of his hand. Now, how is it that you know the ship's missing piece is called a Fabricator and why is it your son can start up my ship?"

Carl looked up from the table, his jaw slowly dropping, his eyes vacant and mind racing.

"You didn't know Cooper could do that, did you?" Roberts said suddenly intrigued. "Or better yet, maybe you didn't know he was your kid."

Carl looked away, trying to hide his eyes.

"It's time, Carl, time to start telling me what's going on. What is this Fabricator thing and what is your connection with my ship?"

Carl didn't answer, leaning forward and still hiding his face, trying to think.

"Talk to me, Carl, or we can do this all day long," Roberts said, picking up his coffee, holding it up off of the table, and Carl noticed.

"OK, ok," Carl said with a quick glance at the soldier behind him. He slowly turned back to Roberts, thought for a moment and then asked, "How do you know Cooper started it up?"

"Got witnesses, got it on video." Roberts leaned back in his chair and studied Carl for a moment and frowned, "You know what? All I care about is finding out how Cooper turned my ship on and I'm sitting here wondering why the hell I'm even talking to you."

Carl looked back at Roberts, knowing exactly who the ship belonged to. "You have Cooper here?" he asked. "Let me talk to him. I can get to the bottom of this right now."

Roberts clasped his fingers behind his head and groaned, "Oh come on, Carl, give it up."

"What do you have to lose?" Carl persisted.

Roberts looked at him doubtfully. He had hoped for something a bit more concrete but maybe this sorry old man could show him something he had missed. "All right then, you'll have your talk."

Chapter 21

"Oh, come on, what's the big deal?" Aunt Margie said.

"Come on yourself, are you trying to say I was made by the Fabricator?" David said as he looked down at his body. "Or am I some sort of android?"

Aunt Margie laughed, "Oh, David, there aren't any androids around here. Well, at least in the immediate area. There are some very primitive attempts going on in the lower levels of…what would you call this?" she held out her hands, "a bunker?"

"A *bunker*…this is a pretty gnarly military base if you ask me, but, wait a minute. Back it up and answer my question," he demanded.

Aunt Margie winked at him. "Don't worry, David, you're special and these guys digging their tunnels out here in the dirt aren't doing anything but making a big ant farm. Someday I'll show you what a real base is," she said, nodding her head convincingly. But after a moment of him staring unimpressed at her, she waved her hand. "Okay," she said, and leaned back in her chair, "What do you want to know?"

"Was I made by the Fabricator?"

"No, David, you were born just like a normal human."

"Then how? How'd I start the ship?"

"You can thank your mom for that and Rishi when he made it possible for your grandmother to conceive."

"My mom…What does my mom have to do with this?"

Aunt Margie kept looking at him as if contemplating something when a knock at the door interrupted them. Kim poked her head in and when she spotted David she was visibly relieved. "There you are," she said and joined them.

"Perfect timing, my dear, I was just wondering how you were doing," Aunt Margie said and turned to David. "Bring that over for her, Hon." She pointed to a nearby chair. She wasn't really wondering how Kim was, she already knew but said it to make her feel welcome.

Kim took the chair from David and positioned it closer to him. Aunt Margie settled back and watched them like an old favorite movie as she had done so many times before and wondered if this was going to be the time they would finally make it. She was pulling for them, of course, as she always did but couldn't help but remember the dramas in the past that stopped them dead in their tracks. Some were sad, some were horrific, and some just plain stupid, but this time circumstances were unique and she knew they had to survive the approaching challenges. There were some monumental hoops they had to jump through, and one of them was about to make itself known.

Chapter 22

Roberts entered the monitoring room and stopped at the two-way mirror. "What is Nichols doing in there?" he demanded.

One of the soldiers glanced at a log sheet. "She didn't check in with us before going in, sir."

Roberts watched her for a moment. It wasn't out of the ordinary for an agent to investigate a person of interest informally, but from her body language, this appeared to be more of a social call. "Why can't I hear what's going on in there?" he snapped.

The soldier behind the monitor shook his head. "We can't find it, sir, some kind of glitch. The techs are looking into it right now."

Carl came in escorted by two soldiers, the freckled red-haired soldier being one of them. They stopped behind Roberts, and Carl quickly looked down to hide his sudden exuberance at the sight of Aunt Margie. Staring at his feet, elated, he realized he could finally be at the end of his nightmare.

"Well, we can't do shit out here," Roberts blurted, glancing around, irritated, his attention finally settling on Carl. "Now tell me again, what's going to happen when you go in there?"

Carl was slow to look up at Roberts. "Oh, you're not going to believe what's about to happen."

"I better be thrilled, Carl," Roberts forewarned and looked at the red-haired soldier behind him. "Go in there with him, make sure he behaves."

Chapter 23

David was first to see Carl walk in, leaping from his chair in disbelief. Kim saw him frantically backing up, eyes fixed toward the door behind her and didn't wait to see who it was. She sprang to her feet, alarmed and baffled at the same time as to what could bring on such a reaction until she saw Carl. She backed into the corner with David, reaching for her weapon but left it holstered when Carl didn't seem interested in them.

Aunt Margie sat calmly smiling while he approached, raising her right arm straight up, open-handed as if she had a question. She clenched her hand into a fist, twisting it with a flick of her wrist and the atmosphere in the room changed.

The lights dimmed in the eerie silence, and to David, the air seemed dead. He felt something at his side. It was Kim facing him with her forehead pressed against his shoulder. He gently held her face in his hands and looked into her eyes. They seemed vacant as if she was in a trance. He put his arm around her, pulling her close and then looked at the other three people in the room. They were all motionless; the soldier, stopped in midstride as if frozen in time and Carl standing with his arms folded, towering over Aunt Margie as she slowly began lowering her hand.

"Well, hello, Carl. How long has it been?" Aunt Margie said in a harsh whisper.

"I did my part, now you do yours," Carl demanded, his voice also gruffly muffled.

"Well, of course, I'm sure you are eager to return to your normal life, if you want to call it that."

"Thirty Earth years I sat in that pit. That was not part of the deal."

"Oh, Carl, what's a few years to you? Besides I didn't put you there. You did that all on your own."

"Spare me the lecture and don't ever call me that name again."

"You're the one who picked it," she shrugged. "Okay…hold still."

"Whatever," he grumbled and then held a hand up. "Wait! There's one thing I have to do first," he said slowly turning around and thrusting his fist into the solar plexus of his red-haired escort. He gleefully watched the soldier crumble, dishing out a barrage of kicks into his helpless body on its way to the ground.

"Oh, Carl, when are you going to learn? He's not going to know you're the one who did it," Aunt Margie reasoned, but Carl ignored her.

"Hey!" David's voice boomed in the room, startling Carl who turned around just as David hit him with a massive body block, sending him flying.

Carl hit the ground hard, sliding to the wall and smacking into it below the mirror. David looked down at the soldier and tried to help him but saw he, too, was in a dazed condition, much worse than Kim's. At least she was numbly looking his way and seemed to be coming out of it. Carl groaned, glancing warily at David while slowly getting up. "What have you done here, a hybrid?" he groaned as he gingerly walked back toward Aunt Margie.

She smiled with a tinge of pride. "No, Carl, the question is, what have *we* done here?"

Carl looked David up and down with contempt. "Not me. This body maybe, which I'm done with," he exclaimed and faced her. "Give me what's mine."

"You will get your body back now and then you will leave," she said and in the stillness of the air, the Fabricator appeared. Spinning with its lights active, the hovering object began creating a form in the center of the room. At first David thought it was a child, but with its grayish color and oversized head, it quickly became apparent, the form was an alien. The photographs he had seen never showed their fragility; the lifeless paper-thin skin, the measly array of tiny muscle groups or the translucent eyelids covering the two huge black orbs.

Carl stepped up behind it, his hand reaching, trembling and touched the crown of its head briefly, then collapsed.

Moaning in a death roll onto his back, Carl took his last breath and at the same time, the alien took its first. A shallow, faint inhale with its upper torso barely moving and then it opened its massive eyes. David felt himself being sucked into an abyss of black and heard the alien as a thought in his head, *"So much easier in this body."* A strange pulling sensation tugged on David, drawing him into the center of his body, and was accompanied by a powerful feeling of inner strength. He realized he was experiencing what the alien was experiencing.

It was studying him, rocking its head side to side. *"Different, but still human."* David heard it surmise in his head before it abruptly turned away and walked out of the room.

David wheeled around to Aunt Margie. "What just happened, why did you let it go?"

"It was our agreement."

"What agreement, and why is it so hard to breathe in here?" David asked, turning to Kim, facing her, moving his eyes in front of hers. He put his hands on her shoulders and gently shook her. "Kim…Kim," he whispered.

"Not much to it, really," Aunt Margie continued. "The alien you know as Carl was dying from injuries it sustained in the crash your grandfather caused. It was about to die and we merely offered it a body to live in until it could be rescued, with a slight catch."

"What catch?" he said, halfway listening, still trying to get Kim's attention. Then he stopped and slowly turned to her. "Wait a minute…" he looked down at Carl's lifeless body, "wait a minute…"

Aunt Margie stood up, "I know this is probably a shock to you, David, but it's for the best, and really, it's no big deal. Now, unfortunately, it's time for me to go."

"No, no, no you don't! My father was a clone?" he said, grabbing her arm and staring at her for a moment. "Was my mom human?"

Aunt Margie looked up at him, her expression warmhearted. "Not just any clone, David, a very special clone and yes, your mom was totally human."

"Somehow that doesn't seem very impressive at the moment," he said, looking back at her. "So what does that make me?"

"Special, David." She picked up her purse and slipped it over her arm. "Now, there is something you should know before I leave."

"Wait…special, how?"

She quietly studied him for a moment then said, "I'm excited for you, David. You're going to learn about the side of you that's been dormant all this time." She smiled warmly and said, "Now I must say goodbye."

"Take us with you," David said, putting his arm around Kim. "Why not? Let's just all go together."

"My work here is done," she said smiling at him, "but yours is not."

David shook his head, "No, I disagree. I think I'm done here. Besides, how are we going to get out of here?"

"There is a way for you to leave this place," she explained.

"How?"

"There is an important discovery you will make if and when you find it."

"What do you mean, *if*? Wouldn't it be better to just tell me so we can all move on? We are wasting so much time here."

"It's all relative, David," she said as her image began to sparkle and fade.

He grabbed her again. "Whoa, just a minute, you were going to tell me something, something I needed to know? Remember?"

"That was it, you have a way out of here, but you're going to have to find it," she patted his arm. "It's time to open your intuitive eye, David...wake up!" and she vanished.

David's eyes slowly wandered down to the body on the floor. He began studying the hands, elbows, nose. "Oh, my God," he mumbled, suddenly realizing why Carl looked so familiar. He had been seeing himself in the whole body structure.

Chapter 24

"You okay?" Kim asked stepping in front of him. She gave him a quick once over, and then knelt to the floor to check on Carl.

David hadn't noticed the room had returned to normal; the lights, the sounds. The air was lighter, easier to breathe again.

"What happened? Did you see what happened?" Kim asked, coming back to him. But he didn't respond, his mind felt like mush. "David!" she bellowed.

"What…" he stammered disoriented.

"What *happened*?"

"Uhh…I saw Carl collapse. I think he's dead,"

"Oh, he's dead alright," she affirmed and looked at the place where his aunt had been sitting. "Did you see where your aunt went?"

"I don't know, one second she was here and then she was gone," he replied.

The door flew open and Cathcart burst in, stepping over the groaning soldier and kneeling next to Carl's body. Roberts was right behind, his eyes darting around the room. "Well?" Roberts snapped.

"He's gone," Cathcart muttered, slowly getting up.

"Where's the old lady?" Roberts demanded and turned to Kim.

"She must have gotten out," she replied.

Roberts motioned to a couple of soldiers standing by. "Go find her!" He then turned to Cathcart who was thoughtfully rubbing his chin over Carl. "What happened to him?" Roberts asked.

"Heart attack maybe, nothing obvious, I'll have to open him up."

"Damn it, I wasn't done with him yet," Roberts grumbled disappointed and glanced at David. "Well, Cooper, looks like it's all you now."

"What? What do you mean *all me*?" David protested.

"Well, you started the ship all on your own and we're going to help you figure out how you did that so we can do it again. Simple as that. Isn't that so, Professor?"

Cathcart managed a vacant glance and nod but his mind was clearly elsewhere.

A couple of soldiers came up, grabbed David and led him away.

Roberts watched them go for a moment then turned to Kim. "What were you doing in here?" he demanded.

"My report, Sir. I had to do a few follow up questions." She was lying but presented it convincingly.

"Then I expect it within the hour," he replied.

"Yes, sir," she said and watched him walk away. She wasn't expecting a deadline for her report and worried for David now that she couldn't keep an eye on him. It did bring about a sobering question, though. What was she prepared to do if he was in mortal danger? She thought about it and realized David's wellbeing had just become very personal.

Chapter 25

The room was cold and sterile, except for a few stainless steel tables and ominous equipment looming from the corners. Everywhere David looked he saw white; cabinets, floor, walls and ceiling. In the center of the room was a chair, very much like a dentist's, and as soon as he was placed into it, techs began attaching sensors to his head, face and neck. Another one slipped thin gloves on him with wires attached along the back. He held his hand up, looking at wire leads embedded in the translucent material, running along his fingers to paper thin sensors at each fingertip. A female tech smiled at him while pulling his hand down and then strapped his wrist to the arm chair. "Is this really necessary?" he asked, but she kept smiling and walked off.

Cathcart came in, hovered over him and supervised the preparation in such a detached and impersonal way that David had to protest, "Can you tell me what the hell you guys think you are doing?"

Cathcart actually looked startled as if surprised that David was able to talk. "Oh, this?" he said picking up some of the sensor wires. "It's no big deal. We're going to create your digital profile. We'll be showing you a series of images along with sounds of association, all the while recording your neuro feedback. Just look at it as a glorified electroencephalogram."

"*Oh*, why didn't you say so?" David muttered, "It's lucky you have one here because I forgot mine at home."

Oblivious to everything but himself, Cathcart continued, "Once we build your profile we'll be able to help you control how you activate the vehicle and hopefully create a program to do it without you. This is for your own good, you know."

"Awesome, thanks a million, that'd be great. Oh, by the way, why am I strapped down?"

"It's just to keep you from moving if you accidentally react to the stimulus, which could disrupt the readings," Cathcart said. For a brief moment, the professor stared at David, seemingly through him, then blinked and ventured an awkward smile. This caught David so much by surprise that he wasn't sure if he should smile back or start screaming.

Cathcart turned away and David tugged at the straps in vain. A couple of lab techs approached him and he recognized the girl in front. She had smiled at him in the hallway earlier. Now she was carrying a headset, smiling once again. It was always nice to see a friendly face. David couldn't see the other tech who stayed out of his line of sight, but he did catch a glimpse of a muscular, hairy arm with tattoos that he was sure had a skull with some knives on it. The girl smelled good. She leaned over him with a giggle when their eyes met and carefully placed the headset on him. "OK, just relax," she whispered, reclining his chair and carefully lowering the viewing screen over his eyes. He felt a scratchy hand gripping his forearm and yelped from a jolting, sharp pain.

The nurse looked behind her and saw a burly hand holding an empty syringe. "What is that? This is a non—"

"Shut up and move it, sweet cakes!" the gruff-looking tech snarled. He grabbed her by her lab coat with one hand, nearly picking her up off the ground. He tossed her aside and she went stumbling toward the door. He then looked down at David and adjusted his viewing screen. "There you go, Mr. Cooper. Have a nice trip," he snickered, patting David's shoulder and walking off.

***

"Professor!" the tech blurted, pointing at his monitor.

Cathcart was next to him entering the last of his data and looked over at his monitor. "What the hell?" he muttered in disbelief.

"He's all over the place," the tech said, following one of David's brain waves jumping erratically. The nurse that witnessed the injection came in and went right to the professor's ear, whispering. When she was done, she left the professor fuming and Roberts passed her at the door as he came in. He stopped behind Cathcart, set his feet slightly apart, folded his arms and began bouncing his attention between the monitors. "Well, Professor, you about ready to get going?" he asked impatiently.

"No wonder," Cathcart growled and slowly turned around.

Chapter 26

David closed his eyes and felt the room moving. He knew he had been given a powerful drug and was already at work trying to keep some sort of stability, but with every breath it seemed his frame of mind was hopelessly slipping away.

Through his eyelids, he saw the viewing screen come to life, and cracking them, peeked into a world of virtual reality. He was standing at the edge of an ocean with waves of blue-green water breaking toward him and the sounds of the surf surrounding him. He heard seagulls off in the distance and could almost feel the breeze on his face and ears. Directly overhead, the sun shone brightly, but the sky was dark as night, filled with stars and planets, a sharp contrast to the bright, white sand around him. Low vegetation and palm trees lined the beach in both directions. Some leaned toward the water. Their fronds shaded the sand below and he felt himself relax. It was soothing and peaceful. He felt like he was on a vacation. He breathed in deeply and as he exhaled, he heard a strange noise behind him.

***

"What did you do?" Cathcart said, standing up and towering over Roberts. "What'd you give him?"

Roberts smiled mischievously. "Something I use for special occasions, something that can show me what a soldier is really made of."

"You're meddling with my program? How am I supposed to reach any credible results?" Cathcart lashed out.

"I don't give a rat's ass about your credibility! I am only interested in *results,* and I'm the only one around here who knows how to get them," Roberts fired back.

"Professor…" the tech interjected while staring at his monitor.

Cathcart kept his attention on Roberts. "The idea here is to see what he does naturally without any other influences. None of this means anything until I know what it is you gave him."

"Like I said, something we use to turn a man into a soldier. Either that or he'll end up thinking he's a chair in a psych ward."

Cathcart's eyes went blank as he thought for a moment, "Let me guess, lysergic acid diethylamide."

"Well, congratulations, Professor," Roberts conceded with a twisted grin.

"Oh, god," Cathcart scoffed, disgusted and turned to his tech, "Mike, we need to factor in—"

"—you'd better take a look at this," Mike blurted, tapping his finger on his screen.

Cathcart sat down, scooted his chair up next to him and froze. "How's that possible?" he muttered and sat back in disbelief.

Roberts came up behind them, peering over their shoulders. "What…what does it mean?"

Neither one responded to the colonel as they both stared, mesmerized, at the monitor.

"Look!" Mike pointed at another graph. Cathcart tilted his head toward the other monitor then, perplexed, took out his pen and began making notes.

"Will one of you two lab rats tell me what the hell is going on?" Roberts finally broke in, irritated.

"Delta…he's in Delta. And he's staying there," Cathcart explained while scribbling.

Roberts stood quietly behind them for a moment, hands on his hips, thinking it over then abruptly bellowed, "Even though I like the sound of it, what does it mean?"

Cathcart reluctantly stopped what he was doing and turned to face him. "Cooper jumped right into it, a Delta brain wave, straight through Alpha and Theta in an instant. Nobody does that…it's just not done."

***

David turned around to see what the noise was and saw his virtual reality had suddenly changed. He saw an image of himself standing in the ship with the console in front of him. The beach was gone now and so was the tranquility he had been experiencing. He found his image strangely odd, moving awkwardly, jumpy like a glitch in a digital program.

His image made a deliberate adjustment to one of the spheres, rolling it to a different setting and then turn toward him, waiting for something. The words "lift off" appeared on a monitor. David didn't remember any monitor in the ship. He saw his hand reach out to touch a different sphere but stopped. Something was wrong. An unsettling feeling swept over him. The image did it again, repeating the same action, followed by the text and the unsettling feeling.

It was like a loop, a repetitious GIF. He had a hunch what the correct action was for lift off and when he thought of showing it, a wonderful feeling charged through him. He would have complied except he had an aversion to being manipulated.

"Fuck you," David responded. His virtual image suddenly stopped, turned to him and approached. David put his virtual hands up to stop it. Their hands met in midair and became fused together. His image seemed just as surprised as he was as their arms kept melting into each other, drawing them closer and closer. They stood inches apart, face to face, and every expression David did, his image mimicked: leaning his head to the side, scrunching his nose, raising his eyebrows…and that's when David noticed his image didn't have any eyebrows.

He thought that was weird and then he began to notice more differences. The crinkled skin on his forehead seemed unhealthy and frail. He looked sickly and his eyes were all wrong, too. They were so big…they were so big…and in horror David looked down at the tiny alien mouth opening and heard himself scream.

Chapter 27

"Mike, it's the LSD. It must be," Cathcart said.

"But still," Mike protested, "we've never had a subject on acid do this."

Roberts leaned forward, looking hard at David's face in the monitor. "Wait a minute. Does that mean he's asleep?" he barked.

"The deepest sleep we can achieve," Cathcart explained. "It's impossible to be awake at this wave length."

"Son of a bitch!" Roberts bellowed and turned to his aide standing by the door. "Jackson! Get in there and wake that little shit up!"

Jackson quickly slipped out of the room and within seconds had his feet planted at David's side, winding up, preparing to execute the "gong." It was a maneuver he had done many times to opponents during his college football days. Taking a bead on David's headgear, the action came naturally. He swung his muscular arm toward David's head but he never made it. Startled, he looked down at his arm in disbelief. It was stopped in mid-air by David's hand firmly gripped around his wrist.

Jackson leaned forward to peek under the headgear. There's no way Cooper could have seen it coming and then was really baffled when he saw David's eyes were closed.

"God damn it, Jackson, smack him!" Roberts yelled over the intercom.

"Wait!" Cathcart waved a hand at Roberts. "He's still in Delta. He just did a cognitive action without wavering out of Delta."

Cathcart paused to think for a moment, his eyes opened wide and mind racing. "Tell Jackson to use his other hand."

Roberts looked at Cathcart like he was ridiculous but relayed the message anyway. "Jackson, Cathcart wants you to hit him with your left." It seemed appropriate to Jackson since it was usually his secondary mode of attack anyway. He wound up and brought his left fist around at David's head but it, too, was met with the same result.

Jackson peeked again and saw David blinking and that's when he noticed all of the straps were hanging undone. David abruptly sat up, let go of Jackson's arms and removed the headset. "You okay?" Jackson asked, rubbing his wrists and leaning forward to look into David's face. He caught a glimpse of David's eyes and jerked backward, "Whoa, Jeeze!" he said in disbelief. He had never seen eyes so dilated. David's irises appeared to be gone.

***

Cathcart frantically pounded at his keyboard, entering data as quickly as he could.

"What are you doing?" Roberts asked.

"I got it! I recorded it! The way his motor nerves and his Delta waves worked together. I'm mapping both sides of his brain and creating a program of it, a program that I believe will run the ship," he said excitedly.

Roberts turned away and looked at the monitor and saw Jackson trying to talk to David.

"Well, that would make my day. What about Cooper? You done with him for now?"

"Yes, hopefully for good," Cathcart said.

Roberts yelled over the intercom, "Jackson, get him outta there," and then turned to Cathcart with a sly grin. "Oh, and you're welcome, by the way."

***

Jackson helped a disoriented David down the corridor to his holding room, passing Kim along the way. "What happened, what'd they do?" she said, careful to seem clinically concerned in front of Jackson.

"Had him on the rack, " Jackson said.

"Yeah, but what else?" she said, putting her face in front of David's, trying to catch his eye.

"Oh, the Colonel broke out his secret stash for this one."

"Oh," she feigned indifference "and where is the Colonel now…I have to turn in my report."

"He's still with the professor in the observation room," Jackson answered, struggling to keep David on his feet.

Kim watched them walk away, worried. She knew David was in trouble, fearing it was only going to get worse if they didn't get what they needed.

She made her way to the observation room and was about to give the partially opened door a shove when she heard Roberts say, "An organic bridge?"

"Yes," Cathcart replied, "In a nutshell, we use Cooper's body, keep it alive, get his brain out of the way, use our software instead and hook the whole works up to the ship. Now that's plan B. Let's do plan *A* first, ok? We may not even need to go there."

"Why isn't plan B plan A? I like the sound of that better," Roberts said.

"Of course, you do. That's because you're a morbid son of a bitch. Now let me finish."

Kim heard feet shuffling and suspected Roberts might be leaving, so she quickly pushed the door open, almost bumping into him. If Roberts was surprised, he didn't show it and just stared at her blankly. She looked away, then down at her folder and held it out to him. "My report, sir."

He kept staring through her, "Put it on my desk," he said and turned back to Cathcart.

"Yes, sir," she replied and abruptly stepped out of the room but wavered outside the door. Down the hallway, soldiers were headed her way. She flipped open her folder, leafing through papers, all the while listening.

"One more thing," she heard Roberts say, "What's the shelf life on plan B? How many times would I be able to use him?"

"What, are you kidding? The first time will probably kill him or at the very least, turn him into a vegetable," Cathcart stated.

Kim started walking, having heard enough. Her legs were numb and shaky with every step as she believed she had just heard the end of David. She knew Roberts, and from the sound of it, even if plan A worked he wouldn't release David. He couldn't have someone on the loose that could interfere with his ship. She got a sudden chill of dread when she realized David fit the perfect scenario for a disappearing subject. He was from a small town with few community ties, no family members except a kooky aunt who lived abroad and wouldn't be a problem for Roberts. Queasiness engulfed her when she realized she couldn't let that happen. She had to decide what to do.

Kim stepped into Robert's office in a daze, her mind racing as she envisioned a way to save David. She laid her report on the desk and knew her plan was preposterous, but it was the only way. She went to the receiving department and headed to the back room where the service elevator was located. She had to know how many guards were posted there today. Privately she had always considered this section of the base as the Achilles heel to the department's security system and was now glad she never mentioned it. To her relief, there was only one guard and she knew him from her many unauthorized passages through this back way. His lackadaisical demeanor was perfect for her plan. She saw him with his hands busy as usual, one holding coffee, the other a bagel as he munched over a newspaper in front of him. He looked up when she came in. "Hey, Nichols, what's up?"

"Oh, hi, Andy. I'm trying to track down my cell phone, thought I might have left it on your desk." The guard raised his forearms off the paper, did a courtesy scan of his desk while chewing and shrugged.

"Thanks," she said and left, checking the first thing off of her long, crazy list.

Chapter 28

Cathcart paced behind the row of techs manning their computers, occasionally pausing to look over their shoulders, checking their progress. "Mike, your status?" he called out to his assistant, sitting at a separate desk positioned in the center of the floor. He was fitted with headgear specially created for the procedure displaying the ship's instrument panel in virtual reality.

"Good to go," Mike answered while he fiddled with the fit of his special wired gloves. They had sensors at each fingertip with their leads strapped along his forearms, draping from his elbows to a cluster of massive computer towers. Bundled wires, the size of docking ropes, ran along the floor like jungle vines from his chair all the way to the ship.

Behind everyone, Roberts stood in the center of the room with his arms folded, looking very much like a crazed dictator. He struggled with his impatience while the professor went agonizingly slow through his steps before pushing the button. *Here…let me push the goddamn button for you,* he wanted to yell at Cathcart, but instead took a deep breath and went back to grinding his teeth.

Cathcart peered into a monitor that displayed the feed going to Mike's goggles. "Check your movement, Mike." Mike stroked the metallic joystick in front of him with his left hand and when he moved it, the professor saw the curser in his monitor move over the spheres in the ship. "Ok, check adjustment," Cathcart said.

Mike's right hand rested on a rolling mouse to best replicate the action of a sphere for the most accurate interaction possible. He set the curser on one of the spheres and rolled the ball in front of him and the sphere spun in the monitor.

Cathcart stood upright. "Great! Now all I want you to do is a short lift off and hold it there for sixty seconds."

"Roger, that," Mike answered, wiggling his gloved fingers over the joystick in anticipation.

Cathcart took a quick glance at the ship through the safety glass and then to the row of techs and nodded to one of them. "Start the sequence," he ordered.

The tech hit a computer key and a thirty-second countdown began.

Cathcart walked over to Mike and did a last check of the wires clipped to his head and earlobes and followed them to where they gathered at the power plant. Satisfied everything was in order, he turned to watch the ship through the glass.

A buzzer sounded off, filling the domed chamber with an irritating sound while the monitors were checking around the ship for an all clear, and when the countdown reached zero the buzzer stopped.

"Ok, Mike, initiate the startup sequence," Cathcart said, earnestly watching the ship.

Mike looked at the ship's instrument panel as if he were standing in front of it and saw one of the spheres had a digital circle blinking around it for the first adjustment to make. He moved his curser on top of it and then went to his right hand.

Everyone in the room felt the immediate shuddering, vibrating in their chairs, and a few gasped as the ship moved.

Roberts unfolded his arms, his jaw dropped and he took a step forward.

"Yes! Yes! That's it, Mike, lift off!" Cathcart blurted, his eyes locked on the ship as it rose up in the air. But then it stalled, did a little wobble and settled back down, shutting off.

"Mike, what are you doing?" Cathcart asked, reaching out and touching his assistant's shoulder.

As if overtaken by demonic forces, Cathcart flew through the air backwards. The occupants in the room stared in disbelief as he twitched on the floor. A few techs rushed over to help him sit up as he groaned and rubbed his head. "What the hell happened?" he muttered. He glanced at Mike and saw him slouched over the joystick, his body quivering and his head smoking. "Pull the plug!" Cathcart yelled, pointing.

A tech initiated the power disconnect and Mike's body relaxed and fell sideways out of the chair to a heap on the ground. Cathcart was slow to get up, all the while looking at Mike as another tech was kneeling by him, checking his vitals. "He's gone," the tech announced and everyone stared for an awkward moment of silence.

"Let's get him to the infirmary," Cathcart finally said. A couple of techs clumsily tried to lift Mike up and Roberts motioned to some soldiers to help. Cathcart somberly watched his assistant being carried away as Roberts came up next to him.

"Too bad about Mike," Roberts said and stepped in front of him. "Now, you done dick'n around?"

Cathcart grunted with a frown, "I guess we're doing plan B after all."

Chapter 29

David took a deep breath and tried to open his eyes but every time he did nothing looked right. He knew he was high on something, a hallucinogenic, maybe psilocybin, but he suspected LSD…or…maybe both. He just wanted to sleep. They must have tranked him, too, he thought.

What are they doing out there? He cringed at the sound again. It was coming from the other side of the door, out in the hallway, and was the same sound that woke him up. He got up on an elbow, saw he had been sleeping on a couch, and desperately wanted to put his head back down. Again with the noise! He glared at the door, irritated, just as it opened and someone poked their head in. Even though his eyes were messed up it looked like Kim was standing there.

He blinked and heard her voice, "Come on! I'm getting you out of here!"

It sure sounded like her, he thought. "Okay, okay, just a minute," he managed to say, hesitating for a second, then his head started to fall to the cushion.

"No, no, no…David! David…you have to snap out of it…*Right now*!" she yelled and he felt a sudden stinging on his face.

"What the…" he said, blinking erratically, pawing the air in front of him as she pulled him upright. "Did you just sla…"

He felt it again. "Whoa…stop that!!" he said, reaching for her arms.

"We have to go!" she said, frantically struggling to get him up. Her sense of urgency was for a good reason; she was way past the point of no return.

She managed to get David out the door but in the hallway he tripped and fell. He looked sideways into the face of a soldier unconscious on the floor next to him. "Jeez! Did you do this?" he said, getting up and seeing three more soldiers scattered about.

"They'll be okay, just stunned! Come on!" she said, dragging him down the hallway. They had seconds to get 100 feet to where the labs were, duck through them into the auditorium, past the ship to the other side and then there would be a short burst back into the hallway to the receiving department. It was a desperate stretch, but David's life depended on it and if she could get him to that service elevator and up to the surface they might have a chance.

They stumbled down the curving hallway, her running and keeping David as steady as possible. When she saw the doorknob to the lab, she began to believe. Closer and closer they got, but when they were within twenty feet her heart sank as a stream of armed soldiers burst into the hallway up ahead.

The soldiers stopped and looked their way just as David fell. "Come on! Come on!" she said, grabbing and pulling at him, dragging him toward the door. Suddenly Roberts stepped into the hallway behind his men and the look on his face surprised her. He didn't seem angry, even when he pointed at them, and yelled out orders.

The soldiers ran toward them and Kim realized she wasn't going to be able to drag David to the door in time, so she did the only thing she could do and pulled her weapon.

She didn't shoot to kill and it worked as the solders immediately stopped and fell to the ground to take cover. Then, in a chilling shriek, she heard Roberts order them to return fire, being sure not to hit David. It was both of their lives on the line now.

In the seconds following, David managed to get to his feet. The soldiers aimed their rifles and Kim opened the door as the first rounds were fired. The bullets hit the door with metallic thuds. Built to handle lab explosions, the door served well as a protective shield. She slowly rose up from her crouched position to sneak a peek through the door's observation window and saw one of Roberts's snipers looking for a shot.

David pulled her into the lab just as the glass shattered. He had finally come around enough to grasp what was happening. "They're shooting at us?" he said in disbelief.

"Me! They're shooting at me!" she responded as they braced a chair against the door. They bolted through the lab but as they went out the door into the auditorium, they heard the barricade give way. David held the door closed pulling fiercely on the knob while Kim looked for something to wedge against it. He heard her scream, "Move!" He jerked his hands away just as the blade of a fire axe sheared off the knob. Kim kicked in what was left of the knob and they heard it fall to pieces on the floor inside.

"Come on!" she yelled, pulling at him. They ran from the soldiers pounding on the door and headed down the aisles toward the ship. A few techs holding tablets watched like deer frozen in headlights as they approached. When the soldiers broke through and began firing, the techs scurried off and David and Kim had to take cover under the ship. She pointed up the aisle to the rarely used side door and yelled, "We have to go for it!"

"Wait!" David said, grabbing her. "They'll shoot you!" He knew they would never make it, running up hill with so many soldiers firing at them.

"We have to! It's the only way!" she yelled in the gunfire, bullets zipping and snapping all around them.

Roberts's voice suddenly rang out, booming loud and clear. "Hold your fire! Don't shoot my ship, you morons!"

Kim desperately turned to David, "This is our last chance! We've got to get to that door!"

He nodded and they braced, preparing to bolt for it together when the door opened and to their horror, soldiers began pouring in through it. Then the other doors began opening up and more soldiers entered, taking up positions around them. They were surrounded. Kim knew this was the end and then looked at him. She feared she would never see him again.

David tugged on her with a slight nod and she saw he wanted to go up the stairs and into the ship. "Why not? she thought, it was better than getting shot down here on the floor. She went with his idea and ran ahead to the stairs. She raced into the ship, screaming and yelling, flushing out the techs hiding inside. She frantically searched for something to barricade the opening as David breezed in seemingly carefree.

"I can't block the door!" she screamed, not understanding his aloofness. The soldiers were on the ramp now, running toward them. Their pounding feet filled the ship like thunder. Kim realized it was hopeless. "David, I'm so sorry, if I'd known…" she said looking into his eyes, but he put his finger to her lips.

"Wait, it's ok…everything's going to be fine," he said.

She looked into his eyes as if he'd totally lost it and barely noticed him reaching for the console, touching one of the spheres. The soldiers were screaming profanities, flashing their weapons at the ship's entrance when the door closed on them.

Chapter 30

Kim wheeled around and stared at the door, "How? How did you…" she asked in disbelief.

"I don't know. I can't explain it. It just came to me," he shrugged.

She listened to the muffled noises of the soldiers banging on the side of the ship. "Can they open the door?" she asked, anxiously.

"Nope, not if I don't want them to."

She took a deep breath, something she had not been able to do for a long time, and glanced around the ship. "So now what…what'll we do?"

David smiled, cracked his knuckles and faced the console, "I don't know why but I have a feeling I can fly this thing," he said, pausing to study the instruments.

"What…out of here?" she said, looking on in disbelief.

"I think so," he said, reaching out and touching a sphere. A slight mechanical noise could be heard around them and a viewing screen dropped down from the ceiling. It was a wraparound, 360 degree view of everything going on outside. They could see soldiers scurrying about, trying to get organized with Roberts standing in their midst barking out orders. Kim noticed their viewing angle of the soldiers changing and realized they were lifting off. The ship jerked suddenly, tilting slightly when the tethers became taut, followed by a loud crack. All of the soldiers suddenly stopped outside and looked at the ship in disbelief. The shortest tether had snapped free.

Kim saw Jackson pointing under the ship as it leveled out, yelling something to Roberts. Then they stood still, watching as three more loud snaps could be heard.

Roberts looked up at the ship and Kim got an eerie feeling he could see her, especially when they both looked toward the auditorium's huge doors at the same time. David was moving his hands fluidly over the controls as if he were conducting an orchestra, lights coming on and holograms popping up.

"David...we're a hundred feet underground and the only way out of here is that way," she said, pointing to the massive solid steel doors, at least twenty feet high. He paused to look at them with her, seeing Roberts positioning his men in front of them, weapons poised and taking aim. "Oh, God, this could get messy," Kim said dreadfully.

"Seems kinda silly, don't you think?" he said, "The two of us in this ship waiting for an elevator door to ding and open up?"

"What choice do we have?" she said, watching him turning back to the controls, "What are you doing?"

"Getting us out of here," he said, looking up at the screen and smiling.

***

Roberts looked at his ship, grimacing with the thought of it being rammed into the steel doors but became perplexed at it levitating upward toward the ceiling.

"What does he think he's doing?" Jackson said, standing next to him.

Roberts glared at the ship and growled, "I have no idea, but they're really pissing me off. I'm going to kill them myself when I get my hands on them."

A sudden low rumble filled the auditorium and everything around them began shaking.

They held on while Roberts flagged down one of his sharpshooters and pointed at the ship, "Shoot that son of a bitch down!" he yelled.

The soldier shook his head, trying to keep from falling. "I can't get a shot, sir."

"Just hit the God damn thing!" Roberts ordered, impatiently.

The shooter shouldered his weapon but hesitated when he saw a blue glow appearing around the ship.

"What the..." Roberts muttered then yelled, "Fire! *Fire!*"

The sharp shooter wedged his elbow into the sling, took a wild shot, then peered over his rifle. He looked bewildered at the spark in the blue shield, dissipating where the bullet had been stopped. It hadn't penetrated.

"Again!" Roberts yelled.

The sniper brought his weapon up but the shaking jerked him violently, making him fall. A loud snapping from above turned their heads upward and they saw jagged cracks spreading in the ceiling toward the walls. Dirt began pouring through, creating a swirling dust cloud, filling the auditorium.

Roberts turned to Jackson, yelling under the noise, "Scramble the surface!"

Jackson looked at him puzzled, then at the ceiling in disbelief while slowly pulling his radio to his mouth and ordering the gunships up top to get airborne.

"Fire! Fire at will!" Roberts yelled to his men. Bullets began spraying up to the ship from every direction but disintegrating in the blue shield on contact. A deep boom shook the entire base to its foundation and chunks of concrete the size of cars began dropping from the ceiling. Then the ceiling gave way, slamming to the floor in a deafening concussion, erupting in a horizontal shock wave. The blast sent splattering chunks of soil and rocks against the walls, taking with it everything in its path.

Roberts found himself coughing and gasping for air on top of the transport doors as they lay flat on the floor in the hallway. A handful of soldiers around him were shaking off dirt while desperately covering their mouths. Jackson was among them, and getting up next to him, they all looked into the dust storm where the ceiling used to be.

"What's that?" Jackson said pointing up at a dim glow.

Roberts moved his head, side to side, thinking out loud, "Looks like sunlight…" He then yelled in disbelief, "They're out!"

Chapter 31

Major Springer had his gunships positioned high over the base and was at a loss for words when the ground began to move. An area on the desert floor below them, larger than a city block, pushed up into a mound and quivered. From their vantage point they could see the earth shaking and cracking with rocks tumbling down. Then with a last, giant convulsive jolt the mound dropped into a vast chasm of a sink hole. They hovered, their radios silent as they milled about scanning the rising plume of dust, not knowing what to expect.

"Major, what's your visual on the ship?" the voice on his radio crackled. "We have it right in front of you."

"Negative…That's a negative, Base, we have no visual…the horizon is clear," Springer replied.

There was a brief silence then the voice came back on. "Major, be advised the target has cloaking ability. Refer to your guidance system. We have the target painted…I repeat, the target is painted."

Major Springer flipped a switch that engaged his ICU with the base's computer. "Roger that, Base, I have acquired and locked on target without visual…permission to engage," the Major said.

"Engage!" the voice on the radio crackled.

The Major initiated one of his AIM-92 Stinger Missiles and fired. The advantage of this particular weapon was that it had the "fire and forget" feature and could steer itself to follow a moving target once it has been "painted". In his many years of experience, he had witnessed some very unusual paths a missile had to take in order to hit its mark. One time he saw it do a corkscrew pattern but nothing compared to what he witnessed today. His missile went straight out and then turned to go straight up and continued out of sight. He scanned his controls and assumed a malfunction had occurred. "Base, I have lost contact with the target," he reported.

There was a brief hesitation on the radio, then the voice crackled back, "That's affirmative, Major. Target has left the area."

Chapter 32

David turned away from the console and saw Kim staring intently at the viewing screen. "What's the matter?" he asked.

"Look…" she pointed.

He came up next to her. "Wow" was all he could muster as they silently stared at the image of their planet. It looked like so many pictures he had seen before but it seemed very different now. Maybe because he wasn't on it while looking at it. He put his arm around her. "Thank you," he said.

She smiled at him, visibly relieved. "You're welcome," she said, her eyes wandering over his face and lingering on his mouth. Slowly their bodies pressed together as their lips drew close, but an odd rustling sound made them stop cold.

"What was that?" Kim whispered, looking toward a dark crevice in the wall at the other side of the ship.

"I…I don't know," he whispered back. They were hushed, eyes searching, and then something moved in the darkness, looming as it slowly emerged.

Kim shuddered as David recognized the alien that used to be Carl, but he also saw something he never would have imagined in his wildest dreams. In its frail arm, stretched out with tiny little fingers wrapped around it, was an army issue .45 automatic pistol.

"You can't be serious!" David shouted. The alien moved toward them, awkwardly holding the heavy weapon, taking small steps. "Carl, put the gun down," David demanded and glanced toward Kim who was way too quiet. "Kim," he said gently, pulling her face toward him. She was hardly blinking, struggling to focus and appearing confused.

"Stop it! Stop it now!" David yelled at the alien while trying to catch her eye.

Again, this human won't hibernate. David heard the voice in his head and abruptly turned to the alien. It was watching him, slowly rocking its head side to side, and then he understood why the gun.

This specimen must be analyzed.

Again, David heard the alien in his head and got an idea. As if hearing himself say the words, he thought them in his head: *Put the gun down.*

The alien recoiled and lowered the weapon, staring at him. It had heard him. David repeated the message, *Put the gun down,* but this time the alien slowly brought the weapon back up and leveled it at him. David messaged differently this time, *I am unarmed. You don't need to point the gun at us.*

How is it you can communicate to me this way? the alien messaged.

David thought for a moment, realizing he really didn't know the answer. The alien turned away, analyzing, but still holding the gun on him.

David kept an eye on the alien while sliding his hand down Kim's back, feeling for her pistol, and paused with his hand on the holster.

The alien looked back at him and stared for a moment then messaged, *What is your interest in the female, the way you were touching her…is it part of your mating ritual?*

David realized its question was clinical, but it also showed that this alien had no understanding of intimacy.

She's special…that's how I show it, he messaged back, moving his hand around the pistol's grip.

Special for mating? the alien persisted.

David looked at the creature with such a huge brain and wondered how it could be so stupid. *Your species doesn't show affection when mating?* he messaged the alien.

We have done away with such organs of hormone-driven acts, the alien answered.

David stared at the alien, afraid to ask why. *How do you reproduce and evolve as a species then?*

We clone our bodies, making them better each time.

His curiosity aroused, David relaxed his hand on Kim's gun and asked, *What was it like when you were in the human body?*

The alien paused for a moment to think, then messaged, *Primitive, overly stimulating, cognitively limiting and repulsive.*

Is that the way you felt when you raped my mother? David snapped, taken aback at his sudden emotion, then realized the gravity of his words. He thought of the being inside this frail body and wondered if it meant something to him. After all, it was in the human body during his conception. He cringed at the thought…was it in some twisted way…his father?

I didn't rape the female… I didn't have to.

That's a lie. David glared at the alien, wanting to yell it out loud but was surprised by its reaction as it curiously looked him over.

Why would I lie? The female knew of my agreement with the Entities and initiated it.

David's mind raced, trying to remember what Aunt Margie had told him about his mom and something Rishi had done to her. He glanced back at the alien and saw it staring at the monitor behind him. He turned around just in time to see a huge ship gliding toward them with its forward section open, gobbling them up. The screen went dark. He whipped back around to see the alien had shuffled sideways to the door.

The alien raised the pistol, pointed it at Kim and messaged, *Release your hand from her weapon, open this door and I will not send a projectile into her.*

"Okay!" David bellowed, holding his hands up, "I'll open it now." He then touched the instrument panel, opening the door with a hiss of equalizing gases. Through the billowing mist, a ghostly trio entered the ship. The two aliens on either side were almost identical to Carl, but the taller one in the middle had a longer face and carried itself differently.

Carl lowered the pistol as the tall alien stopped and they faced each other. It stood with a posture of an individual being answered to and David heard an exchange of greetings. They were getting caught up without a handshake, hug or a touch, all done mentally. *What a heartfelt bunch,* he thought.

The aliens stopped their interacting and slowly, all at the same time, turned to look at him. Evidently, they had heard him.

It can communicate in our way, David heard Carl message, and suddenly felt the tall alien's attention on him. It was strong, running around inside his head, much stronger than Carl's. There was no hiding from it and he felt naked as it turned toward him. The two aliens on either side of it had weapons up now, pointed at him.

David put his arm around Kim, pulling her close and stepping in front of her.

How is this possible? the tall one communicated to Carl. *It repels hibernation.*

It can also operate the Entities' craft...I am planning a thorough dissection to find out how it is possible, Carl messaged.

You know I can hear you, David messaged, looking at them irritated.

Yes…acquiring this technology will be most useful, the tall one said, glancing around the interior of the ship, then looking at David, *and the secrets this one has.*

David suddenly knew what it felt like to be a lab rat as they stared and ignored him, making their plans. Finally, the tall alien messaged clear as a bell; *Come…bring the female with you.* The message carried weight. This creature was even more complex than he thought, and as he had guessed, it was the leader.

No, thank you, David messaged, bluntly but to the point. He didn't know if he was looking at surprise on the leader's face but he sure felt something. It was a sort of bristling under his skin and running up his back into his head. His ears suddenly got hot. Apparently, it wasn't a request. The leader's next message was direct and forceful with the alternative now pointing at his stomach. Carl dropped the .45 on the floor, since it was of no further use, and stepped behind the trio, watching and waiting.

David knew he would have to be out of his mind to go with them and stalled, pretending to be thinking about it. He had moved Kim behind him and her pistol was impossible to get to without being obvious. He was exploring different scenarios of melee where he could somehow get to it when the two aliens holding weapons took a step forward. They extended their blasters, showing deadly intent, and he knew he was out of time. He figured they wouldn't kill him and decided to call their bluff, hoping to withstand a stunning blast. Somehow, he had to get to Kim's pistol and defiantly messaged, *No.*

To his surprise, the weapons flashed immediately, not giving him a chance to do anything but contort awkwardly and freeze in disbelief. The pulses streaking toward his abdomen had stopped short in midair. They quivered, pancaking out as if splattered on an invisible wall. David reached out and felt a clear partition absorbing the energy. There was a barrier between him and the aliens. More flashes followed with the same result. The aliens stared perplexed at the blasts dissipating in the barrier and then realized it was moving toward them. The wall was pushing them out of the ship. Reluctantly they retreated with the leader, who was the last to leave. It stared at him as the door closed and David noticed something in the alien's eyes he hadn't seen before—anger.

Chapter 33

"Kim…Kim," David said, gently shaking her shoulders. She sleepily brought a hand up and began rubbing her eyes. He smiled, relieved she was okay as she stared at the controls, blinking. She shook sense into her head, reached past him under the instrument panel and abruptly pulled on something. He stepped back at the mechanical sound and watched an object swing out and unfold into a chair.

Kim promptly plopped herself into it and gazed around, "What happened? Did I fall asleep?" she asked.

"What the…" David bent over, peering under his side of the dash and groping around aimlessly.

"Like this!" she said, reaching her hand past his, and with a quick jerk another chair popped out. "There were a few things we were able to figure out about this thing," she said.

He sat down and sighed, looking her over. "You okay?" he asked.

She nodded, then remembered and her eyes widened, twisting around toward the dark crevice in the wall.

"It's gone," he said.

"I did see an alien," she muttered. "I hate that they can do that."

"Do what?"

"Ghost us. They can make us sleep. The department has been trying to find out how for years," she said, looking at him puzzled, "You were awake while this happened?"

"Yeah."

She studied him for a moment then said, "So, where'd it go?"

"Back on its ship," he paused and mumbled, "I wonder how they knew it was on this ship?" He curiously turned back and stared at the console.

She looked around, confused. "Isn't this its ship?"

"Nope, this belongs to…" Suddenly he realized he wasn't sure what to call Rishi and Aunt Margie's kind.

"David," Kim said, clearer headed now, "you need to tell me what happened here. What is going on?"

"Aliens came on the ship and took alien Carl away," he said.

"Alien *Carl*?" she said frowning, even more confused.

"Oh, that's right" he scratched his head, not knowing where to start, "you didn't know Carl was an alien."

She leaned back into her chair perplexed. "That can't be. He's your fa—" She cut herself off and looked away.

"I know all about that," David groaned.

She looked back at him and curiously said, "What do you mean he was an alien? Our DNA results had him as human."

"He was an alien *inside* a human body."

"And how do you know this?" she scoffed.

"Saw it leave Carl's body and go right into the alien's body," he said.

"And where did this body come from?"

"It was made for him, or it," he said, ignoring her look. "The Fabricator, that thing you guys were looking for, can make bodies."

She glanced at the docking station. "We thought it was just part of the ship, to make it run," she muttered, her voice trailing off. She slowly turned back to look at David. "So...the device made Carl's human body too?"

"That's what I was told," he said, noticing her distant expression. "What..."

She didn't say anything but began looking him over like he was damaged goods.

"Oh, get outta here," he said folding his arms. "I'm perfectly normal."

"The human body that was your father was made by a machine. That's normal?" she argued. "You know, what you are saying...is that you're genetically modified."

"I'm a GMO? And here all along I've been trying to avoid that stuff," he chuckled. He knew she was messing with him to a certain extent but how much he couldn't be sure. It was possible it really did bother her or maybe she just didn't believe him. He looked over at the console and decided to find out, putting his hand on one of the spheres.

"What are you doing?" she asked.

"I'm asking the ship."

"You're asking the ship," she said in a monotone.

"Yeah, I'm asking the ship if it's true," he said, seeing her skeptical. "I know it sounds crazy, but if I just rest my hand on a sphere with a question in my mind, I get an answer…try it," he gestured toward the sphere in front of her.

She looked at it, remembering the feel of it. She touched the controls once when Roberts was showing her the docking station and the outline of the void for the Fabricator. The sphere was as cold and smooth as it looked.

David glanced at her with a startled expression, then quickly averted his eyes and pulled his hand away.

"What, what'd it say?" she pried.

"You're right, I'm engineered," he said, still avoiding her eyes and leaning back in his chair, exhaling. He glanced and saw her watching him, so he forced a smile and faced her.

"Are you going to tell me what's going on?" she asked.

He pointed to the sphere. "You might want to find out for yourself."

She did a double take at him, glanced at the sphere, and reached out and set her hand on it.

To her surprise, it wasn't smooth or cold this time, more like warm and fuzzy as the energy surged into her. "Wow, this is amazing!" she exclaimed, looking at him. Her eyes narrowed as she listened. "Aunt Margie, Rishi, the Fabricator, I understand now…all about them, but what's this, an ancestor?"

"That's who I'm supposed to meet. The ship's taking us there right now," he said.

"Where?" she asked puzzled.

"It didn't say, it just keeps saying *Origin*."

She was nodding, "Me, too…*Origin*. What could that mean?"

"Not sure, but that's mostly my stuff. Try asking it about yours," he said.

She closed her eyes, listening deeply, her head slowly bowing forward and her face becoming grim. He watched her, intrigued, and put his hand on his sphere.

Kim's jaw muscles flinched and she was gritting her teeth when she abruptly pulled her hand away. "That's bullshit!" she blurted, folding her arms, glaring at the dash, "I don't believe it."

David stared at her in disbelief. "I heard it, what it told you," he stammered, "Your parents, are they still alive?"

She didn't answer, slowly turning her back to him.

"Kim, your parents."

"I don't know who they are!" she snapped, then mumbled under her breath, "I was adopted."

He quietly stared at the back of her shoulder, giving her time to process. After a few minutes, she turned back with a quick look and began fiddling with her jacket buttons. He knew she was trying to say something but was too upset. "Wow," he said, breaking the tension, "you wake up in the morning one day, meet a special person and start thinking of the possibility for a normal life together and then something like this happens."

She looked at him, her eyes sharp. "Are you talking about me or you?"

He laughed, "Look, I'm not interested in being a normal couple anyway, that's boring."

Her hard look suddenly turned soft. "You said couple…we're a couple?"

"Well...I, uhh..." he hesitated, searching for the right words, "I think I should meet your parents first."

"Good luck with that," she frowned.

He shook his head chuckling, as if to say it really didn't matter.

"At least you have one normal parent, your mom," she offered, "Didn't she ever tell you about your father?"

He thought for a moment and shook his head. "Back then I could never get a straight answer out of her. She would always end up yanking my chain, telling me I was the result of some love affair she had with a god...Greek or Roman and usually Hermes. I think he was her favorite," he muttered and was surprised when Kim laughed. He had never thought of it as funny before.

After a quiet moment, Kim sighed, looked at her buttons again but left them alone. "I was around fourteen, looking for something to wear in my mom's closet. There was a file on the floor with my name on it. For the first time, I saw my birth certificate and found out she wasn't my mom and my dad wasn't my dad. It was such a shock. I was numb. I kept reading *"unknown...unknown"* where my parents' names were supposed to be. It explained a lot, why I always felt an odd fit with my family. I was not like my mom or my sister and definitely not like my dad."

David nodded, he was a good listener. "Your adoptive parents didn't know how to reach your real parents?" he asked.

"I was dropped off anonymously at the orphanage."

"Wow..." David muttered.

"I know, right? They could have been drug addicts or illegally in the country. How could people do that to a baby?" She then faced him. "I don't think I'm ever going to have kids. This world is too screwed up to bring an innocent child into it," she said, pausing, measuring him, "How about you, do you ever want to have kids?"

David exhaled big and long, "I think you're supposed to be a grown up to be doing that sort of thing," he shrugged. "It's too late for me anyway."

"What? You're not too old to have kids."

"No, it's too late for me to grow up," he laughed alone.

"That's an old one," Kim groaned. "So you are one of those confirmed bachelor types, huh?"

"Been one a long time," he admitted. "I wouldn't rule out having kids though, if I met the right person." He glanced at her, "How about DNA, did you ever do one of those tests?"

"I'm a mutt," she said. "I have the most even distribution of human racial genetics they have ever seen," she stated proudly.

"How does that happen?" he said amazed.

"That's exactly what I said and they pretty much didn't have an explanation for it…just coincidence is all they said after doing it three times."

"Kind of makes it pointless to be prejudiced, doesn't it?" he said.

She smirked at him then said, "How about you, ever get your ancestry done?"

"Nope…wouldn't even know how to go about it," he said, still curious. "So, what did you do after you found out?"

"At the time, I was learning martial arts and found it a great place to channel anger. I started to win tournaments. One day this guy in fatigues came up to me and after assuring me I didn't have to join the military, talked me into trying out for a job at the Agency.

They were interested in my fighting skills but moved me to agent when they saw I had a knack for reading people, especially when they lie."

"Yeah? What am I thinking right now?" he said, and put on his best poker face.

She studied him for a moment and finally said, "Not much."

"It's called mindfulness," he chuckled, and glanced up at the viewing screen. "Whoa…land ho!"

Kim turned around and they slowly got up together, staring at a flat desolate landscape on top of a massive sheer cliff looming straight ahead.

Chapter 34

"Do you have any idea where we are?" Kim asked, panning right and left at the dark ominous coastline.

David looked down at the moonlit jetties protruding from the wall of black with the ocean pounding on them and then walked back to the console. He sat down, rested his hand on the sphere and listened. "Southern tip of the African continent," he announced, then chuckled.

"What?" she said.

"This is where I'm supposed to meet someone."

"That's nuts," she said, swinging her hand toward the screen, "there's nobody out there."

He got back up and stood next to her, watching the foreboding silhouette growing larger, becoming mesmerized by the full moon's reflection zigzagging on top of the rolling swells, and wondered who he was to meet.

"Is it me or is that a light over there?" Kim blurted, pointing down the coast.

"Yes!" He saw it right away, a warm amber glow in the cool moonlit landscape and it was getting brighter and brighter. "I think we're headed for it."

Soon they were viewing it clearer and Kim spoke first, "Looks like you're meeting at a fire, a fire at a cave."

"And look—there's somebody there," he added.

The ship slowed to a stop, hovering in view of the fire with a figure sitting by it. It was a boy. He looked their way and then stood up alarmed and ran off into the darkness.

"I don't think he was expecting us," Kim observed.

David squinted at the screen, "Where'd he go?"

They both stood quietly, searching the darkness while the ship centered itself on the cave, enabling them to see into it. "Look!" Kim exclaimed.

"That's a big one," David murmured at the flashing light on the back wall. A huge fire burning deep inside the cave behind a rocky silhouette was giving them glimpses of the interior. There was a large clearing toward the front of the cave that appeared to be of sand, covered with divots from a lot of human feet. Apparently the boy was not alone.

A sudden huge shadow streaked across the back wall in the flashing light. "Holy shit...did you see that?" Kim exclaimed.

"I saw it, relax," David said, turning to the instrument panel. "Whatever it was, we're safe, it can't get to us." He reached for the controls but stopped talking when he realized the ship was rotating on its own, slowing to a stop with its opening pointed toward the cave. They looked at each other as the door opened and the ramp began deploying to the cliff's edge.

"You were saying?" she said as the thunder from the pounding surf below flooded into the ship.

"I hope that's not who I'm supposed to be meeting," he muttered.

Kim looked down and picked up the .45. "Here, you know how to work one of these?" she asked, holding it out to him.

He took it, pulling the slide back partway and saw it didn't have a round in the chamber but the magazine had bullets in it. He pulled the slide all the way back and let it go, loading the chamber. While easing the hammer down he realized the alien didn't know how to arm the pistol. "I could have jumped that alien," he growled.

He took note of the weight of it in his hand and glanced at Kim. She was watching him and looked relieved, realizing she probably wouldn't be shot by accident. She reached for her Glock but he stopped her.

"Wait a minute, this is supposed to be a meeting not a fight. The ship brought us here to meet someone, so I say we have faith that it did so for a good reason."

She studied him for a moment with her hand still on her weapon. "So, you're leaving yours here?" she asked.

"Hell, no, I'm just saying better to appear peaceful looking." He tucked the pistol behind his back and added, "Who was it that once said aggression toward the unfamiliar is an indication of inner weakness?"

She nodded, amused, "I have no idea, but did this certain somebody happen to differentiate between reckless abandon and a cautious survivalist?" He chuckled and shrugged as if he wasn't really sure what it all meant anyway.

Standing at the top of the ramp as wisps of salty air buffeted their faces, they waited, for what, they weren't sure. Something moved in the shadows and the boy came up, stopping next to the fire and beckoning to them. They could see him clearly now, covered with a white chalky coating over his dark native skin except the area around his eyes. They walked down the ramp and couldn't help but notice how freakishly similar he looked to an alien.

Their feet sank into the cushy sand as the boy walked up to David, talking in a strange language. He spoke with intermittent clicks of his tongue off the roof of his mouth, earnestly attempting to convey something very important.

"That sounds like the San people," Kim said.

"The what?"

"You know, the Bushmen, they talk with that clicking sound, they're the oldest people on the planet with the most DNA of the first humans."

"Looks to me like a kid pretending to be an alien," David muttered.

The kid suddenly grabbed David's hand and tugged on it. He wanted them to follow him into the cave. Glancing at each other — *here we go* – and they began walking into the darkness. They hadn't gotten very far when they started to hear a lot of people deep in the cave.

"Sounds like someone's having a party," David said, suddenly wishing he didn't have to worry about some pistol stuffed in the back of his pants. Kim heard them but she didn't say anything. She was checking around as they walked. They passed a cave painting of an animal and then another and then a lot of them, paintings of herds running and being stalked by hunters. One beast was painted in remarkable detail, like it was some kind of tribute. There were strange objects painted on the walls, too, almost like they were done by a different artist and difficult to identify. One looked a lot like an alien ship. It was odd how it was placed overlapping another painting, almost rudely and must have been the result of some overwhelming inspiration. It even had the outline of a hand nearby. Perhaps it was the artist's signature.

He glanced at Kim who was staying close to the wall, and when he noticed the next painting behind her, he stopped cold in his tracks. It was probably done by the same person that drew the other strange objects because it wasn't of animals or humans. It was a painting of three figures with pale thin bodies and enormous eyes, and the one in the middle was taller.

Aliens, he thought with a chill.

Kim stopped and came back to him. "What do you think of that?" he said, pointing. The boy also joined them, and together they studied the painting.

It suddenly occurred to David that Kim wouldn't recognize them because she wasn't aware enough when they came on the ship. "It's them," he said, "Carl's rescue party." Kim looked back now while the boy began talking loudly, waving his hand toward the painting. He grabbed David's hand, pulling him earnestly this time. "Ok, ok," David said, letting the kid lead him away, thinking the pistol tucked behind his back didn't seem like such a bad idea after all.

Deep in the cave they came to the rocky barrier where the sand was cool, lit only from the reflection off the ceiling as the fire roared on the other side of the rocks. They could almost feel the warmth of it.

They followed the boy around the barrier to the side of the cave where there was a pathway, and single file, they walked through the rocks into another spacious opening—a huge room with the fire burning in the center of it.

There was a dozen or so women seated around it, clapping and singing in a tribal chant. Three men, naked except for a skin covering their genitals, were dancing in front of them, slowly working their way around the fire. The women smiled as they approached and made room for them while the men kept dancing, occasionally glancing their way. They were fun to watch, feeling the music, moving their sticks and arms symbolically to tell some tribal story, their knees bent, pumping their legs and pounding their feet on the ground. Their shins were wrapped with strands of thumb-sized dried pods, shaking with every stomp, filling the cave with a racket that closely resembled the sound of rain.

A woman next to Kim suddenly got up and broke out into a spontaneous dance as if she couldn't hold it in anymore, and once expressed, unceremoniously sat back down. A few moments later, another woman in the circle bolted to her feet, dancing to her heart's desire. As she moved around the fire, her shadow flashed ominously against the wall. David and Kim looked at each other and smiled.

There was a new sound in the cave, a tapping noise getting louder and louder, but it wasn't coming from anyone around the fire. It was coming from the back wall. They leaned sideways, jockeying to see past the women across from them. They saw a man sitting at the far end of the cave against the wall. His head was covered with plumes of white feathers that shook while wielding a stick, smacking something on his lap.

He stopped and was slow to stand up. He was elderly with an eclectic array of beads and pouches swinging around his neck. He kept his head bowed over a large animal leg bone cradled against his chest as feathers and strips of leather hung from his arms and legs. He started smacking the bone again while raising his head and looked toward them with solid white eyes.

Chapter 35

"That's a Sangoma, a witchdoctor," Kim said.

"I don't think he can see very good," David mumbled.

The men stopped pounding their feet, moving out of the Sangoma's way as he entered the circle. He walked with purpose around the fire, hitting the bone as he did. He stopped in front of David and turned to him, dropping the stick to the ground. Reaching out with both hands, holding the large bone over David's head, he began chanting. David glanced at Kim and saw she was watching intently.

The Sangoma stopped his chanting and sat down, facing David, his blank eyes pointed in his general direction. David wondered how it happened or if he was born that way. He braced to not freak out if they were to suddenly unroll from inside his head. It was strange how he had this eerie feeling the Sangoma could somehow see him.

The Sangoma sat quietly and seemed to be waiting. The natives stopped their singing and all turned his way, watching. The Sangoma then picked up the bone and extended it to David, as if it were an offering. David glanced around and saw everyone was expecting him to accept it. He reached out, palms up under the bone, and the witchdoctor surprised him by lowering it into his hands. It was heavier than it looked, appeared ancient with a grayish patina and polished golden brown where handled the most. But its most remarkable feature was the areas of delicately carved animals and figures, very much like the cave paintings. There were scenes of hunters stalking herds of leaping animals similar to antelope and women gathered together with children playing around them. Someone had spent a lot of time on it, creating what appeared to be a ceremonial piece, but for what?

The natives had started their singing and clapping again, carrying on with their fun, ignoring him. The witchdoctor also appeared to be in some sort of meditative state, ironically with his eyes closed.

David rolled the bone over in his hands. There were two figures sitting by a fire under carved dots as stars. David's eyes drifted past them toward the heavy knuckled end of the bone and he froze. He stared at the three oddly familiar figures seemingly floating in the stars. The frail bodies, huge eyes and pointy chins, all looked to be done by the same artist. Whoever carved this bone had met the aliens.

The Sangoma reached into one of his pouches, dug around and pulled out a bird's foot with black and white spotted feathers attached to it. He began shaking it over the bone, mumbling and chanting. David ignored the plume of dust in his face with the musty smell of clove and kept studying the ancient bone. He felt dizzy as the bone took on a different look. In his hands, it was strangely familiar. His eyes were dry. He rubbed them as a nauseous chill came over him. He needed some fresh air. He thought of going outside when the bone moved in his hand and he looked up.

A hairy figure sitting in front of him was trying to take the bone. There was an awkward moment of wrestling, both tugging on it, and then the man stopped and glared at him. David looked into the eyes under the heavy ridged face, and found them oddly familiar.

"Do I know you?" David asked, feeling the silliness of his question. *How would I know a caveman?*

The primitive hominid abruptly let go, curiously looking at him. Tilting his head, he began gesturing toward the bone and speaking in a language David couldn't understand. But it was clear he wanted David to know this was his bone.

It happened all at once. His hands were not his anymore, they were covered with hair, holding tightly to the bone. It was not old anymore, it was fresh, without carvings and bloody with flesh hanging from it. A pale hand suddenly gripped the bone, pulling, trying to take it away. They stood up, continuing to wrestle over the bone, and glancing up he saw the alien leader. He pushed the alien away and it stumbled backward, falling to the ground in the midst of hominids, lots of them. One of them looked familiar. It was Kim, a primitive Kim. She was in pain, blood running down both her legs. All of the hominids were in pain with blood on them and, somehow, he knew the alien did it. He took a step and cringed from a jolting pain in his abdomen. There was blood everywhere, his crotch—it was cut and bleeding. The alien got up smiling and, enraged, David swung the bone.

The alien's head shattered like a ripe watermelon as screams of horror came at him from all around. The hominid Kim came up to him, holding his arms down, looking upset and screaming words he didn't understand. He looked down at the dead alien and was shocked to see a fellow hominid, dead, his head smashed in.

Confusion swept over him as he saw angry, screaming faces. Among them he saw the alien again, smiling. He attacked, holding the club high over his head, but the hominids mobbed him, pushing him down, flat on his back. He lost sight of the alien, unable to move, struggling…he had to kill the alien.

***

"DAVID!"

David opened his eyes to see Kim peering down at him. She was kneeling at his side, looking very concerned. "We should go!" she said, loudly. "Are you ok?"

He got up on an elbow to the sound of screams filling the cave. He saw a crazed woman, shaking violently, circling another woman that appeared confused as did the other tribe members standing by paralyzed.

"Why are they fighting?" he asked getting up groggily.

"I don't know, one of them just started going crazy," she said.

The woman under attack became angry, reacting with a violent push against her aggressor, sending her to the ground. The tribe members now looked at both of the women, even further perplexed.

"Let's go," Kim said, pulling on David's arm, but he was frozen, staring up at the ceiling. "What is it?" she asked.

He watched it, ghost-like, subtly flicking over the woman's head. It looked like a distortion of the air, similar to what heat does to images when looking through it. It was shaped like a thin wobbling tentacle, snaking out from the far side of the cave, deliberately touching the top of one woman's head, then the other, seemingly escalating the confrontation.

"Can you see it?" David asked.

"What, see what?" Kim questioned.

One of the men stepped up in an attempt to stop the fighting, grabbing the shoulders of one woman from behind. The tentacle let go of her, flicking up and then settled on him. He paused, distracted, and while trying to understand what was happening, the woman in front of him jerked back, hitting him in the nose with her head. Enraged, the man violently punched her and stood over her unconscious body, screaming angrily. The men around him took a step back in shock. David recognized the screamer as one of the dancers, but the joy in his eyes was gone.

It came from his blind side, a brutal striking blow, sending him to the ground. He rolled over, unable to breathe, his wind gone and his stomach locked in spasm. He looked up into the barrel of Kim's pistol pointed at his head.

"Kim-Don't-It's me-David!!" he gasped, terrified at her cold, vacant eyes, and then he saw it, the vapor-like tentacle pulling away from her. Paralyzed, he stared, expecting to be dead in an instant, but Kim's hand began to tremble. She cried out and fell to her knees.

He sat up, putting his arm around her and took her pistol. She collapsed, stunned, and he watched the tentacle backing away. It moved about the room, touching those watching, and he saw the transformation as they turned into angry monsters. Fighting began breaking out all around them. They had to get out of the cave.

Kim reached for her pistol. "We've got to get out of here!" she yelled. David was startled and relieved to see she had recovered and gave her weapon back to her. He picked up the old bone and they rushed under the menacing tentacle as David kept an eye on it. Just as they reached the passageway he saw what he was looking for. It was about three feet tall, narrow and transparent like the tentacle sprouting from it, distorting anything behind it. "Look! There, can you see that?" he said pointing.

Kim looked and shook her head. "What…what am I looking for?" she said.

He got close, stiffened his arm so she could look down it. "There, next to the Sangoma." Together they saw the Sangoma standing next to it, staring at it as if he knew it was there but only David could see the vibrating image. Then the witchdoctor turned their way, gazed in their direction and began to disappear.

"Holy shit! What the…" Kim said, losing her words, staring stunned where the Sangoma had been.

Fighting broke out close to them. "Come on!" David said, and pulled her toward the passageway. They raced through the rocks into the sandy area, alone and glad to be leaving the madness behind them. Kim paused at the paintings of the three aliens. "Was it them?" she asked.

"I…I don't know," David said, glancing at the images, then staring, considering the idea for the first time. He hadn't seen any sign of the aliens. He turned back to her and to his horror saw the tentacle flicking over her head. He grabbed her, pulling her to his side and tracked the wavering tentacle to its vibrating mass against the far wall. He didn't know if it would do any good but pulled his pistol anyway and fired a round across the sand into it. He wasn't surprised when it merely hit the wall. But the quivering did seem to jar to the side briefly. The tentacle withdrew and the mass streaked upwards into the rocky ceiling.

"Is it out here!?" Kim bellowed, clearly upset, her weapon out.

"It's gone!" he reassured her, but his mind was racing, trying to understand what he had just seen. In the split second he shot it, an image blipped in the mass. It was subtle and vague and so quick that he wasn't sure of anything except that if he were to describe it, he would have to say it had two big eyes.

"Come on," Kim said and now she was pulling him toward the mouth of the cave. The boy was gone and his fire nearly out with no sign of the ship.

"Now what?" Kim asked peeking over the cliff's edge to the shore far below. She then grimly turned back to the darkness of the cave. "You're going to have to tell me where it is," she declared.

"Wait, look!" David pointed out over the ocean.

Something was materializing out of the haziness…the ship. The ramp emerged and he pushed her toward it. "I'll be right behind you!" he yelled and turned his back to her. He didn't have to wait long. A vibrating mass dropped from the ceiling about twenty feet away and he brought his pistol up. The bullet went through it and this time it didn't care. It began slowly moving toward him.

"David, come on!" Kim shouted. She was at the top of the ramp straining to see what he was shooting at. David turned and ran as the tentacle sprouted from the mass, chasing him up the ramp. He dove through the opening and rolled over to see the hatch close in time, but not before noticing something more disturbing. The sand was covered with the transparent images sprouting tentacles in his direction.

Kim was standing at the control panel, her hand on the sphere. "Can they get in here?" she yelled, and after a tense moment, she relaxed and fell into the chair. She stared at David and blurted, "What the fuck!"

Chapter 36

David slowly turned the bone in his hands, lost in thought. Kim glanced at him, still struggling to make sense of what just happened.

"David, can you tell me anything. Was it an alien?" she asked, looking back and forth, between him and the bone in his hands.

"I don't know. I got a glimpse of something but can't say for sure."

She noticed a strange, distant look on his face. "What are you thinking about?" she asked.

He looked at her, pensively for a moment, then asked, "What were you feeling?"

"What do you mean, when?"

"When you had your gun pointed at my head."

She blinked, staring blankly into his eyes as the blood drained from her face. "Oh, my god," she mumbled bringing her hands up, covering her eyes. "I can't believe I did that. What is wrong with me?" she asked, her voice muffled through her hands.

He waited, giving her time to think. "You don't remember?" he finally asked.

"I do now, that's what's so disturbing."

"No, I mean, couldn't you tell?"

"Tell what?"

"You were being manipulated."

She stared at him, speechless.

"What *do* you remember?" he asked.

She took a breath and exhaled. "Anger, like I've never felt before. I was so angry at you and something kept telling me, *Do it, don't think about it, just do it*. My god, how could something so terribly wrong seem so right?" She thought for a moment and turned to him. "David, it wasn't me."

"I know, I know," he assured her. "Was there any thought as to a reason why?"

She shook her head. "I can't remember." She thought hard for a moment, then looked at him in utter disbelief. "I remember feeling it, a powerful reason but it's crazy. Now I can't remember what it was." She looked away perplexed.

"But, Kim, you stopped yourself. Do you remember how?"

She shook her head, her mind too scrambled to say anything.

"Okay, let me ask you this," he said. "Somehow you sensed you didn't really want to shoot me. Now, if you had *known* you were being manipulated…do you think it would have been easier to handle the anger?"

She cleared her throat and looked uncertain. "I want to say yes, but I'm not sure. It was so convincing," she said and then whispered, "*I thought the feelings were mine.*"

"Was it more like an impulse?" he persisted.

"Call it what you want. It felt real and turned to outrage fast. What has that kind of power?" she asked.

"Wish I knew. Those poor natives didn't have a chance, except the Sangoma."

She abruptly looked at him. "I saw him disappear. Was that what you were talking about, the way Aunt Margie vanished?"

He nodded. "Yeah, looks like the Fabricator gets around."

"Could it have been the Fabricator doing the manipulating?" she asked.

"No," David said, shaking his head. He didn't even have to think about it.

She looked curiously at him. "Why go all the way to Africa to have a meeting? Couldn't the Fabricator just make the Sangoma here in the ship?" she asked.

"The Sangoma wasn't the one I was to meet," he said, adjusting himself in his chair and then holding up the bone. "I met the guy who carved this and I probably had to be in Africa to do it."

"What? I didn't see you with anybody else but the Sangoma," she said.

"Well, I did," he said, sighting down the bone while pointing it across the room. "I know you probably think it is all in my head, but I went somewhere else. I met an ancient hominid." He glanced at her and noticed her look. "I'm not crazy. I know what I saw...I saw a caveman."

She nodded. "I don't think you're crazy," she said and had no problem accepting his version as something he believed since she suspected he was drugged. As the Sangoma was shaking the ceremonial feathers in front of him, the plume of dust it created must have been full of some airborne drug.

"So, why a caveman? What was the meeting about?" she asked.

David frowned and looked at the bone in his lap. He had been wondering the same thing. "I'm not sure, other than the fact that he was abused by the...," He stopped and thought of the natives in the cave. He thought about the painting of the three intruders on the wall. He looked back at the bone wondering how old it was. Then all he could think about was, how long has this been going on?

Kim reached toward the sphere and set her hand on it, listening.

"You asking if it was the aliens?" he said.

She kept her head bowed while listening and nodded.

"It's my turn," she announced. "The ship is taking me to meet someone."

"Where?"

"All it's saying is *Home to Grimalkin*. What's a Grimalkin?"

"Cat...I think," he guessed.

"Oh, great," she said chuckling, "I'm off to meet a cat."

"Well, I hope your meeting goes better than mine," he said, and glanced back at the bone, "What did it say about the cave?"

"It was the aliens hurting the people, and it also said there's going to be more of it."

He looked up and stared at her for a second. "Worse than what we just saw?"

She shrugged. "I hope not, I mean, how bad could it get, a meeting with a cat?"

David nodded. "Yeah, I guess we should plan on scouting out all the pet shops when we land," he joked.

"There's going to be a lot of pet shops to look at," Kim said under her breath with an ominous look at the viewing screen behind David.

He twisted around. "Holy crap!" he blurted. Two huge green eyes were looking at him through the viewing screen and it took him a moment to realize he was face-to-face with the famous gaze of Lady Liberty. "My god, people down there must be freaking out right now."

David put his hand on the sphere while Kim stood up, looking through the viewing screen down at the people below. "They seem all right, I don't think they can see us," she said.

"We're cloaked, invisible to them," David confirmed.

They both stared for a few moments and wondered what was next.

"Hey, maybe we're supposed to go see Cats on Broadway," David quipped.

Kim chuckled, "Right, I never did see that show."

"Kim…," David said, his voice changed now and she saw him gesture behind her.

She turned around and saw it, a lit-up circle on the floor, not far from the door. She walked over to it, gingerly probing the outer edge with the tip of her shoe.

"It's a portal," David said, listening to the ship, "We're supposed to get inside it."

She looked stunned. "Are you serious?" she mumbled.

"It's going to beam us down!" David exclaimed, "What's it like to be transported?"

She looked at him as if he was crazy. "David, nobody on Earth is doing any transporting," she said, then looked back at the ring and said under her breath, "I have no idea what this is going to be like."

"Oh, come on, you guys are doing secret stuff like that all the time, everybody knows it," he stated. He paused to stare at the gun on the panel and the bone leaning next to it.

Kim said, "The only classified stuff I've ever been briefed on was the Roswell incident and that other one I'm not supposed to be talking about," she said.

He turned to her, grinning, "You realize we're standing in an alien ship now, right. I think we're way past the whole *keep the UFO's a secret* thing."

She laughed, "Good point."

He walked to the transport ring, leaving the pistol and club behind. She raised her eyebrows at him and he shrugged. "I don't think I'll be needing a gun down there and can you imagine me walking the streets of New York swinging a caveman club?"

She cocked her head, "Have you ever been to New York?"

"Very funny," he chuckled. He stepped into the ring facing her. "Are you bringing yours?"

"Always do, never leave home without it," she said, looking up at him, wondering if he disapproved.

He shrugged. "Doesn't bother me, but why? What are you expecting?"

"It's for the unexpected," she said, carefully straightening his shirt collar, and as she did the compartment around them began to blur. "Whoa, what's happening?" she asked, looking side to side. He kept his eyes on her, his arms around her waist, and pulled her close. She faced him, staring at his lips, letting hers draw closer, and as their bodies sparkled and began to disappear, they kissed.

Chapter 37

Roberts emerged from his office, spit-shined boots glistening against the polished floor, and with a quick twist he was marching, his pounding heels echoing down the long hallway. A soldier at a door marked CONTROL snapped to attention while another opened the door for him and he paraded in without breaking stride. "At ease," he barked and walked up to Jackson. They stood over a soldier seated at a monitor. "Where are they now?" he demanded.

"They just entered the air space on the east coast," Jackson said, pointing to the screen.

"Well, it's about god damn time," Roberts snapped with contempt. "What the hell took that thing so long to kick in?"

A nerdy tech standing in the proximity explained, "The computer on our tracker kept rebooting because it was locked onto something that it wasn't programmed to understand, so we had to reprogram it. But we had to wait until it stayed still long enough for us to update it. Holy Moly, with the way that thing was zipping around, faster than we have ever seen before, it was amazing we were able to get it updated at all. But we finally did and now it can report its location from anywhere in the world!" the tech finished, smiling proudly.

Roberts stared at the tech and was sorry he asked.

Cathcart burst in, out of breath, holding his notes high against his chest. He had been running and looked around the control room panting like a dog. "Where are they now?" he managed to gasp.

"They're approaching Manhattan, Sir," the soldier next to Jackson announced.

Roberts glanced at Cathcart. "Any idea why they'd be going there?" he asked.

Cathcart shook his head.

"They've stopped!" the soldier monitoring declared.

Roberts stepped closer to look over the soldier's shoulder "Where?" he said.

"Right on top of the Statue of Liberty, Sir," he said with his index finger on his monitor.

Roberts looked up from the monitor grinning.

Cathcart looked at him puzzled. "What?" he said.

Roberts glanced past Cathcart to another soldier across the room with a headset on. "Well…anything?" he asked.

The soldier shook his head. "All frequencies clear. FAA has normal chatter and NORAD is quiet."

Roberts nodded, as if confirming his hunch, then turned to Jackson. "What about Nichol's tracker?"

Jackson shook his head. "No sign of it yet, she's still out of range or maybe the ship is shielding it."

Roberts considered this for a moment while rubbing his chin, then ordered, "Get'em scrambled, heavy, and I want everyone in civvies. We'll take the jet to Kennedy," he said, looking back at the monitor. "They think nobody can see them."

"What's going on?" Cathcart persisted.

Roberts turned to him, displaying a rare smile and said, "Well, Professor, it appears you are going to get a crack at your organic bridge theory after all."

Chapter 38

"Hey, get a room!" the kid howled as he zipped by on his bicycle. David and Kim opened their eyes and had to squint from the bright sunlight. They were outdoors, standing on grass next to a stone wall with shade trees nearby filled with chirping birds. It was as if they had just walked into a wonderland of normalcy.

People were everywhere, living their lives, walking and talking, laughing with their kids…there was lots of laughing. They gladly absorbed the civility, realizing how much they had missed it. Some people were obvious visitors, tourists in action, standing in awe, craning their necks to gawk up at the monument behind them. They turned to look and were so close they could barely see her head.

David felt Kim's hands on him. She was brushing dirt from the cave off his clothes and he stood still, arms out while she did. She suddenly spun around. "Do me," she said and he began brushing her, lightly at first, stealing subtle feelings of the curves of her body as he did and was the perfect gentleman until he got to the end and finished with a playful pat to the bum.

She whipped around and looked at him, loving the way she could read him. "Thank you," she said, teasingly.

"You bet, any time," he answered with a little grin, their eyes locking, both acknowledging their growing magnetism for each other. To avoid making an awkward spectacle of themselves, they looked away. They walked together to the edge of the grass, mingling with people, enjoying the feeling of meandering among them.

Kim grabbed David's hand. "Come on, let's catch the ferry!" she said, pulling him toward a line of people. They shuffled with the tourists toward the boarding ramp like a crowded column of slow moving penguins.

"Do you have any money?" Kim asked.

David shook his head, "Goons at the base took everything."

She nodded, not surprised. "I have some but we'll have to stop for more."

"I'll pay you back," he said, then muttered, "God, I wonder how my restaurant's doing."

Kim had enough money to get them on the ferry. They stood at the stern in the afternoon sun and watched the massive monument shrink while they motored away. David looked at the space around the statue's head and couldn't see any sign of the ship. He had no way of knowing if it was still there or if it had left and didn't care. He turned his back to it and studied the other people on the boat. Most of them were seated, some in conversation, sharing and joking, some with kids busily playing with each other. He saw an elderly group sitting off to the side, three couples that appeared to be visiting together. One elderly man had his eyes closed, letting the ocean gently rock him while the woman next to him gazed out on the horizon.

They were all travelers, passing through, looking for experiences, something he had seen many times in the diner. He gazed out over his tourist boat companions and realized, for the first time in his life, he was one of them.

He looked at Kim. There was so much he wanted to learn about her. He studied her profile while she gazed out over the ocean. She casually looked over at him and smiled as if she knew his thoughts. A gentle breeze buffeted a lock of hair into her face, and without taking her eyes off of him, she let it happen. It didn't have to be said. They were both thinking the same thing…if they could just keep on going.

The ferry's motor went into reverse, shuddering as it drifted sideways, and the skipper threw it into neutral just as the boat bumped the dock. They slowly herded off with the people and when they got onto dry land, they paused, looking around while the crowd fanned out. David felt Kim's hand in his, pulling him toward a nearby pushcart. An intoxicating whiff of baked bagels greeted him as they walked up, and hunger hit him hard. He vaguely heard Kim ordering while his mouth watered over the golden delights covered with sesame seeds, onions, and some with black poppy seeds. He hadn't eaten anything in a long time.

Kim tugged at him again, and he saw her holding a steaming bagel and followed her like a zombie. They sat down along the boardwalk and she split it, a water bagel stuffed with a schmear of cream cheese, sliced tomatoes and basil. For the next few seconds they made no attempt to talk.

"Thank you. That was awesome," David said through his napkin.

"One of my favorites growing up here," she said.

"You what?"

She dabbed her mouth with a napkin. "Grew up in the projects until I was sixteen, then we moved to LA when my dad got a better job."

"So, this is all familiar to you?"

"Sure, it's been a while but not much has changed."

"Your old stomping grounds," he said, looking around with a new appreciation. "You've probably been to the Statue of Liberty a million times."

She scrunched her mouth, trying to recall. "Actually, I can only remember once, when I was a kid."

"Really..." David said, mildly surprised but then he wasn't. He could recall visiting only once the famous U.F.O. museum in town, and the only reason he remembered was because his mom started acting so weird when she got startled by a wax figure of an alien.

"So, where do we go from here?" he asked, looking around.

"You feel like a walk?" she gestured toward the skyscrapers.

"A walk sounds great," he said standing up and breaking out into a stretch, "You have any idea where to look for this Grimalkin thing?"

"Not a clue," she said joining him and sounding as if it were the furthest thing from her mind. David, too, quickly forgot about their mission and turned toward the city, excited to see it for the first time. They started toward the skyscrapers under a clear sky and the afternoon sun. It was a beautiful day in New York, and they walked away without noticing the white cat sitting on the nearby wall curling its tail up and down, watching them the whole time.

***

They entered lower Manhattan, the sounds of bustling vehicles bouncing off the walls of the massive buildings. A sudden blast of a horn echoed around a corner, surprising David with a sense of being underground. He looked up, relieved to see blue sky but shuddered anyway, remembering the base.

Kim led the way, obviously having a destination in mind, and David was glad. He wanted to be distracted, craning his head around, trying to catch every detail while soaking up the hustle bustle of the city.

Kim stopped, standing in front of a store window and David realized she had found what she was looking for. He looked at the mannequins with their outfits displayed in inviting poses and felt an old familiar feeling of dread creeping up on him.

"You want to go in with me?" she asked.

And there it was…a dull wave of fatigue began sweeping over him, its paralyzing effects taking hold. It's a phenomenon that takes the strength right out of a man's legs and makes him desperately want to find a chair. He had always thought a savvy clothing store would have a few comfortable chairs and a game going on a wide screen TV to keep a man busy while his woman shopped. It could be off in a corner and even have some token men's items for sale, and the ultimate would be if they served beer.

He hemmed and hawed but there was another reason for him hesitating—he didn't have any money.

"Come on, let me buy you some stuff," she offered. "Pay me back later."

He glanced at her, looked at his pants and did a quick futile brush at some of the stubborn dirt. "It would be nice to get a change of clothes," he admitted.

"Great!" she responded. That was all she needed to hear and promptly dragged him into the store. She went ahead of him and he wasn't surprised when she made a beeline to a specific rack. Before her feet were set, she had an outfit out in one hand and was sliding hangers with the other.

David watched the familiar shuffle unfold; unhook, hang sideways, compare, put back, bring out another, hold up and maybe look in mirror, peering over it…it was numbing.

He looked around and saw the men's department and went straight to it. He would show her how it was done. He grabbed a couple of shirts, a pair of pants, a change of underwear and some socks, and proudly piled them up on the counter. *Bam*! he thought. It only took a few minutes and he was done.

He looked over and saw she had only managed to move to another rack and headed toward her, prepared to brag about his efficiency. But as he got closer he paused and noticed the look on her face. She was really enjoying herself. He watched her, hovering like a hummingbird delicately landing and sampling a colorful flower, then proceeding to buzz over another cluster of colorful clothes. It surprised him how good it made him feel to see her happy.

She saw him coming and held an outfit in front of her with raised eyebrows. "What do you think?" she said, pausing for a second, then quickly swapping it with the one in her other hand. "Or maybe this?" She looked so cute he would've nodded approval for anything she was considering. "Come on, you have to choose one," she said.

"Get'em both…I like both," he said and he honestly did. He watched her holding the blouses up, scrutinizing them, and realized this might take awhile. He didn't want her to feel rushed and started backing away. "I think I'm going to wait outside for you," he said.

"Oh, okay…I'll hurry up," she said, clearly having trouble deciding.

"No-no, I'm not in a hurry. I just want to see what's going on outside," he said.

"Wait," she said, "what about your clothes? We have to get something for you."

"Already got them, up there," he said, pointing to the register, "and thanks, I really appreciate it."

"You sure?" she said, slightly leaning her head to the side.

He smiled at her and for once he was doing the reading and saw how much she needed more time. "I'm sure…I'll be right out in front."

"Okay," he heard her say as he walked toward the store's entrance knowing exactly what she was doing. She was escaping, and why not? With every second they spent in civility, memories of what they had been through were becoming more and more surreal and distant. He wanted to escape, too. He wanted to forget about the ship and the bone and the hominid. He pushed the door open, wondering what the hominid would think of the shopping experience in this store, and chuckled, thinking surely they would have this in common.

Chapter 39

Colonel Roberts sat in a C-21a military version Learjet, one of two his department had for transporting high profile people and cargo. He opened a folder to a map of Liberty Island and thought about the Blackhawk helicopters he had staged in a nearby tourist's helipad. He would have a lot of explaining to do if all did not go well.

He intended to hit the areas so fast that the local authorities wouldn't know what hit them. If need be, they would be informed later that the activity was the result of reliable intel about a pending terrorist attack. Hang gliders, loaded with explosives or possibly a dirty bomb and not enough time to alert them.

The plan to capture the cloaked ship was both innovative and simple but it was untested, and this bothered him to no end. He had to rely on the contraption Cathcart and his engineer's came up with, and without seeing it work with his own eyes, it was unsettling. They had designed a steel net, strung between his helicopters, that would snag the vessel and run a programmed pulsating electrical current through it to create a force field, supposedly neutralizing the vessel.

Hopefully, it would stay cloaked and they could merely scoff it off as a false alarm. That would be ideal, but if the ship became visible to the public, well, he tried not to think about that. One thing he did know is that possession of this asset was the most important thing to him in the world.

Across the aisle, Jackson's phone buzzed. "Roger, that," he said, then turned to the Colonel. "Sir, Nichols is on the move. GPS has her in downtown Manhattan."

Roberts looked up from his notes. "Bout time, call ahead and give them a heads up we're going into town first."

"Yes, Sir," Jackson replied and got back on the phone.

Roberts sat back. This new scenario changed things and the more he thought about it, the more he liked it. If he could capture the two thieves that stole his ship, he could make them fly it to the hanger he had arranged.

He tried not to get too excited; he would bide his time. It was good that Nichols didn't know about the tracker. He had them installed in the pistol grips of all his agents, mostly to avoid misplaced weapons but also to eliminate surprises. If an agent was down or turned up missing, he wanted to know about it. He knew how avid she was about keeping her weapon with her at all times and was counting on her doing the same with Cooper. Yes, he would find her and as soon as he spotted Cooper with her, he would take them into custody. Things were looking up.

Chapter 40

David leaned against the front of the clothing store and gazed up at the massive buildings. He felt like an ant looking up from the bottom of a canyon. He watched people as they filed by, coming and going. Most of them seemed preoccupied with their minds elsewhere. It was a sharp contrast to his home town where eye contact on the sidewalk was the standard. He looked around and shuddered. Couldn't do that here, he thought, there are just too many people.

Kim emerged with a broad smile and bags in both hands. "Got a special surprise for you." she said playfully.

"What? What?" he said, following alongside, trying to see into the bags, but she was walking way too fast.

"It's a surprise. You'll just have to wait," she said, appearing to have a destination in mind. He kept up with her and couldn't help but notice everyone else was walking about the same speed. Must be the New York way, he thought. They turned a corner and found themselves entering a hotel lobby. He glanced at her and she was smiling coyly. "Wouldn't you like a shower before getting into these clean clothes?" she asked.

"Ohh, that sounds good," he said and reached for the bags. "Here, let me help."

"Don't peek now," she handed them over and headed toward the check-in desk. He watched her go to the counter, and when she began to talk to a clerk, he glanced into the bag. His heart leaped at the glimpse of lacy lingerie slipping out of a box. He quickly closed the bag and looked up, glad she didn't see the expression on his face. She would have known for sure that he had looked. He managed to compose himself by the time she came back, grinning, waving a door card.

"Where to?" he asked, his hand hovering over the elevator buttons.

"39th floor," she replied, "we should have a spectacular view from up there."

He nodded approvingly as if he was thinking about it and not her prancing around in a teddy.

He held the door open for a talkative group and then backed away, joining Kim in the corner. They were squished and, of course, he didn't mind having an excuse to get closer. They stared at each other as the group piled in, glad they were keeping their backs to them. They sounded German or possibly Austrian and kept exchanging boisterous expletives of something they did or were about to do.

A girl in the group squealed. David looked to see why and saw it was nothing but silliness. He felt Kim's finger tapping on his shoulder and assuming she wanted to whisper something, lowered his ear to her. A sudden gush of hot breath filled his ear and he felt her teeth nibbling on his ear lobe. He pressed her against the wall and they kissed.

When the elevator stopped and the door opened to the 39th floor, they were alone. They laughed, realizing they hadn't even noticed the group leaving. David picked up the bags and they followed the signs to the room, their feet barely touching the ground in anticipation.

Kim reached for the door card, her hands fumbling and jittery, inserted it into the lock and managed an impromptu grin while holding the door open.

"Thank you," he said, breezing in with his hands full, trying not to show his giddiness. He passed closet doors and a large bathroom, then entered into a generous bedroom with a king-sized bed overlooking the city. "Nice room," he said, taken by the view. Kim took the bags from his hands and blindly tossed them behind her. Then she stepped in front of him. "Let's take this dirty shirt off of you," she said, tugging on it, pulling it up and out of his pants.

He ducked as she pulled his shirt over his head and stood in front of her half naked. She paused, studying his chest with a slight smile and tossed his shirt to the floor.

"Well then," he countered, "let's take this dirty jacket off of you," and started peeling it off her shoulder. She pulled her arm out and he felt her hot breath on his neck while reaching around her with his other hand for the jacket. Their eyes locked and they kissed, holding each other tightly while he let her jacket fall to the floor in a heap. She pushed him away, reached for her pistol, unclipped the holster and dropped it on her jacket.

She went for his waist. He fumbled clumsily with the buttons on her blouse, wanting to rip it off of her. His hips suddenly yanked to the side. She was having trouble with his belt. They tore off their own clothes and within seconds were naked, falling into each other's arms.

Their lips brushed in passing, then returned kissing deeply, rolling onto the bed, exploring and receiving. They stoked the passion they had for each other, unveiling and revealing a shared lust for life they had only imagined before. She held him tightly, taking him and keeping all of him. He discovered an incredible new world and found it was full of infinite possibilities. They held each other, first to catch their breath and then just to be together, quietly sorting their feelings and stayed that way for a long time.

Kim woke up first and saw it was dark outside. She untangled their arms without waking David and got out of bed. She stood over him for a moment watching him sleep, then lightly kissed him on the cheek. She covered him back up and looked around, realizing she felt hungry. After looking over the dinner menu, she quietly ordered room service, and seeing David hadn't stirred, tiptoed off to the bathroom.

***

David was in the grassy meadow, dreaming he was among his friends again but this time not the center of attention as he was before. He was mingling with them when he noticed his mom off in the distance and walked to her. She was bent over, holding a stake to the ground with one hand and pounding it with three distinct hammer blows. "Mom, what are doing?" he asked.

"Hello, sweetie," her face lit up when she saw him. "I'm making a pen," she said, positioning another stake to the ground and with the same three blows, pounded it in.

He scratched his head at the circle she was making in the grass. "A pen for what?" he asked.

"For the critters," she said, straightening up, stretching, her hand pushing into the small of her back. Her belly was huge and he realized she was pregnant. She gestured behind him, "Hand me one of those, honey." He turned around and stared in horror. Holding a stake for him to take was an alien with Carl's head stuck on it.

He bolted upright in bed, panting profusely, not knowing where he was. He rubbed his face. He could still hear his mother hammering on the stakes. He heard them again coming from the door...someone was knocking. He heard the shower running in the bathroom with Kim softly humming. "Just a minute" he yelled out.

He grabbed a robe, slipped into it and peeked through the peephole.

"There must be a mistake," he said, looking down at the cart.

The porter glanced at his ticket, "Nichols in 39?" he verified.

"Oh...right," David said, and backed up to let him in. He watched the parade of silver domes with shiny flatware and white linens go by with a jiggling red rose that seemed to be waving at him. He caught a whiff of something roasted, meaty and delicious and there definitely was sauce involved.

He followed the cart, hovering over it, waiting for the porter to leave but he kept fidgeting with stuff as if it wasn't perfect enough. "Oh," as David realized why. "I'm sorry I don't have any cash," he confessed.

The porter put his finger on the bottom of the tab. "That's okay, you can catch me right there," he said and headed for the door.

"You bet, will do," David said with as sincere a nod as he could manage, closing the door behind him and locking it.

He lifted the first silver dome, and the aroma of garlic, roasted chicken, mushrooms, white onions and carrots filled the room. Fluffy mashed potatoes were under the next dome and more garlic. He loved garlic. He reached for a taste, hand inches away, but hesitated at Kim's gentle humming. Her voice, softly mingling with the water, tugged at him and he looked down at the dish. He suddenly wasn't hungry for food anymore. He covered it back up and walked toward the bathroom as if succumbing to the irresistible sound of the siren's song.

Chapter 41

"Roger, that," Jackson said and turned to Roberts across the aisle. "GPS has pinpointed Nichols in a hotel."

Roberts nodded thoughtfully, not surprised. "I want floor plans to that hotel by the time we get there, and get somebody over there to watch their room," Roberts directed and turned to look out the window. It was getting dark outside. He looked at his watch. They would be landing in a couple of hours and hopefully his two people of interest would stay put. He hoped to get in, take them into custody and get out without a fuss. They would have to be delicate about this with the locals.

Chapter 42

Kim stopped humming when David stepped in the shower. "Wash my back," she said turning around. He had never seen her with her hair up before and it gave her an air of elegance that he reacted to with a nibble to her neck. She moaned then turned to engage in some playful sparring.

"Okay...*Hey*," David said, with his hands up, "that's not a safe thing to do in the shower."

"Oh, I see, now you're *safety Dave* all of a sudden?" she giggled and turned back around.

He chuckled while he ran his soapy hands over her, taking his time, soaking up every inch and memorizing every curve.

"What are you doing?" she finally said, turning to him. "You're supposed to be washing my back."

He tried to pull her close but she put her hands up, resisting. "Maybe that's how I wash backs," he said.

"Oh, yeah?" she said, then whispered, "I had a wonderful time."

"Me too...why are we whispering?" he whispered.

She shrugged. "Not that anyone is listening, but it's a message just for you," she said as her eyes sparkled and then she started lathering him up.

***

They stepped out of the shower with pruned toes. Kim took her towel to dry a spot on David's back while he grabbed their robes off the hook.

"Dinner came," he said while draping a robe over her.

"Oh, do you like Coq Au Vin?"

"Coke a what?"

"You telling me you have a restaurant and you don't know what Coq Au Vin is?" she said in disbelief.

He studied her for a moment then said, "What'd you call it?"

"Coq Au Vin."

He finally nodded, "Of course I know what it is. I just like the way you say it. Besides, who doesn't like Coq Au Vin?"

She smirked, "Well, I didn't know if you were a foodie or not…you could be a vegetarian."

"Nope, I have my moments though. Usually I have to feel sick before I start eating healthy," he admitted.

"Me, too," she laughed as they walked into the bedroom. David lifted one of the silver domes. "Bring it over here," she said sitting on the bed's edge. He rolled the cart over and they sat side-by-side, tentatively nibbling at first but soon all talking ceased until most of the dinner was gone.

"I was so hungry…even cold it was good," Kim said, falling back onto the bed.

David fell back, too, and looked over at her. "I'm stuffed," he said, pushing his stomach out, smacking it a couple of times.

"Oh, my God, how do you do that?" she said scrunching her nose. "Looks painful."

He laughed, letting his stomach relax. "Must be a guy thing," he said, and tried to push the cart away with his feet. The wheels weren't cooperating and he got up to push it by hand to the door. He turned around and saw Kim under the covers, watching him with just her eyes peeking out. He crawled in and they relaxed in each other's arms, talking less, breathing deeper and soon falling into slumber.

The caveman, the bone and the ship had all faded away to a seemingly distant, surreal figment of their imagination. As David drifted off, he became aware of a new-found strength and knew it was coming from Kim. It was a feeling of confidence that he could handle any challenge set before him, and little did he know how soon he would need it.

Chapter 43

David pushed the dinner cart out into the hallway while Kim locked the door behind them, and they walked toward the elevator arm in arm. It was a new day. They looked and felt refreshed and were feeling adventurous. They stopped in front of the elevator appearing as if they were on vacation as David reached to push the elevator button.

"Excuse me, I'm sorry but the elevator is out of order," a voice from behind them said.

They turned to see a hotel employee, sitting in a chair around the corner with an open magazine on his lap. "You'll have to use the one in the other wing. Our apologies," he said, pointing down the hallway and flashing a cordial smile.

They thought nothing of it since they were more occupied with each other, but might have thought differently if they had seen the way the doorkeeper watched them walk away.

***

The hotel lobby was more crowded than usual but not enough to draw the clerk's attention. However, the security guard's suspicions were raised by the handful of businessmen wearing heavier jackets than the weather dictated. As a retired cop, he had participated in many stake outs and began to suspect he was witnessing one on his watch. He counted six men, strategically placed. He knew the bigger the coat, the bigger the guns, which usually went hand-in-hand with the amount of danger involved.

Was it a team for some incoming celebrity? Most likely not. Their security usually arrived with them with a couple of men running lead. No, these guys were waiting for someone, someone important and dangerous. Then he noticed their ear pieces, state of the art, almost undetectable, and reached for his radio. He unclipped it from the top of his shoulder but hesitated when he saw one of the men staring at him, index finger pointed straight up, wagging it back and forth. Another man nearby, stood up slowly and stared sternly as he approached, stopping to face him. "You need to stand down on this one," the man in black said with such a tone that the guard knew it was not a request.

"I think I should have been told about this," the guard protested.

"You would have been told if what you think matters," the man said coolly.

The guard glared, weighing his next move, when an officer in fatigues walked into the hotel as if he owned the place. The guard looked the man over in front of him, "You guys military?"

The man didn't confirm nor deny. "Look, we don't want a scene, and you know what? Nobody needs to know we were even here," he said. The guard slowly returned his radio to his shoulder clip. "Thank you," the man in black said and turned away.

Roberts nodded approval to his man leaving the exchange with the security guard, who was now leaning against the wall frowning. Roberts scanned the room and his men, and liked what he saw. He concluded he was ready when his radio crackled. "Talk to me Jackson," Roberts mumbled into his communicator.

"They're stepping into the elevator right now, sir," Jackson said.

"Copy that," Roberts acknowledged, and nodded to his men. Four of them got up and positioned themselves in front of the elevator, prepared to be the greeting party.

"Nice and easy, gentlemen," Roberts muttered over his communicator. "We don't want to draw any attention, but don't forget they are armed."

***

"I wish I had my phone," David said while they rode down on the elevator. "I have no idea where we can go for breakfast."

"It's probably best we don't have them anyway. I know Roberts would have been tracking mine," Kim said and then looked at him excitedly. "Besides, I remember this great place, a mom- and-pop diner. I think you'll love it. I just hope it's still there," she said.

David nodded. "Sounds great," he said as the elevator stopped and the doors slowly opened.

Kim looked out the door, surprised. "That's odd," she said.

David looked, too. "Are we on the right floor?" he said, craning his neck, looking above the door. "Ground floor," he confirmed.

"Seems more like the service elevator to me," Kim said, looking around at an informal area of the hotel. She glanced out the glass door and recognized the top of a building in the distance. "I know where we are. Come on!" she said and grabbed his hand, pulling him outside and they walked together down the side alley toward the street.

***

In the lobby, the elevator doors opened and a couple emerged looking very similar to Kim and David. They walked past Roberts' men, oblivious to the pouncing they narrowly escaped.

"Jackson! I'm not seeing them!" Roberts said impatiently into his communicator.

"What?" Jackson said from the 39th floor and glanced at the soldier with him. They walked to the elevator looking at the number panel above it. "We saw them get in and the elevator didn't stop once," he said forcefully and weakly added, "sir." He waited in the silence that followed, expecting a berating barrage from his superior. He glanced around, down the hallway both ways and saw they were alone. The hotel was spotless except for a magazine on the floor nearby, a gossip rag with a headline "I Saw an Alien! Am I Crazy?" Jackson chuckled and bent over to pick it up when he heard Roberts voice in his ear: "Jackson! Front and center…now!"

Chapter 44

David and Kim wound their way through the crowded sidewalk, traversing the masses with Kim leading the way. They had stopped at a corner, waiting for a light to change when Kim excitedly pointed across and up the street, "There…there it is!"

David looked at the line of tall buildings and saw a sign sticking out of the bottom of one that read, *Nepeta Café*.

"That's it?" he said. "That's a hole in the wall."

"Oh, come on…give it a try," she begged, and tugged for him to join everyone else crossing the street.

They entered a bustling atmosphere of clanking coffee cups, busy utensils and breakfast chatter. It was packed and noisy, but David was enjoying every second of it. They looked around and it appeared their timing was good as only a few people were waiting ahead of them.

David welcomed the familiar feelings rooted deep in his upbringing, and while they waited, he put his arm around Kim. He noticed a strange feeling and looking past his arm saw an attractive woman looking at him. He realized he was doing something he had never done in the past. By putting his arm around Kim, he was essentially taking himself out of the "available" market and he didn't care.

Kim sensed him looking at her while he slid his hand to her lower back and looked directly at him when he noticed something missing. "I didn't bring it," she said.

"Really…why?" he said surprised. "What about the unexpected?"

She turned to face him, looked at his chest then up into his eyes. "It just didn't feel right…that kind of energy mixed in with us…with this," she said, gesturing heart-to-heart.

"If it makes you more comfortable, then I'm glad," he expressed and pulled her close.

"Two for breakfast?" a little voice said.

It came from a young girl about eleven years old, holding a pad in one hand and wiggling a pen back and forth in the other.

"Yes, how long is the wait?" Kim asked and noticed a couple getting up from a table by the front window.

The girl flipped the front page over and ran her finger down the scratched-out names. "There are only two parties in front of you, so it won't be long," she said, noticing Kim looking toward the window. "Is that the table you guys want?"

"That would be nice, but…" Kim said, glancing at the people ahead of them.

"Let me see what I can do. We have a few tables opening up out in the back courtyard and these people said they wanted to be outside," the girl said and walked off.

They both watched her go. "She's cute, so efficient, too." Kim said amazed.

"She reminds me of what I think my mom would have been like, working the diner as a kid," David said.

"I'll bet that's *her* mom," Kim said nodding toward a woman working the register.

"Yeah, I see a resemblance," David said, and fell into an old habit he had when in a new restaurant. The first thing he did was to make a quick study of the kitchen to give him a feel for the type of management running the place. He noted the breakneck pace of the two cooks and one helper for all these people. It was impressive and, for a moment, he missed working his diner. One thing about that kind of work, once you got into it, there wasn't much time to think about anything else. Maybe that was the draw for him; periodically getting lost in the busyness and then having new eyes on his circumstances, a new way to look at them again.

He thought of his diner and his employees. He wondered if he should be worried. He had to assume that if they wanted to work, they would run it as they had when he was off doing things for his mom's estate. There wasn't enough money going through the business to be too concerned about it but, still, it seemed he should give them a call.

"Your table is ready for you," the girl said, holding menus and gesturing toward the table at the window.

"Oh, great!" Kim said. "Thank you."

"You've been here before," the girl stated to Kim. She was looking at her with her head slightly tilted and had a strange expression on her face.

"Yes, how did you know?" Kim asked.

The girl grinned while she handed them their menus, then looked at Kim and declared, "I've been told I have a knack!" and skipped away.

They watched her go and from behind the register, her mom was watching her, too. "Sophie," she called out, waving the pad of names at her while pointing toward a couple at the door.

David slid his empty cup toward their waitress as she came with a pot of coffee. She poured and smiled at Kim. "Coffee?"

"Yes, thank you," Kim replied and slid her cup over.

A chanting crowd passed by their window and caught their attention. "What's going on?" Kim asked.

"Construction workers protesting the remodel up the street," the waitress said with a dip of the pot for the last drop. "Treated unfairly or something like that," she added, and walked off.

Chapter 45

The security guard saw it in the officer's face first, the way he was glaring around the room. The men in black, on the other hand, were alarmed, checking every person around them as discreetly as they could. The guard knew the feeling of a blown stake out. They had missed their person of interest. He braced for the impending, uncomfortable confrontation he knew he was about to have as the officer approached him.

"I need to see the recordings from your surveillance cameras," the officer said.

The guard wavered for a moment. "You don't have any authority here without a court order, so unless marshal law has been declared, I'm afraid that's imposs—" The guard stopped at an F.B.I. identification dangling in front of his face.

"We are in pursuit of two escaped criminals that are armed and dangerous," a man in a brown suit standing next to the officer flatly announced.

"I'll need to take a look at that," he said, taking the I.D. and squinting hard at it for a moment. It was authentic and he was required to cooperate with domestic agencies. He handed it back, "Right this way."

***

Roberts stood in the middle of a dozen monitors rerunning their recordings for the last ten minutes. "Keep replaying them," he said as Jackson came into the room. "Where is she?" he demanded.

Jackson shook his head. "She left it in the room. I think she's trying to escape," he said and had never seen such a look of surprise on his commander's face.

Roberts slowly turned back to the monitors and quietly studied them for a while. "There!" he abruptly yelled, pointing, "Where is that camera?"

"North-side entrance," the security guard said, freezing the image of David and Kim walking arm in arm down the pathway leading to the street.

Roberts turned to Jackson. "Does that look like they are trying to get away?" He then glanced at the monitor. "This time of day, I'd say they are going for breakfast."

Jackson was dumbfounded. Staring at the monitor he turned to the soldier at his side. "That's impossible!" the soldier reacted, looking at the monitor, perplexed.

Robert's jaw clenched, "We don't have time for this! Obviously, they don't know we're here. I want a man in every restaurant in that direction," he growled and pointed to the monitor.

Chapter 46

"These guys are known for their egg toasties," Kim said while David studied the menu.

"Sounds good, but I have a habit of ordering the same thing for a first meal at any new place," he said, flipping it over and scrutinizing the back of it.

"Really," she said, "what are you looking for then?"

"Just curious," he said.

"So, what do you always order?"

"You'll think it's boring, but it's what I was raised on…it's sort of my benchmark for a place," he said, finally putting his menu down and pouring cream in his coffee.

"What is it?" she persisted.

"Bacon and eggs over easy with a short stack," he said, offering her cream.

"Does sound boring," she said, with her hand over her cup.

"Is that what you want…the two by four?" the waitress asked, having overheard him while finishing up at a nearby table.

"Uhh…two by four," David said, glancing back at the menu.

She pointed at the menu, "Two eggs, four pancakes with any of these," she said circling with her finger.

"Sounds good to me—with bacon," he said, handing his menu to her.

"What do you recommend?" Kim asked.

"Any of the toasties…we're known for them," the waitress said as if she had stated it a million times.

Kim didn't have to say it but her smile had *I told you so* written all over it. She ordered one with avocado, bacon and a schmear. The waitress left with their order and they settled back, sipping coffee and glancing around.

David was watching the foot traffic passing by the protestors outside when he felt Kim's foot rubbing his shin. He turned to her and saw it staring at him, over her shoulder. Kim noticed the startled look on his face and twisted around. "Aww…where'd you come from?" she said, cooing, stroking the furry head of a white cat sitting on the window sill.

David smiled at the way the cat fell into a euphoric trance, purring so loudly he could hear it vibrating in the glass next to him.

"Sophie!" the receptionist blurted from behind the register. The girl was talking at a table nearby and when she looked their way, her jaw dropped.

"Grimalkin!" she hollered from across the room and raced toward them.

Kim and David looked at each other with their mouths open.

"Is this your cat?" Kim asked, shifting her intoxicating scratching to the underside of the white feline's chin.

"No, she belongs to our neighbor, Alice."

"Ohh, I see, and what did you call her?" Kim asked following the cat's chin now pointed upward.

"Grimalkin, that's her name, Grimalkin," Sophie said, reaching for the cat. It was a large cat for the little girl but, somehow she still managed to hold it in one arm while petting it with the other and talking. "She must really like you because she's usually very ornery out here. She's supposed to stay in the back room when she visits. My dad says she's the best mouser we've ever had!" The girl's eyes turned into saucers. "Oops! I'm not supposed to tell you that," she said lowering her voice.

Kim laughed, "Oh, that's ok, don't worry about it. Where does Alice live?"

"Upstairs, she's a fortune teller, she can tell the future," Sophie declared.

"Oh, I see. Can I meet her?" Kim asked.

"Oh sure, her door is next to ours out front," she said and pointed out the window. Then she leaned closer and said in almost a whisper, "You can go up the back way, too, by the bathrooms. That's how Grimalkin gets down here."

"Oh great, I would like that. Maybe after breakfast we'll go visit her," Kim said glancing at David, and then smiling at Sophie.

The little girl was gazing out the window with a vacant expression and said in a low, ominous voice, "She knows you're coming."

Kim and David glanced at each other, speechless, then stared at Sophie, when she abruptly smiled and announced, "That's what she says every time someone visits."

They watched her skip away with the cat bouncing in her arms and then looked at each other, chuckling.

"A fortune teller, huh?" David said, picking up his coffee and sipping. "How are you with mystics?"

Kim held her coffee up in front of her and frowned. "Not very good. She's going to have her hands full trying to get me to believe anything she's got to say." She then blew hard and took a tentative sip and added, "You know we could get lost here. I know places we could go. I mean, do you care about the ship and the aliens?"

David shook his head. "I don't, I would just as soon leave it all behind," he said, looking out the window and feeling troubled.

"I have money stashed," Kim said watching him, "so don't worry about that."

"No, it's not that. I was just thinking about my house and restaurant, and what about Roberts?"

She scoffed, "Roberts wants the ship, which we don't have any more. I'm thinking that if we just disappeared for a while, a year or two, you could have someone run your diner for you and let things cool off," she said. "And if we had to, I know how to change our identities."

"You do?" he said impressed.

She nodded, "Oh yeah, I've been using a special credit card. I'm sure Roberts has all of my regular credit cards flagged." She looked to the side and pulled her elbows off the table. The waitress came up with her arms full and in a flurry, filled the table with steaming, delicious-looking offerings.

David took a sip from his refreshed coffee cup, set it aside and began his routine. First, he peeked under the eggs for grill burn, then cut one in half looking for cooked yolk, then cut into the pancakes to check their centers for consistency.

Kim smiled while watching him, then looked down at her breakfast and dug in, took a bite, closed her eyes and welcomed the explosion of flavors. She let a moan slip while she swirled the morsels in her mouth, savoring them as long as she could, and then finally swallowed. She opened her eyes and saw David staring at her. He gulped down his pancake. "Can I try that?" he asked.

"Sure, get a bit of everything if you can," she advised, nudging her plate toward him.

He maneuvered around her breakfast until his fork couldn't hold anymore, then looked it over, took it in and rolled his eyes as he expertly appraised the skills of the cook.

She grinned, watching him with confidence. She knew what she had.

Finally, he swallowed, looked down at his breakfast and poked at it with his fork. "I'm getting that next time," he muttered.

He offered her some of his breakfast but she politely shook her head. "No, thank you."

David grabbed a bagel, tore off a piece and chased his egg yolk around the plate. "What about the fortune teller?" he questioned.

Kim glanced at him while chewing and did a short headshake.

"Aren't you even curious?" he pried.

"Not really," she retorted while using the edge of her fork on her toastie.

"It's up to you, but it is kinda crazy how that cat had the name you were told to meet up with," he noted as he corralled the last of his egg against the edge of a pancake.

Kim's fork dropped to her plate with a loud clank.

He looked up and saw her staring at him, her hand paralyzed over her plate. She seemed afraid to look to the side.

David looked outside and a chill ran down his back as he saw Roberts standing in the midst of the crowded sidewalk staring at them through the window.

"David, we've got to get outta here!" Kim gasped.

Roberts's smiled morbidly as he watched them get up from the table and retreat. He took a step toward them right into the path of a fast-walking construction worker and they bumped hard. Roberts spun around, ending up with his back slamming against the window.

The muscular man followed Roberts, thumping a meaty finger on his chest. "Watch where you're going, you gung-ho muthafucka."

To everyone else the commotion appeared the result of a mild skirmish to be dropped, but David knew better. He was watching the translucent tentacle hovering over Roberts' head, slowly descending and touching him. Roberts' posture changed with an awkward twitch. "They're here," David said, pointing to Roberts' hand reaching around his back.

They watched in disbelief as Roberts pulled out a serrated commando knife and plunged it into the worker. A woman screamed. The worker looked down in shock at the knife handle sticking out of his shirt, a red patch growing around it, and fell to his knees. Roberts kicked him violently, knocked him to his back and leaped on top of him. With ferocious savagery, he pulled the knife out and plunged it back in, again and again and again. The worker's legs thrashed about, desperately kicking the air, then fell still.

David saw the tentacle release from Roberts's head and withdraw somewhere behind the crowd. Roberts's men were looking on baffled and confused. They knew something was terribly wrong but didn't know what to do.

"Oh, my god!" someone in the restaurant yelled. People stood up at their tables, talking loudly. Some rushed past David and Kim to get a closer look.

Roberts's men took positions in front of the growing, angry crowd surrounding their colonel. Roberts had stopped his attack now and was slowly standing up, and when he turned toward the restaurant, David saw the look of a man lost. Roberts looked down at his bloodied hands, at the mutilated body at his feet and his shoulders slumped.

"What is going on with people these days?" their waitress said, coming up next to Kim. "I'm so sorry you had to see that. How terrible!"

Kim nodded. "I know, it makes no sense. Is one of those ours?" she said noticing some checks in her hand, "I think we'll be going."

"Can't say I blame you. I feel like leaving, too," the waitress said, thumbing through the checks.

As Kim handed over her money she asked, "Ok if we go out the back way?"

"Oh sure," the waitress said and saw Sophie standing nearby, watching them. "Sophie, go ahead and show them the back way out," she said, then turned away and drifted over to look out the window. Roberts stood among his men, confused while they argued with the crowd, holding them at bay.

Kim felt Sophie's hand take hers. "Come with me," she said, and started leading her away.

Kim noticed they were heading toward the stairs. "Sophie, we want to leave through the back door," Kim said.

"Alice is waiting for you," the girl said, pulling harder.

Kim stopped, her arm stiffening. "Uhh, I don't think so," she said.

Sophie turned around and looked squarely at Kim, the innocence in her eyes gone, her voice low and guttural. "Alice has a message for you."

Goose bumps swelled up on Kim's body as she numbly let Sophie lead her along.

David noticed Kim acting weirdly and followed her to the stairs. Sophie abruptly let go, her feet pounding on the wooden steps as she raced up. Kim slowly turned to him, bewildered. "Did you see that? That kid freaked me out," she mumbled.

"That freaked you out?" David said, "What about what happened outside with Roberts?"

She looked and saw the police were on the scene now, interviewing Roberts. "Don't forget that's Roberts you're talking about. There's nothing he can do that would surprise me. Although, that was really stupid on his part and the poor guy he killed, jeeze, that was terrible." She grimaced at the crime scene for a moment then added, "I don't think we have to worry about Roberts anymore and probably not for a very long time." She then glanced up the stairs after Sophie. "I'm getting to the bottom of this right now," she mumbled, and began climbing the stairs.

David looked back out the front window, captivated at how different Roberts was now. He was leaning against a police car, head bowed, staring at his feet while a cop questioned him. Another cop displayed his contempt while he looked on, hands anchored on the gear around his waist. The police had formed a perimeter holding back the crowd, some looking on in horror while others were busy gossiping.

Then David saw it, translucent, quivering and shaking. Two people fervently talking over it were unaware it was right in front of them, in front of the whole crowd, and then David realized why it was there. It was absorbing and gloating over the carnage it had caused. Suddenly it streaked up, gone, and no one noticed but him.

Chapter 47

David caught up to Kim at the top of the stairs where Sophie was holding the door for them under a sign that read:

Enter and believe it or not

It's all an Illusion

They entered into the musty smell of incense and the hazy air it made. Sophie led them down a dark hallway past rooms with hanging beads for doors to an opening covered with bohemian drapes. She parted them and slipped through, turning into a bright light coming from around the corner. The drapes fell closed and it was dark again in the hallway. Kim and David looked at each other and then they slowly parted the heavy curtains, peering into a large room.

They saw Grimalkin sitting on top of a small table against the back wall that was covered with gypsy fabrics. The cat was watching them, her tail hanging down with the tip of it slowly curling up and down. They looked toward the bright light coming through a window and saw the silhouette of a woman sitting in front of it.

"Please come in," she said warmly. Her hair was curly and a bit frizzy, illuminated around the edges from the back lighting, giving her an eerie halo effect. She appeared to be older which was in sharp contrast to her youthful-sounding voice. She patted the chair next to her. "Sit here, Kim," she said. It was the only chair available.

"How do you know my name?" Kim questioned.

"Oh, honey, that's what I do," she said, bubbling with inner enthusiasm. "I've been looking forward to meeting you for a long time."

Sophie came up to them and gave Alice a hug. "Thank you, Sophie," Alice said, kissing her on the cheek.

"You're welcome," Sophie said, looking at Kim, mindlessly twirling her dress back and forth before scampering off.

Alice noticed David, looking around uncomfortably. "Hello, David," she said, shifting in her seat, looking him over with nods as if confirming what she already knew.

"Oh, hello, Alice. Listen, Kim, I don't think we should stay long," he said.

"They won't come here," Alice said flatly.

David looked at her for a moment and said, "I'm sorry, but you can't know what I'm talking about."

"They won't disturb us," she said assuredly.

Another moment passed as David studied her. "Are you sure we are talking about the same thing here?" he finally said.

"Of course, we are. They don't come around, because I stop them when they do," she said.

"How do you stop them?" he asked.

"I see them when they appear and they don't like it. You can stop them, too, when you let them know you see them for what they are. It disrupts their pleasure, sort of like you did before."

Kim looked at David. "What's she talking about?" she asked.

David shrugged, "In the cave, remember? I shot at one and it left."

"It wasn't the bullet that made it leave," Alice said. "It hadn't realized it was being observed." She then glanced toward the kitchen and exclaimed, "Good idea, Sophie!"

Sophie came up holding a plate of oatmeal cookies she had made.

"You will want to have one. Sophie's quite the baker," Alice said.

Sophie proudly looked on as they each took one.

"Thank you," David said, tasting, glancing at his cookie and giving her a nod.

"You're welcome," Sophie said.

"Sophie, dear, take David and show him the kitchen," Alice suggested. "Maybe let him in on one of your secret recipes while Kim and I talk."

"Sure!" Sophie said, taking David's hand and leading him away. He curiously looked back over his shoulder as he left, still munching on his cookie.

Kim watched them go and Alice was waiting for her when she turned back. "Someday I will arrange for you to be reunited with your parents, but today is about you and your future," she said.

Kim's eyes narrowed. She never showed surprise to a stranger and held still, smelling a cheap trick. A con sometimes leads with a personal statement and while you are trying to figure out how they knew it, they are reading you, looking for your tells, creating a baseline for manipulation. Kim was focusing, accumulating her own observations, seeing an older lady claiming to be psychic, sitting with her hands folded, beaming like a sweet granny, and she wasn't seeing anything.

"You're a tough one," Alice said. "Are you finished yet?"

Kim decided to accept the verbal challenge and engaged, "How do you know about my parents?"

Alice chuckled, "Oh, sweetie, they were created just like I was."

Kim showed her best poker face and kept silent.

"You don't believe me. What about the Sangoma?" Alice asked.

Again, Kim kept her candid reaction to herself. "What about him?" she said flatly.

Alice smiled slightly in admiration of Kim's persistence. "He was created just like me and your parents. You saw him dematerialize and return to our world. Do you believe that?"

"I don't know what I believe," Kim said, then quickly added, "Why were my parents created and not born naturally?"

"They were created to make a special baby…you."

"Why not just create me?'

"It was important for you to grow into this body."

"Why?"

"There's nothing like firsthand experiences."

"Experiences for what?" Kim persisted.

"The future."

"Okay, here we go, nobody can tell the future," Kim said flatly.

"That's kind of true," Alice agreed. "But don't you think it's possible to predict probable outcomes depending on scenarios and people involved?"

"Oh, you mean reading people? You think you know me?" Kim challenged. "Go for it then, tell me your prediction."

Alice grinned patiently. "I understand your skepticism, and it would be easy if everybody just did what I foretold, but that's not how it works. It's really all about choice. You always have a choice," she said.

Kim thought it over and said, "I'm listening, but more out of curiosity than anything else."

"Good!" Alice said, leaning back in her chair and clasping her hands over her stomach. "As I see it, you need to choose between one of two paths. Ironically, no matter which one you choose, the eventual outcome will most likely be the same, except one will be much more agreeable with the entity inside you."

Kim frowned impatiently. "Get to the point, will you? What are these choices?"

"You either go and hide, letting the world unravel as it will, or take a stand and stop them," Alice said, pausing, giving Kim a chance to absorb this.

"I can't stop them, I can't even see them!" Kim protested.

"You will when you learn how to open your eyes."

"And how am I going to do that?"

"By closing them first."

Kim nervously glanced around. Closing her eyes in unfamiliar surroundings was not one of her favorite things to do.

"It's okay, Kim, you're safe here," Alice said. "Close your eyes."

Kim reluctantly closed her eyes, trying to relax, and in the blackness a sudden, freakish image flashed in her mind.

Kim abruptly opened her eyes with her hand over the sudden, familiar knot in her gut. "Are you doing that?" she glared. "Stop it!"

Alice kept her attention on Kim and said, "I won't let go until you feel better."

Anxiously squirming in her chair, Kim appeared ready to get up and leave. "I don't have to take this," she fumed.

"Kim, you will feel better when you close your eyes and start telling me what you see," Alice encouraged. It was more the way she said it that was so compelling than the words themselves.

Her breathing labored, Kim gave Alice a shaky look as if on the verge of a panic attack. She had to do something. She closed her eyes, took a deep breath and tried to relax. She felt a slight surge of relief and began looking around in her mind's eye. "Sandy…" she muttered.

"That's better, tell me what you see," Alice said.

"The sun is shining. I'm sitting on the beach, looking out over the water. It's calm, waves lapping on the shore, it's beautiful," she said breathing comfortably now.

"Kim, this is your safe place. Look around and embrace it," Alice elaborated. "Somewhere you will find an area where you can put bad things, where you can observe them and they can't touch you."

"There's something close to shore, a platform surrounded by water," Kim said.

"That's it, that's where you put anything you don't want in your sanctuary."

Kim looked down the beach and saw she was alone. "There's nobody here."

"There will be and, remember, they must do as you say."

Kim turned the other way and saw something right next to her. "Whoa!" she blurted, reacting suddenly.

"Kim, you are safe. If you're afraid of it, tell it to go to the platform," Alice said.

Kim froze, her body rigid for a moment and then mumbled, "It's going."

"It has to," Alice said. "In your sanctuary, you have absolute power. But remember, it will try many distracting tricks to make you forget to keep it there."

"It's extremely angry," Kim observed.

"Look at it, Kim, and tell me what you see."

"It's shaking, quivering, distorted when I look through it," she whispered. "It almost disappears but flashes back, really mad. What is this?"

"Whatever it is, it has no interest in your well-being and you have it trapped," Alice said.

"What do I do now?"

"Study it. Learn all the ways it tries to manipulate you so you can better identify it next time. And there will be a next time."

"And then what?" Kim asked.

"Then you let it go."

"Let it go? Why not keep it trapped or *kill* it?" Kim said irritated.

"Its energy cannot be stopped, only redirected, and keeping it trapped will consume you. Letting it go away from you and avoiding it in the future is the best way," Alice said.

"It's gone, I let it go," Kim said, exhaling in relief and opening her eyes. "Oh, my god, that feels so good."

Grimalkin jumped up on Alice's lap. "I knew you'd like it," she said, stroking the cat's head.

Kim took a few deep breaths then looked at Alice. "You mentioned one of the choices to make would be bad for my entity. Which one?" she asked.

Alice smiled, continuing to pet Grimalkin. "Oh, I wasn't talking about *your* entity," she said looking up at her. "I was talking about the new one growing inside you."

Chapter 48

"What's this?" David asked, peering into the bowl of thick, milky batter.

"That's for my magic pancakes. I make'm from scratch," Sophie announced proudly.

David grabbed a clean spoon and held it up. "May I?"

"Sure!" she said, stepping up to watch, her nose barely higher than the bowl.

He dipped and tasted, rolling his eyes in decrypting analysis. "Flour, eggs, sugar, pinch of brown sugar, dash of vanilla and something else," he said looking at her while chasing the last of it around in his mouth. "Is that ginger?"

She jumped excitedly. "Yes! What else? What else?"

He squinted thoughtfully. "Wait," he said, savoring the last of it with a hand up and then glancing at her. "Lemon?"

She jumped again. "Zest!" she bellowed.

"You want a job? If you ever want to run away from home—," he said, setting the spoon in the sink.

She laughed and put the bowl in the fridge. "Someday I will serve them in my own restaurant," she stated.

"You could be serving them downstairs right now," David declared.

She suddenly turned to him, alarmed. "I gotta go!" With a playful hop and skip she headed for the door and hollered, "*Bye!*"

Listening to her feet clomping all the way down the stairs, David shook his head amused and for the first time in his life he had a strange desire, a tinge of something he had never experienced before. He had always believed he would be a good dad and suddenly he felt like being one. He thought of Kim while walking out of the kitchen, hoping that someday he would be able to change her mind.

Chapter 49

David peeked out from the kitchen and saw Kim sitting by herself, staring off in thought. "Where's Alice?" he asked walking up to her, glancing around. "Meeting not go like you'd hoped?"

"She had to go," Kim said, standing up. "David, she told me something I need to tell you." She faced him and began fidgeting with the buttons on the front of his shirt.

"What's the matter? Is something wrong?" he asked.

She took a moment to collect her thoughts. "I didn't believe her at first, but when she disappeared like the Sangoma, I knew…she's one of them."

"Believe what?"

She kept looking at her fumbling fingers. "According to her, I'm going to have a child, a son," she said, slowly looking up at him.

"Really, wow, you should be excited about that…I'm happy for you," he said and then chuckled with a sly smile. "Let me know if I can help out."

She blinked and looked directly at him, her eyes sharp now. "David, I'm pregnant!"

"Ohh…" he muttered, surprised. "But, how, I mean, so fast? Last night?"

She nodded and turned away. "I'm sorry, David, I don't know how I could have let this happen."

"Wait a minute," he said, taking her by the shoulders and gently turning her back to him. "I think I had something to do with it, too, remember? I was there."

She looked at him for a moment with foreboding. "What are we going to do?"

He smiled. "What, are you kidding? We're going to be parents!" he said excitedly, but she looked away.

He tried to look into her eyes. "Is that Ok?" he asked.

She twisted away even further. "Don't." She held her face away, struggling for words. "I…I wasn't going to do this. This wasn't going to be a part of my life." She couldn't look at him.

He was stunned, not knowing what to say. It was amazing how the timing was unbelievable, yet seemed so right for him.

Kim agonized, remembering what she had decided to do many years ago if this were to happen to her. But she looked into David's face and instantly knew she could never abort his child. She stared at him for a long moment, then reached up and held his face in her hands and said, "Are you sure…absolutely sure?"

He grinned at her. "I would love to raise a child with you, and I know you will be an awesome mom."

She stood tense for a moment, then relaxed and fell into his arms. They held each other, lost in thought for a long time. Finally loosening their embrace, David mumbled, "I'm the dad, right?"

She pushed him away, glaring at first, then remembering his twisted humor, punched him on the shoulder. "And I suppose you want a DNA test, too," she retorted.

He laughed at the thought then suddenly they looked at each other, alarmed, surprised and excited. "This is going to be a special baby," he said.

She nodded, looking down at her hand over her belly. "That's exactly what Alice said."

Chapter 50

David and Kim left Alice's place, taking the main stairway to the front door, and once outside, leaned against the building. They were both deep in thought about the sudden detour in their lives. Sure they were having a child together, but there was something else, too. They both felt it. Something was making itself known and was now a part of their new relationship.

Two policemen chatted next to their patrol car while supervising the wrap-up of Roberts's crime scene. People milled around the safety cones as passersby mindlessly comb through them.

David looked at Kim with concern. "Don't you think we should get you someplace safe?"

"According to Alice," Kim said with a glance, "we need to make a decision…either run and hide or stop them."

David looked miffed. "Really. Did she happen to mention how we would go about doing that before disappearing? And what exactly is going to happen anyway?"

Kim chuckled. "She said we would figure it out or something along those lines."

"That sounds familiar. I'm starting to have a problem with the way these guys insist on just observing but are always ready to put their two cents in."

"I know it's pretty obvious they aren't going to do it for us," she said. "Plus, I have new concerns now, responsibilities to keep in mind," as she patted her tummy.

"That's right," he nodded, "we should probably lay low with your condition and all."

"My condition?" she said, defensively. "You think I'm handicapped or something?"

"You *are* carrying our child," he said smiling at her.

She smiled back, "Yes, I am and if anything, I am now more determined than ever to create a safe place for our son."

"I get that," he said thoughtfully. He looked out at the people walking by as a homeless man walked across the street, unconcerned for the cars zipping past him. "I guess I'm processing being a new parent, too," he said.

"That's a good sign. At least I'm not alone in this."

"I'll figure it out," he said. "And besides, I'm with you. We have to do something. I just don't know what." They both watched as the bum stepped up on the sidewalk and paused to stare at the headlines at a newspaper stand.

"We should probably go back to the island and see if we can get back on the ship," she suggested.

David frowned and appeared troubled by the thought. "But when we get there, how are we going to contact the ship?"

"It knew when to come to us at the cave," she reminded him.

"True," he agreed, watching a man in a suit pushing the vagrant aside to get a paper.

"That was rude," Kim remarked as the homeless man got up with a clenched fist.

"Uh, oh," David said as the bum took a wild swing and smacked the businessman's close-shaven jaw. The man in the suit went to the ground and a few people turned to look but didn't bother to stop walking.

The businessman got up rubbing his jaw, yelling, trying to get the attention of the cops down the street.

"David, look!" Kim whispered, grabbing his arm, pointing at the homeless man. A translucent tentacle stretched out over him, flicked side-to-side, then settled on the top of his head. They both saw the transformation as the man's anger quickly turned to rage.

"Can you see it now?" David asked.

"Yes, look, there's another one," she said, pointing at the businessman. He, too, was being touched.

They realized they were witnessing two humans being orchestrated like puppets: one to drop his briefcase and the other his paper bag. They flung themselves at each other, punching and clawing, tumbling to the ground. Bystanders had now stopped to gather around, watching in disbelief as the businessman began screaming. The homeless man pulled his head back and spat a chunk of bloody flesh on the sidewalk. The crowd fell into a state of quiet shock with the sound of gasps here and there. The businessman pushed the vagrant off and got up enraged, holding his hand to the side of his bleeding face.

"Break it up! Break it up!" one of the policemen yelled as he rushed to grab the derelict from behind.

The businessman stared at them apparently in shock, blood streaming down his face onto his suit, then he lunged for the bum's throat.

The second policeman seized the businessman and turned the foursome into a scrum on the sidewalk. A pedestrian stepped out of the crowd seemingly to help, but hesitated behind one of the officers.

"Uh, oh," David muttered.

"I see it," Kim said.

The tentacle hovered over the pedestrian tasting the air like a reptile's tongue and then gently dropped, touching his head. He abruptly reached out and pulled the policeman's pistol from its holster.

The other officer noticed and pulled his pistol. "Freeze! Drop the gun…now!" he ordered. The pedestrian didn't respond, standing in a daze with the pistol hanging at his side.

The policeman, whose weapon had been taken, spun around and charged at the pedestrian who callously brought the gun up and shot the officer in the face. More shots rang out and the pedestrian fell to the ground, his body bleeding and contorting.

The tentacle released as soon as the man died, rising up in the air, darting and flicking about, searching for its next victim. It finally touched a woman protestor grasping a sign in front of her. She abruptly dropped it and began screaming, "What is wrong with you people? Do something!" She then ran at the policeman.

"Get back! Get back!" the policeman yelled, leveling his weapon at her.

David saw Kim had her eyes closed and then to his horror saw a tentacle attempting to attach to her. It instantly recoiled in discomfort, flicking back and forth over her.

"Go away!" he yelled, pawing the air over her head. It slowly backed off but didn't leave entirely. It hovered menacingly nearby, lingering for a moment as if making an observation before streaking upward and disappearing.

"You okay?" he asked, gently holding her arms.

Kim slowly opened her eyes. "I got this. They can't touch me," she said defiantly.

David took a deep breath. "Well, that's good. You're going to have to tell me how you did that."

Suddenly more shots rang out. Pedestrians were on the sidewalk, dead and dying while the policeman kept screaming, "Obey! You must comply!"

"They've got him!" Kim yelled.

David saw it attached to the officer and pulled Kim away. "Come on, let's get outta here!" he yelled.

They backtracked to avoid the chaos, turning at the end of the block. They rushed faster than the crowd and were almost to the next street when they saw it and froze. It appeared to be waiting for them while the crowd moved through its transparent, quivering image without realizing it. They edged toward the buildings and it mirrored them. Then they moved toward the street and it did the same.

"What is it doing?" Kim asked.

"I don't know. This is new to me," he said, glancing to the side and noticing one had moved between them and the building. "Hey, hey!" he said, pushing her toward the curb.

"David, there's one in the street!" she said. It was slowly drifting toward them with cars passing through it. They looked at each other, then behind them. There was one there, too. They were surrounded.

David noticed a man pass through the one on the sidewalk in front of them. "Let's go through it like everybody else!"

She grabbed his hand and they fell in with the crowd. They still tried to veer out of its path but it matched their moves, intent on a collision course. David went through it first, not feeling a thing, but Kim's hand was suddenly ripped out of his. He saw her standing in front of it. "Kim, come on. Don't screw with it!" he warned.

"I can't. It's blocking me!"

David tried to reach through it but his hand ran into something. "What the…" he said, moving to the side but it moved too, staying between them. He angrily thrust his hands at it but he still couldn't get through. "I don't get this," he said, and this time he felt around, following the invisible barrier around Kim. It curved trying to surround her. He tried grabbing it, but there was nothing to hold onto and then he noticed the other three images had closed in around her. He circled them, realizing the barrier was complete now and enveloped her. She had her eyes tightly closed. "Kim! Can you hear me?"

"I'm going to stop them!" she declared.

The four sprouted their tentacles in unison, quivering and vibrating, reaching up and joining together over her, forming a bridge.

A woman walked by close enough to bump into the barrier around Kim and looked for something she couldn't see. She kept walking but not before giving David a puzzled look. He didn't try to explain.

He waited for Kim to repel the tentacles but noticed the air around her was changing, becoming misty. "Kim! Are you okay?" he asked earnestly.

Her eyes opened, looking panicky. "David," she sounded weak.

"What's wrong? What is it?" he yelled, pushing at the barrier and the images around her. "Damn it…let go!"

"David!" Kim screamed.

He froze, looking at her and for the first time saw her totally frightened. She reached for him, her hand becoming transparent like the images. "I don't understand," she said, her voice fading. Her whole body began vibrating transparently. All of a sudden, the images streaked upward as he grabbed for her but she was gone.

Chapter 51

"NO, NO, NO…KIM!" David screamed, desperately searching the sky for her.

Powerless and terrified at the same time, he frantically looked around for help, but only saw indifferent faces passing by. Desperation grew with every second that passed as he feared for what she must be going through and couldn't help her. He had to do something.

At that moment he saw one, standing off to the side, vibrating and searching for its next victim. He charged, putting his hands through it and hitting the building. He stood like an angry boxer, punching and swinging his arms at it from all directions but couldn't touch it. "Take me! Take me!" he wailed in frustration. He brought his fist down on top of it and finally felt something, a subtle thud as his hand went through it, and he sensed its pain.

"You don't like that, huh?" he yelled, pounding on it again and again until it made a shrill sound and streaked away. He looked up after it and paused in horror. The sky was full of them, silently drifting to the ground like huge snowflakes.

"Get out of the way, bitch!" a voice rang out from behind and he saw a fat lady shaking her protest sign at a woman sprawled out on the ground.

"What the hell is wrong with you?" the woman cried, getting up. "Why'd you do that?"

"You're one of them! You work for the company!" the fat lady roared and swung at the woman. "You're crazy!" she screamed and darted away.

David saw the tentacle attached to the fat woman, and when she glanced at him he got an eerie feeling. "Holy shit," he murmured as she turned toward him. He looked around. People had stopped walking. They, too, were being touched. He caught the eye of one angry man, "You look'n at me, asshole?" The man bellowed at David.

"No, no, wait, you're being played man, *stop!*" David yelled, backpedaling, but saw it didn't matter to the angry man. He turned away and ran for his life with the painful sense of leaving without Kim. He worried more for her than the clomping feet racing behind him. He bore down as he headed for Liberty Island. He had to save her, and getting back on the ship was their only hope.

Slicing his way through the crowded sidewalk, he passed confused people being touched and then saw them turn angry at anything and everything. Some glared at him, pointed and most yelled inaudibly, but he did manage to make out some absurdities: *Thief! Terrorist! Mother Fucker!* He glanced back. What insanity, he thought, as the newly possessed mindlessly joined the growing mob running after him. He turned around just in time to avoid running into a man while dodging his grabbing arms.

He looked up to the sky while he ran and wondered if they were watching him or even worse, trying to cut him off. He heard a crash and saw there had been a wreck up ahead. He came alongside untouched bystanders taking in the surreal scene. Another driver came around the corner, shot across the intersection and plowed into the crowd.

Chaos ensued as perplexed onlookers swarmed like ants. David saw his pursuers closing in fast and darted across the street. He had to leap out of the way of a speeding car that intentionally veered to hit him. It missed, bounced off a parked car and mowed down some of the crowd chasing him. He sprang to his feet and continued barreling down the sidewalk, passing more people agitated by the sight of him. He realized they were being touched farther ahead now. He *was* being cut off.

David moved fast, shoving through the hostile crowd, and then there was nobody in front of him. He emerged onto an empty sidewalk, looked up, and saw they were waiting. The wall of people rushed toward him and he glanced toward the street. Angry faces were charging toward him, recklessly crossing from multiple spots.

He had nowhere to go but into the alley behind him. It was dark, deeply set in the middle of the block, and there wasn't a soul in front of him all the way to the other side. He sprinted for it and from the middle of the block saw a body in the street ahead. Someone ran past it, a blur to him, then two more flashed by. A woman stopped to stand over the body, slightly hunched as if ready to help but then looked up and saw him running toward her.

David waved at her, "Run! Run!" he warned but to his surprise she pointed at him and yelled incoherently.

"What the hell, can't she see…" he muttered, but to his horror, people started to gather behind her, all pointing and screaming at him. He skidded to a stop when they started running toward him and looked around. There was nowhere to go but up and he jumped for a fire escape ladder. His hand missed and he fell onto a stack of wooden crates, knocking them over. Frantically, he bolted to his feet, shoved one of the crates over, climbed up and stretched for the ladder again.

He bounced on his toes until he wrapped a few fingertips over the bottom rung, and felt the ladder start to fall, but suddenly the crate crumbled under his weight. He hit the asphalt, realizing they would be on him in seconds. He reached for a stick on the ground and thrust it at the berserk, psychotic faces as they backed him against the wall. He yelled, bowed his head, bracing for the onslaught and was about to close his eyes when he noticed the circle of lights around his feet.

The mass of deranged bodies hit the wall of energy around him, exploding into rage and began tearing at each other as they faded into nothingness.

Chapter 52

"You're welcome." Rishi said, sitting at the ship's console.

David stood stunned and in shock, still holding the stick. He staggered out of the ring and leaned against the instrument panel. "What…" he started to say but choked, coughed, and had to take a few breaths before he could even clear his throat. "Kim! We have to save her!" he gasped.

Rishi was watching him carefully. "Yes, something will have to be done soon," he said, much too calmly for David.

"Beam her over like you did me!" David yelled, frantically looking back at the ring. "*Now!*"

"She's okay for now," Rishi said, walking to the viewing screen.

"How do you know she's okay?" David asked, desperately searching the monitor alongside him. "Where's the ship?"

"I can see where and how she is doing, and I wish I could beam her over but my access to their ship is limited," Rishi said, and pointed toward Earth in the monitor. "The one you want is the big one, right there."

David only saw the Earth and the stars behind it. Then something caught his eye, something glittering. He looked closer and saw thousands and thousands of tiny sparkling objects in a grid pattern, blanketing his planet. Then, slowly, he realized he was looking at alien ships twinkling in the sunlight. "What is going on…what are they doing?" David said, turning to Rishi who was staring at the monitor. "Rishi, are they invading?"

"Sort of…" Rishi answered.

"Sort of?"

"It's more like a vacation for them."

"Usually, when on vacation I want to have fun. This is no vacation!"

"In some circles, one man's fun can be at another man's misery."

"They're here to kill us, aren't they?" David said. "What do they want, our resources…our water, or…" his expression turned disgusted, "they're here to eat us…"

Rishi scoffed, "Oh, please. This species is way too smart to put such unhealthy things into their bodies."

"Then, why…why are they here?"

"You'd have to look at it from their point of view, living for thousands of years in a safe and secure existence, reproducing their bodies over and over again. They don't remember the value of experiencing a life from beginning to end." He held his hand out to the monitor, "What you are looking at here is the collective consciousness of an entire species that is, simply put, bored."

"Bored?" David blurted.

"I'm afraid so…," Rishi grimly said. "They have evolved not seeing the harm in vicariously experiencing suffering and death through their victim's demise."

David turned away from the monitor and glared at Rishi. "Why did you allow this…why didn't you stop them?"

Rishi thought for a moment, then gazed up at the monitor. "It has always been our way to value the natural course of life's direction, even when we see creatures killing each other needlessly. You see, the moment we impose our agenda, the end result will be tainted, orchestrated and considered artificial."

David gestured to his body, "Tell me I'm not part of an agenda."

Rishi turned to him and said, "You asked me why we didn't stop them and my answer is: we are...*we* are."

"Oh, I get it, so you've finally decided to get involved and I'm it?" David protested.

"You both are but you are not alone, we are in this together."

David stared at Rishi and thought for a moment. "Aunt Margie said you had done something to my grandmother to make my mom different, other than human. What did you do to her?"

Rishi scoffed, "I think your mom could explain that better since it was her idea in the first place."

David's jaw dropped. "What?"

"I know it's difficult for you to remember the decision we made at the beginning. But I remind you we all agreed that if these creatures are not prevented from exploiting humans, we will witness a mass extinction."

In a daze, David slipped into his dream with his friends in the meadow, and saw Rishi among them with Alice, the Sangoma and Aunt Margie. Everyone was watching along with him at his life as David. He turned to the special person he had vowed to search for in this life and saw it was Kim standing next to him. He looked past her and saw his mom, looking back at him with confidence and approval.

"I understand now," David muttered, and walked to the console. He stopped to stare at the pistol. "I remember now, the way of the Aether and how that part of me could never kill." He picked up the pistol, stuffed it into his pants and turned to face Rishi. "Do you know which ship Kim's in?"

"That I do."

"I need you to beam me into that ship."

Rishi stared at him for a moment, slowly nodding. "Hmm, this just might work. You sure that's how you want to handle this?"

"If that's where she is, that's where I have to go."

Rishi eyed the pistol grip peeking over his belt. "You think that's going to do you any good?" he asked, and reached for the bone leaning against the console. "You'll probably do better with this."

David grabbed it. "I'll take anything I can get right now," he said, and walked over to the ring. He stepped in and looked back at Rishi. "What did you mean, *this might work*?"

"Well, it just so happens that the alien you need to deal with is on the same ship."

"How will I know which alien?"

"Oh, you have met before, the tall one with the white streak on top of its head, the leader."

David's mind raced, staring at Rishi. "So I kill the leader," David said, shaking the bone emphatically, "and then the others will…what…go away? Something like that?"

Rishi didn't respond at first but kept watching David, seemingly waiting for something.

"Come on! What am I going to do?" David snapped.

Rishi finally dropped his hand to his lap and frowned. "Well, David, you've been given an ability to solve this problem and I can tell you right now that bashing in the head of an alien isn't the answer."

"What ability? What is this ability I keep hearing about? I'm an Entity? So what! I don't have any super powers!"

"Everyone is born with a gift. You just have to find yours, David."

"Look, I don't have time for any introspection right now, so just send me to that ship."

Rishi nodded. "Ok, but you should know that I can only transport you to one area in the ship and...well, let me put it this way: It's a popular place, so there's a good chance you won't be alone when you barge in."

David clenched his jaw and said, "It is what it is. I have to do this."

Rishi touched the panel and the ring around David's feet began to glow.

"Wait!" David blurted. "You never told me what I'm supposed to do. If I'm not bashing the leader's head in, how am I going to deal with this?"

"Any remedy I tell you won't mean a thing until you realize what it means to you in your life."

"Oh my god! What does that have to do with taking out the leader?" David protested.

Rishi smiled at him. "I guess what I'm trying to tell you, David, is that I don't know the answer to that. It's something you are going to have to discover on your own. But you know what? I know you can do it. I have faith in you."

"Oh great," David said, looking down at the ring. "You're a big help." He thought for a moment then said, "One more thing...how do we get back?"

"That's the spirit!" Rishi chuckled. "Be optimistic. Just don't forget where that room is. I'll be watching for you."

Chapter 53

David braced inside the ring as the energy field dissipated and was horrified to see he had materialized in the midst of aliens. There were at least thirty of them, lounging in odd chairs, staring at him. He spun around, holding the bone out and reached for the pistol. The hammer snagged on his pants and he yanked, desperately pulling up harder and harder, painfully wedging the crotch of his pants into his groin. He froze. *What the hell?* The aliens weren't moving.

In a quirky surreal moment, the aliens appeared as if they were sitting in perm-chairs at a salon and so preoccupied they weren't aware of him. He held out the pistol, edging past their catatonic gaze, wishing they would close their eyes.

He made his way to the door and opened it. Peeking out into a dimly lit empty hallway, he saw grayish green walls with a rubbery, vinyl-like floor. He looked back, checked on the aliens and then closed the door behind him.

Realizing he would have to guess which way to go, he quickly decided to sneak to the next door. He paused, contemplating whether to open it or not when an alien inside the room did it for him.

Bursting through from the other side, David's reaction was instant, a jab into the alien's abdomen followed by a swing to its head. He stood over it, numbly staring at the oozing liquid running out of it, then looked into the room. His heart leaped. There was Kim, unconscious, lying on a table.

He glanced around while dragging the alien inside and grimaced at the slimy trail he was leaving behind. He closed the door and rushed over to Kim, holding her face in his hands.

"Kim," he whispered. She moaned and he dug his arms under her to help her sit up. Her face fell into his neck and then he felt her arm around him.

"David," she murmured.

He gently brushed her hair away from her eyes. "I'm taking you outta here," he said.

"I remember now. They took me," she muttered, becoming more alert and slowly looking around. Her eyes fell on the dead alien. The bone was across her lap and she gingerly picked it up, inspecting the liquid covering the end of it. "So, what's the plan?" she asked.

"Simple. I take you next door and Rishi beams us back," he said but then frowned.

"What…"

"I just remembered the room we have to go to is full of them, but I think it'll be ok."

"It'll be ok?" she said puzzled.

"They're doing something. They're in some sort of a trance. We'll just have to be careful," he said and then pulled out the pistol. "Here, you're better with this than I am."

She took it, swung her legs around and slid off the table. "Have you seen them with any weapons?" she asked.

"Once. Some sort of blasters."

"Handheld, like pistols?" she said, while checking hers.

"Yeah, odd looking things."

She frowned, nodded, and then said, "I'm ready when you are."

They hadn't taken a step toward the door when it opened by itself. They flinched and crouched, expecting an attack. They waited but saw nothing at the open door except the wet trail from the dead alien's body running out to the hallway.

They backed around the table to another door. David motioned to her that he was going to open it and Kim swung the pistol back and forth in an attempt to cover both doors. David opened the door and was suddenly engulfed in silence. He smelled gunpowder and his ears began to ring. He turned to Kim and saw her mouth moving, barely hearing her when she shouted, "They're coming!"

She shoved him through the doorway. Bursts from blasters narrowly missed them as they rolled, pulling each other around the corner.

They were in another hallway and, more importantly, alone. They sprang to their feet and ran.

"Do you know where we're going?" Kim blurted.

David glanced down the first intersecting hallway and saw aliens approaching. "Not that way!" he yelled. The next hallway was empty and they took it, following its gradual curve. They were close to the edge of the ship and hopefully heading back toward the room. But they froze in their tracks when they rounded the curve and came upon a group of aliens waiting for them about forty feet away with blasters pointed at them.

Kim pulled David back against the wall as bursts from the blasters zipped by, missing them by inches.

She looked back. "We're boxed in!" she shouted, raising her pistol at the aliens now flanking them. The .45 flew from her hand and she saw it smoking on the ground. "Fuck!" she yelled and reached to pick it up. David's sudden yank from behind pulled her away and she fell backwards into a room. Bursts from the aliens' blasters streaked past the open door as they scrambled to get up.

"Come on, follow me," David yelled, and they began racing up the stairs. Kim peered over the side, looked down the stairwell and saw at least twenty levels below them and even more above. "This ship is huge!" she said. "Do you know where you're going?"

"Just keep your eyes open for the transport ring and let's hope Rishi can get to us," he said and then paused. "Let's see, we've gone up six levels and the room is in that direction…I think," he said pointing at a door.

"That's your plan? Go in that direction, work our way down to the same level and maybe we might find the room?" she said doubtfully. "That's it?"

"If you have a better plan, let me know."

She frowned, thinking it over for a moment, but a noise nearby drew her attention. They backed into a dark area under the stairs, holding their breath as a group of alien soldiers came up the stairs and gathered on their floor. Now unarmed, Kim looked on as David adjusted his grip on the bone and watched the aliens slowly parade by.

When the danger had passed, Kim looked David over and whispered, "You seem to know your way around this ship better than you think."

He looked back at her surprised. "What are you talking about? I don't know this ship."

She faced him. "How is it you know how to open the doors?" she said.

"I don't know. I don't think about it. I just do it," he said.

"Exactly! I can't open them. I think you might have inherited some of their instincts."

"So what, I can open some doors, big deal," he shrugged.

"Don't you realize that if we can get anywhere in the ship we can stop them!" she exclaimed.

"Are you crazy? There's probably hundreds of them on this ship. How are we ever going to get to the leader?" he asked.

She stared at him for a moment, then said, "What do you mean leader. Who's this leader?"

"Rishi said that the only way to stop them is to get to the leader," David said, shaking his head. "It's impossible."

"What! How long have you known this?"

He looked surprised but also like it didn't matter. "Rishi told me just before I came here to find you."

"And he told you the leader is in this ship?"

David nodded, looking around. "I think we should go this way to get back to the room."

Kim looked at him, her eyes sharp and direct. "Come on, David. We are in the heart of the alien's ship where the leader is. It's up to us to do something."

"With what? An old bone?" he said in disbelief.

She frowned but suddenly they had to hush, someone was coming. They slipped back under the stairs and froze as a lone alien soldier walked past them. Kim nudged David, gesturing toward the blaster hanging at its waist.

David shook his head but she flashed a look of disappointment, turned away, and attacked. Seeing her in a wrestling match with the alien over the blaster, he groaned and joined in. Grabbing the alien from behind, he was surprised at how quickly it stopped struggling once defeat was obvious. It stood meekly in front of them waiting for its fate. Kim backed away, studying the unfamiliar weapon in her hands, being sure to point it away from David while trying to find the trigger.

David stood face-to-face with the alien for a long moment and then did something Kim couldn't believe. He gestured for the alien to leave.

"Are you crazy?" she asked, watching the alien slowly walking away. "Why did you do that?"

He turned to her. "That creature is over a thousand years old and it's a young one in their civilization."

"So?" she retorted, glancing back as it shuffled away. "It would just as soon shoot us than care how old we are."

"That's true," he chuckled and looked at the blaster in her hands. "You want me to show you how to work that thing?"

She handed it over and stepped closer as he pointed at the side of it. "Take this for instance," he said, making a slight adjustment. "This will stun an individual long enough for us to escape." He abruptly swung the weapon out, blasted the creature in the back, and it fell like a cut tree, unconscious before it hit the ground.

"Wow!" she said, reaching for it.

"Here, here," he said pointing out the trigger.

She held it up, blasted the wall a couple of times and admired it in her hand. "I have just made a new friend!" she announced.

David proudly looked on and thought. *There she is, the mother of my child.*

Chapter 54

"You sure you want to do this?" David asked.

"I don't think we have a choice. No human is ever going to have this opportunity again.

He sighed, frowned and turned to the door. "Alright, alright," he droned and moved his hand over to open the door.

Kim raised the blaster. "In and out without being seen. It is possible. We can do this," she declared, then gave David a nod.

They entered the empty hallway, Kim leading, David patting the bone in his free hand and eyeing her blaster. "Man, if I didn't feel primitive before, I sure do now."

They paused at an intersection and Kim looked at him. "It's better to have something like this in trained hands."

He smirked, "You remember I'm the one who showed you how to work it?"

"Don't worry, we'll get you one," she said, looking both ways and sprinting across the intersecting hallway.

"What do you mean…*we*?" he said joining her.

Kim didn't answer and was studying him. "How did you know about the blaster?" she asked.

"Okay, I think you're right. Everywhere I look now, I just seem to know stuff."

"I knew it! So you're sure we're going the right way?" she asked, looking down the hallways.

"I think so."

She turned to him in disbelief, "What were you just saying?"

He rubbed his chin, thoughtfully looking down the hallway, then back. "I think we should go this way," he said, pointing at the intersection they had just gone through.

Kim started for it, leading the way, when a pair of aliens came around the corner, walking right into their path. "Whoa!" she blurted, frantically bringing the blaster up, but David's hand stopped her and everyone froze.

"These are different, philosophers," he said, and faced them.

Kim watched them standing quietly, exchanging stares. She looked at the aliens for a moment, then to David, then back to the aliens again and finally whispered, "What's going on? Are you guys communicating or something?"

David seemed to ignore her for a few more seconds before the two aliens politely stepped around them and continued on their way.

"Are you okay?" Kim asked, pointing the blaster at the alien's backs, "Should I stop them?"

He gently lowered her blaster again, "They told me that they don't agree with what the leader is planning to do to us and they mean us no harm," he said, as he watched them go.

"What is the leader planning to do?"

He grunted, looking back at her, grimacing. "Dissections. First me and you after you have the baby."

"What...they know I'm pregnant?"

"Evidently the whole ship knows...They know all about you," he said with a straight face.

"Oh-shut up."

He chuckled. "They also told me how to get to the leader," he said pointing down the hall, "That way."

Kim looked troubled while they walked. "You trust them? Could be a trap," she said warily.

"Apparently these guys aren't like that. They're not here to participate but rather to observe. They told me their people are following a destructive path of negativity and they actually want us to succeed. They want to go home," he said, stopping at a door and carefully studying it.

Kim looked back down the hallway, leaning side to side, keeping watch, when suddenly she heard a door open. She whipped around and saw David calmly walk through it.

"Jeez! Give me a heads up when you're going to do that," she grumbled. "Weren't you worried some of them might have been on the other side?"

"The philosophers told me they're all on the upper level at an orientation," he said.

"Orientation for what?"

"That thing Alice was warning us about. The party they've been planning for Earth?" he reminded her. "They also told me how to get back to the room." He pointed down the stairs. "We have a choice. We can go that way and probably make it without seeing any of them, or we go that way," he pointed up, "and crash the party."

"I think you know what my answer is," she said without hesitation.

He nodded slowly.

They climbed the stairs to an upper level where David stopped at a door and stared at the sign for a moment. "This is it."

Chapter 55

"I can't hear a thing," David whispered with his ear to the door and staring at the ceiling.

Kim was facing the door, blaster up and knees bent, "Just open it!" she said.

"All right, all right. Look for the taller one. The one with the silver streak on its head," David said, glancing at her, seeing her fixed and ready. "And if you do see it, step aside because I got dibs."

"Wait!" she blurted. She had seen many an agent trying to psych themselves up with such swagger. She studied him for a moment and realized he wasn't compensating for insecurities, but something else was going on, something much more personal. "No way," she said competitively, "You want the leader? You're going to have to get there first." She crouched toward the door again. "Besides, if by some miracle you manage to get there before me, have you decided what you're going to do?"

"Rishi told me it's my destiny to deal with the leader and that I will know how to do it when the time comes," he said stubbornly and reached for the door. "Ready?"

"You're planning to improvise at the last second?" she said in disbelief.

He smiled back at her. "Can you feel it? The entities have spoken. There is a master plan."

"Whatever," she said unimpressed, "You still gotta get there first."

He chuckled, gripped the bone and prepared to open the door. "Are you ready?"

"Ready."

The door opened swiftly in a whisper and David immediately closed it back up.

They stayed poised, seemingly stuck in their crouched positions while in their heads each reviewed the quick flash of images they had just seen in the hallway.

"Was that who I think it was?" Kim asked, referring to the three figures standing about twenty feet away, two smaller aliens listening to a taller one with a white streak on its head.

"Yup." David said, blinking at the door.

"And?"

"And what?"

"Did anything come to you?" she said, slowly rising, turning to look at him.

"Nope."

"Well, I'm sure they didn't see us."

"I don't think so either," he said, scratching his head. "Why didn't I just run in there and bash its head in. The leader was right there," he said frustrated.

"It's not too late, David," she said, grabbing his arm. "It's…not…too…late."

He took a breath and nodded, "You're right. I'm going in there…*We're* going in there and ending this thing right now." He reached for the door. "Ready?"

"Do it!"

The door opened and a reception of blasters was waiting for them. Kim fell first as the aliens neutralized her blaster and then hit David when he reached for it. He fell next to her and they were both unconscious within seconds.

Chapter 56

David could feel the heat and hear the crackling of a nearby fire. It glowed off to the side as he sat on the cool ground of a cave. He noticed someone sitting in front of him but couldn't see who it was in the haze. He squinted, looked hard and finally realized it was the caveman holding the bone, pointing at the carved images he had done. He was running his hairy fingers over them, circling them and talking earnestly.

David had to shrug, not understanding a word. The caveman stood up angry, yelling, hammering his finger on the carved image of the tall alien in front of David's face. He threw the bone down in disgust, yelling with his elbows out, fists clinched at his hips, when a green glow emerged from the center of his chest.

The caveman's face grew huge, looming in front of him, eyes piercing and mouth open, screaming, "Wake up!"

***

…*human mostly*…David heard the voice in his head as a murmur. Groggy and flat on his back, he rolled his eyes under his eyelids, thinking the voice sounded familiar.

They made it, the Entity told me, another voice said and he recognized that one.

He cracked his eyes open and looked through a forest of holograms floating over his strapped-down body and saw alien Carl talking with the leader.

The reason for this specimen eludes me. Did the Entity tell you its purpose? the leader asked.

To begin a new branch of the species without our portal. But something unexpected happened.

Yes, I see, that must be this, it is non-human, the leader said, gesturing to one of the holograms.

The Entity said it was my contribution from mating with its mother, Alien Carl said.

Is that true? Do you recall passing anything along? the leader asked.

No, my participation was mechanical and completely detached.

If you were completely detached, then how are you so certain you didn't contribute?

I didn't think it was possible, Alien Carl replied.

The leader watched for a moment, then said, *What was it like?*

What? Alien Carl asked, turning to the leader.

You are the first of our species to jump to a clone not made by us. What is your impression?

Disgust.

The leader studied the smaller alien next to it then turned to the table and picked up the bone. *Why would it be carrying such an ancient relic?*

Have you consulted the ship's archives for this planet? Alien Carl suggested.

The leader swung the bone around to an opening in the wall and set it down inside. A teal-colored bar of light scanned over it from one end to the other.

David heard the ship's response in his head: *Genetic traces of multiple individuals found to be present with the most noteworthy being the first humanoid selected for portal infiltration.*

The two aliens slowly turned to David. *What does that mean?* Alien Carl asked.

David heard the leader utter a command he didn't understand, and another teal-colored light came down from the ceiling and scanned over him.

It's awake, Alien Carl said, suddenly noticing David's eyes moving. David immediately yanked at the restraints, but they held firm.

The leader looked on, unconcerned as the ship's A.I. reported: *Specimen is a genetic combination from multiple individuals.*

How many individuals? the leader asked.

David stopped struggling to listen.

Three.

Correlate by age, oldest first.

The name was unfamiliar to David, but the way the leader shifted its head toward Alien Carl told him who it was.

The A.I. continued. *Second individual is the first humanoid used for portal activity.*

David went numb, did he hear that right? Was he part caveman?

This specimen will require a thorough examination, the leader said.

Do you want to postpone the procedure? Carl asked.

No, on the contrary, it's imperative to know all the aspects of the integration of our species with this specimen. This will be a complete vivisection, the leader said, then looked down, doing something out of David's view.

A searing pain suddenly ripped through David's body. Arching in spasm and teeth grinding, he jerked violently at the straps lashed over him. It stopped as suddenly as it started, and he glared, panting in anger.

There it is again. Do you recognize it? the leader said, pointing to a hologram.

It is from my world, Alien Carl said, staring in disbelief.

The leader then turned to Carl and said, *Proceed on your specimen and continue the incubation sequencing.*

David strained to turn his head, watching Alien Carl walk to the table next to him, and his heart stopped when he saw Kim. She was on her back, lifeless, and naked. Numb with fear, he frantically looked over her unstrapped body for signs of life and saw her take a breath.

He looked at the aliens. They didn't know she could resist them when awake. If he could only reach her, touch her, he could wake her up. He struggled with the straps, yelling, "Kim!"

The leader turned back, holding an odd spoon-like instrument and swung it over David's body. It paused, curiously watching him as he struggled with the straps while using his body primitively to communicate.

David glanced at the leader but not for long. He was more concerned for Kim, watching Alien Carl selecting from a rack of wicked-looking instruments. The alien retrieved a long, pointed, invasive-looking probe and swung it over Kim's belly button. It suddenly paused and looked at David, fascinated by his urgent need to save her. Then, almost mockingly, with a mere flick of its finger, tiny hooks popped out several times at the tip of the silver point.

"Don't!" David warned. Alien Carl slowly lowered the pointed tip, almost touching Kim's belly button, watching him, taunting him. When he was done playing with David, he began to plunge the instrument into Kim's belly. Frantically, David screamed inside his head, *NO* and a strange thing happened. Alien Carl recoiled backward, pulled the instrument out of her abdomen and dropped it on the floor.

Are you ill? the leader asked, turning to Alien Carl.

This specimen just executed a perfect leverage sequence at me, Alien Carl said while staring at David.

The leader looked surprised at David. *There is only one organ that can do that. I will take a closer look at it,* the leader said, and turned to browse over its instruments.

Alien Carl bent down, picked up the probe, discarded it and then turned to select another. He took a similar instrument from the rack and made a point of retracing its steps, taunting and observing David at the same time.

"I'll do it again!" David warned, but a sudden searing pain in his lower belly made him look back in horror. He saw a laser cutting an incision at his belt line upward, around his belly button.

He screamed in pain and disbelief, yanking at the straps in agony as the cutting continued up his belly and stopped at his ribcage. He collapsed in shock, numbly watching hooks swinging up from the sides of the table, sliding their tips into his flesh and pulling his abdomen open. Excruciating pain clamped his lungs down to desperate gasps as the leader peered into him. David's only thought now, was for Kim. He looked over at her just as the tip of the sharp instrument disappeared into her stomach. "Kim," he yelled, gathering strength for her and pulling at the straps with all his might, one last time, harder and harder until he collapsed, exhausted. She didn't move.

He pushed the pain out of his head, and while laboring, gasping for air, he noticed something. The strap on his arm was loose and it happened to be the arm closest to Kim. He twisted his wrist, wiggled it free and reached out to touch her.

Kim suddenly inhaled and lifted her head. Alien Carl stopped in disbelief just before being kicked to the wall. She whipped the probe out of her stomach, screamed in anger and threw it at the unconscious alien on the floor. David's arm fell as he lost consciousness.

The leader turned to Kim, leaned its head forward and she froze. She slowly faced it, her eyes vacant and lifeless. The alien walked up, reached out to touch her and put her under completely when she blinked. "I know what you're doing," she said in a low, ominous voice. Startled, the alien hesitated for a moment, then shifted all of its energy toward Kim, determined to subdue her.

Kim slightly recoiled, backed up a step and abruptly punched it in the nose. The alien leader fell with little more than a slight thunk. "Take that, fucker!" she yelled, standing over it, fists clenched and wanting more. About to kick the unconscious alien, something made her pause. She looked to the side, saw David, and screamed.

Chapter 57

"David!" she cried out and rushed to him, "Oh my god, oh my god…" Her hands trembled as she grabbed the hooks and tried to pull them away.

"Kim," he mumbled, pointing a bloody finger to the control panel next to her. "Pu…push," he said just above a whisper.

She frantically pushed one, nothing happened. She pushed another one and the hooks retracted. "Oh, thank god!" she gasped, her hands fluttering over his gaping body, not knowing what to do next.

He gulped and with shallow breaths, pointed a shaking finger to the rack of instruments.

She moved to the rack, holding her hand over each one, and watched him shake his head, again and again until he nodded and dropped his arm.

It was a wand-like instrument and she brought it over. "Is this what you want?" she asked, looking at it helplessly. He looked pale, eyes closed and unresponsive. "David!" she yelled, frantically waving it in front of him and squeezing his arm.

He slightly opened his eyes, touching the wand, and it began to glow. He guided her hand, moving the tip of it over the wound, and it began to fizzle and heal his flesh.

"Pu…" he whispered, "put the skin together." He had to close his eyes and breathe while trying to regain his strength.

After a few moments, Kim ran her finger along the pink hairline strip up his abdomen and watched it change into a natural flesh tone. "David, you're going to be fine," she said, looking into his eyes.

He nodded and brought his hand up, resting his palm on his solar plexus. 'Feels weird. Give me a minute."

Kim looked down at the bloody spot on her stomach and swung the wand over it. It fizzled and was finished in seconds. "This thing's amazing!" she said, then realized she was stark naked. Her clothes were piled to the side on what looked like a bench. She began slipping them on. "We should get out of here. Can you move?" she asked.

David sat up slowly, taking deep breaths and testing his stomach. "Almost," he said, grimacing while swinging his legs off the table.

"This is incredible!" Kim said, touching her healed skin before pulling her top over it.

"They've been using it to heal creatures for thousands of years," he said.

"Amazing," she said, slowly turning the wand over in her hands.

David got to his feet. "Not really," he said walking gingerly to the scanner, "They just don't like waiting around for their guinea pigs to heal." He then picked up the bone and turned to stand over the alien leader sprawled unconscious on the floor. He patted the end of the bone in his open palm for a moment. "Funny, but I'm about to do exactly what Rishi said I shouldn't." He then raised the club over his head.

Chapter 58

"You think it's going to make a difference?" Kim asked.

David hesitated, glancing at her. "You're starting to sound like Rishi now."

"Well, do you?" she persisted.

"I think it's a good starting point," he replied and turned back to the leader's head.

"It's just that—" she cut herself off.

"*What?*" he said impatiently, still holding the bone over his head.

"There's just been so much killing, and I'm wondering how we're going to stop it all."

He lowered the bone. "Are you saying you don't want me to kill this thing?"

She shrugged, "It is life, we should respect it."

He turned slightly toward her. "I have never seen this side of you before."

"Even if you don't think it deserves a chance to live, it *is* a life form."

He looked at her for a moment, considering her new condition and figured it was bound to change her perspective on things. He nodded and looked down at the leader. "You know I hear you and agree...except this one time," he said wielding the bone over his head.

"David!" Kim yelled. He turned just as Alien Carl swung a blaster at him and he threw the bone. It hit the alien's arm, knocking the blaster out of its hands, and as it scrambled for the weapon on the ground, David and Kim ran out of the room.

"Goddamn it! *Fuck*! I was so close." David yelled as they blindly hurried away, turning down random hallways, trying to escape. The best they could do now was to find the room and hopefully get off the ship.

They came around a corner and startled an alien soldier with a blaster. Kim surprised it with a kick to its face and took its weapon. David led them back to the stairwell, and they raced down to the lower part of the ship, stopping at the floor they had started on. He opened the door and a lone alien was walking away from them far down the hall, turning into a doorway and disappearing.

"I hate leaving this chance behind," Kim said as they stepped through the doorway.

"Why did you stop me then?" David said.

"I didn't stop you. I just didn't see how killing the leader would make a difference."

He stopped and faced her. "What could I have done then?"

She thought for a moment. "I don't know," she finally admitted.

Deep down he felt she was right. Something Rishi had said about having the ability to do it a better way. He glanced past her, to an open doorway and his jaw dropped. "Oh my god," he whispered and began walking toward it.

"What," she said, trying to look at him while walking along with him. He didn't say anything and once they were both in the room, quickly closed the door.

"What's going on?" she said, looking around at a room full of strange looking chairs.

"These are the ones. The chairs they were sitting in!" he said, waving his hand over them. He panned over them, and his eyes settled on one off in the corner. "Come on," he said and began wending his way to it.

David stood over the odd-looking chair for a moment then turned to sit into it.

"What are you doing?" Kim asked.

"I have to try something," he said.

He awkwardly backed into the chair and gave up trying to get comfortable. It was obviously made for a much smaller body. Cramped, his knees bent and his head jammed into the chair's headgear, he tried to turn it on. "Tell me if I'm doing this right," he said.

"It might help if I knew what you're doing," she said, watching him fiddle with the controls on the chair.

"Never mind, I think I've got it," he said, then took a breath and looked over at her. "Listen, I might go unconscious. Keep a look out for them." He closed his eyes as tiny lights on the chair blinked on.

"Wait a minute. Tell them what… to hang on? You'll be right back?" she said leaning over him. "David…*David*!"

Chapter 59

In a brilliant flash of white light, David left his body. He found himself floating over the magnitude of Earth, stunning, dynamic and beautiful. It was night and the land glowed where the masses lived. Mexico City, Sao Paulo, Shanghai, Delhi, all pulsating embers of a global fire.

He watched as streaks of light flashed into Beijing, Tokyo and Los Angeles. He looked side-to-side and was startled to see he was among thousands of hovering spheres, appearing as bubbles with an outer, translucent shell, moving and swirling around an inner, pulsating glow. They would pause for a moment, seeming to get their bearings, and then plunge to the planet like meteorites.

He realized he wasn't looking at lights, he was looking at humans. The chair was enabling him to see life differently, as a glowing energy source, and he now understood what he was feeling. The chair was beckoning him to choose where he wanted to go on the planet, but instead he turned to face the ship.

He went through the ship's hull drifting back into the room where Kim was standing guard over his body in the chair. She was bursting in vibrant colors shining up the center of her body and on the crown of her head was a purple glow, shaped like a flower. His tentacle deployed, slithering its way over to her, and, hovered for a moment above her portal before gently touching it. She dreamily turned his way and he was overwhelmed by her emotions as they flooded into him.

"David…I see you," she said.

Yes, it's working, he messaged to her.

Kim touched her fingertips to her temple. "I heard that!" she exclaimed.

Good. I'm going to find the leader, he messaged and released the tentacle.

As he left the room he realized the chair was revealing to him Kim's vulnerabilities and the ways he could manipulate her. He could make her do hurtful things and she would never know it was him.

Like a spirit from another world, he drifted through solid walls, scanning for the energy of the aliens. Throughout the ship he saw them, a blue grayish glow compared to Kim's golden tone, and he noticed a large group of them heading toward her. He headed to intercept, emerging into the hallway alongside them. It was the leader surrounded by alien soldiers, marching with determination.

He studied them while maneuvering around corners and down hallways as they did, noticing a dark blue color emerging from their heads. It was so brilliant that he barely noticed the other colors on their bodies, in the same areas as Kim's but nondescript, fluctuating between tiny spots and nothing at all. The closer he looked the more he realized the blue color was emerging from their foreheads.

As he hovered over them, he could see they each had a purple crown, a tiny portal, coming and going, and wondered if it was large enough to get into. He drifted over one of the soldiers and when he saw a tinge of purple, he touched it and was in.

His first impression in the alien's state of mind was a memory from Earth, white racists marching in an air of superiority. He felt a stunning display of indifference for other life forms while marching along as an alien soldier. The intention of the group was obvious, to terminate the inferior barbarians running amok on their ship, to kill thoughtlessly without remorse because they believed it was the proper thing to do. David could see the vulnerabilities of the soldier and determined it was an individual that had another thing coming.

Without provocation or warning, David manipulated the alien to pull its blaster and blow away the alien next to it.

Mental screaming burst from every alien turning to look at the shooter. All of the aliens froze in cognitive disbelief, searching for an explanation for their comrade's action, and while they did, David's lessons continued. A dozen aliens hit the floor before the leader abruptly stopped everything.

David's tentacle fell away, rejected, and he drifted backwards to regroup. He saw a new primary color shining from them, yellow at the center of their abdomens, emerging and joining them together. He also saw the purple color was gone from all of them. The leader's forehead blinked dark blue while each soldier took a turn blinking back as if they were all rebooting. David went to the leader, hovering over it, wishing he had gone to it first but it was too late; its crown portal was closed.

Once all of the soldiers finished the sequence, they continued marching. David circled them, thrusting out his tentacle, searching for their crown portals, but they were jamming him now. He looked ahead through the walls and saw Kim's colors. Heading toward her, he came across a few aliens and manipulated them to fire their blasters, but the leader's group quickly snuffed them out.

The leader's influence spread and every alien he saw from then on was either glowing yellow in the process of rebooting or was already done and had its crown closed.

Kim was ready for them, blasting the first few that came through the door. They fell back and took up positions, periodically shooting blasts at her to keep her pinned down.

David drifted into the room and saw she had taken cover, but through the walls he could see the energy signatures of aliens accumulating outside the door behind her. He touched her, *Kim they are getting ready to come in the door behind you.*

She looked around wildly then saw his image. "David, is there another weapon around? I don't know how many more blasts this one has in it," she said, repositioning to keep an eye on both doors.

I'll look for one. He wasn't sure if she heard him. She was obviously preoccupied.

David looked around at their dire situation. The possibility of getting back to the room was looking bleaker with every passing second. He looked at his body, and even though he could return to it anytime, they still needed another blaster. There had to be something else he could do. He turned back to the aliens.

He was in front of the leader when it ordered another attack on Kim. Fighting his fear for her safety, he focused on the alien, look for an opening. He saw the yellow energy coming from its midsection. It looked like a portal, so he stretched out the tentacle and touched it.

As if an amber light had come on overhead, the atmosphere shifted to yellow. Sensing an odd, strange pause, David slowly looked up and saw the leader looking at him, realizing the identity of its adversary.

David's connection was broken with the leader as it swiftly went past him. It addressed its soldiers and ordered them to fire at his body in the chair.

David felt the first blast and saw his tentacle weaken. He was running out of time. He glanced through the walls and saw Kim fending off the aliens from two fronts while trying to protect his body at the same time. It was too much to ask. Another blast hit his body and his return to it began.

Determined to fight to the end, David turned to the alien, but was startled to see the ancestral hominid standing in his way, staring at him. With vibrant colors glowing up the center of his body, his ancient ancestor gestured to a greenish glow coming from his chest.

Confused, David looked at the caveman as it abruptly dove toward him and plunged into his chest.

David felt a new strength and circled to confront the leader, extending his tentacle, searching for entry. Another blast hit his body so strongly that the tentacle evaporated.

Powerless to stop it, David watched the leader approach the door for the final offensive.

Kim saw the leader through the doorway, pointing at David's body, ordering the soldiers to annihilate him, and raised her blaster. She had a shot but hesitated when she saw David's image hovering in front of the leader's chest. She couldn't know blasters had lined up behind her and never felt them hit. Paralyzed as she fell to the floor, she saw David's image plunge into the leader's chest in an explosion of green and was devastated that she would never be with him again.

Chapter 60

Kim woke up, her body aching all over. She tried to lick her lips but her mouth was dry. Her eyes were crusted shut. Was she sick? Was she alive? She reached to rub her face but her hand was stuck under covers. She was in a bed. She managed to get a hand out and rubbed an eye open but the room was too bright. She closed it and worked on the other eye before venturing a few squinting glances. Where could she be? she wondered, blinking, trying to bring her eyes together and focus. She heard a voice off in the distance, then another. People were talking in the next room. She saw a glass of water next to the bed and grabbed it.

She chugged it, noticing the chatting seemed casual, and then a woman's laughter broke in. She sat upright in bed. She knew that laugh. She froze, listening, hand holding the empty glass in midair and heard the woman again. It was Aunt Margie!

She swung her legs out of bed and a sudden queasy feeling gripped her. She had to take a moment to fight the nausea that rose in her stomach. After a few breaths, she looked down and saw dinosaurs. Her legs were covered with them—kid's pajamas. What the hell was going on? She looked around, clearer now, and realized she was in David's bedroom. She was above the diner!

She stood on shaky legs, grabbed a robe draped over the chair, and pushed herself to the bedroom door. Rishi was sitting on the couch, talking between Aunt Margie and Alice. All three turned to her and smiled. Another person with his back to her turned, showing his profile.

"David!" she cried in disbelief.

He whipped around, "Kim! You're up. How do you feel?" he said springing to his feet and engulfing her in a warm embrace.

She looked into his eyes, baffled. "What happened?"

"Everything's fine, it's ok now. Can I get you something? Water?"

"Yes, I'm so thirsty."

'It's a side effect. It'll pass," he said and paused to look at her a bit longer before heading off into the kitchen.

She looked at the three characters sitting on the couch smiling silently at her. "Why am I not surprised you three are well-acquainted?" she said. "All we need now is the Sangoma."

They chuckled lightly, watching her as if expecting more. A sudden rustling noise came from the bathroom. "What?" she said and glanced back at them, seeing mischievous grins as the toilet flushed. "No, are you kidding me?" she said smiling, shaking her head as the door opened. She turned to see the Sangoma and froze.

It came out head first, almost running into her, looking at her feet. It slowly raised its bulbous white head and its huge eyes sucked her into their black abyss for a chilling moment of terror. Paralyzed, struggling to breathe, she somehow noticed the alien moving oddly as she stumbled backward. She stared in disbelief as it adjusted its jumpsuit.

"Hey, Chief," David called out from the kitchen.

They both turned to look at him.

"You're going to have to shake the handle on that thing and don't forget to put the seat down. There are ladies in the house," he said without looking up.

The alien leader abruptly turned back to the bathroom, diligently complying with the rules of the house.

Kim stared at the alien's backside for a moment, then walked toward the kitchen in a daze. She paused to stare at the lounging trio. "You could have told me," she chided.

"That wouldn't have been any fun," Rishi countered as the ladies chuckled.

"We knew you'd be all right," Alice said, waving her off.

Kim kept a snarky look on them while walking toward David. "Chief?" she said to him, puzzled.

"That's what she wants to be called."

"She?"

"Yeah, believe it or not it's a she, or that's what it's choosing to be."

"But what about the toilet seat?"

David handed her a fresh glass of water. "Yeah, they've got some things to work out, and we're going to help them."

Chief came up to them and Kim studied the huge eyes staring at her and realized something in the look was different. Sure, she didn't feel the painful barrage of mental force anymore, but there was something else…it was empathy, a hint of it coming from a creature she thought incapable of feelings.

The word *sorry* popped into her head and she realized it hadn't come from her. Chief was talking.

"She's apologizing," David said.

"I don't know what to say or how to say it," Kim replied.

"You just say something like, that's ok, forget it. Me too. She has ears—just can't talk."

It was all a misunderstanding, Chief added.

"I'm glad to hear you say that and, I guess, apology accepted," Kim said and was relieved Chief wasn't the hugging type. The alien did a slight nod of acknowledgement as David held out glasses of water.

"Take this to the group for me, will you? One's yours," David said, passing them off to Chief. He gave water to Kim, too, with the same instructions, and joined them in the living room.

"What are we doing?" Kim asked.

"We're going to iron out the particulars," David said as they sat down, completing the circle.

Everyone took a drink except Chief. *I would like to know what assurances I have for the safety of my citizens,* Chief messaged to all.

"Yes, it can be a dangerous planet," Rishi said, setting his glass down.

"Nobody is making you guys visit Earth," David stated factually.

This is true but if we are trading our technology for your planet's experiences, I would need some sort of measures so we aren't targeted by Earthlings. You can see how this would degrade the natural essence of each experience.

"We'll keep it secret," Aunt Margie said. "No one else has to know."

"What are you guys talking about?" Kim asked, looking confused.

Alice said, "Think of it as an amendment to something that's been going on for a long time. It's not a big deal." She then addressed the group. "I agree. We keep the aliens' visits secret and introduce their knowledge to Earth as we have done in the past. This will ease the transition and enable us to select which part of the world will benefit the most."

"Wait a minute!" Kim said. "Alien visits? Keeping them secret from humans? What is going on?"

Alice answered, "We are going to provide them with temporary human bodies so they can document their experiences on a genuine, first-hand perspective."

"You realize," Rishi broke in, "there will be a sudden rash of very naïve, unsophisticated and credulous people appearing on the planet."

"In other words, there could be a bunch of ignorant, selfish people showing up and running around everywhere?" David said, glancing at Chief.

"We have been coming across stupid humans for thousands of years," Chief countered.

"Yes, David, more than usual," Rishi said, eyeing them both.

"This is a good point," Aunt Margie said, rubbing her chin. "We should do something that will help them understand their human vessel. Something we should have done for Carl."

"Wait," Kim interjected, "Shouldn't we be in a more suitable setting for planning the world's future and not out in the middle of the desert above a *diner*?"

"What are you trying to say?" David said.

"Come on," she appealed to the group. "Shouldn't you be including the leaders of the world like maybe running this by the U.N.?" she reasoned.

There was a spattering of laughter around the room. "Mouthpieces," Rishi muttered almost to himself.

"They're not in charge, hon," Alice said, "just figureheads."

"Well then, who *is* in charge?" Kim said baffled.

Rishi's voice resonated low and wise, "The illusion of being in charge is a human construct, held together only by the rules agreed upon. Take the Chief here. She is the leader not because of appointment but rather by qualifications."

"She is the most experienced and is the best at deciding the highest good for all her species in the most efficient manner. As soon as an individual shows they can do a better job, they become the new leader—simple as that."

"You didn't answer my question. Who's in charge here on Earth?" Kim persisted.

"No one is in charge here because those qualified aren't given the platform to contribute," Rishi said. "It is still very much like the Wild West where the fastest gun makes the rules. Only now, instead of pulling a gun out of your pocket, it's people and money."

"No matter how you put it, this whole thing sounds like an invasion to me," Kim griped.

"No, no, no," David assured her. "The aliens have evolved out of their bodies for so long that they have lost all their connections to it, well, except for the obvious one.

"So, we are teaching them to be human?" Kim asked, scanning the group.

Rishi clarified, "All life forms connect to the universe through their bodies and it just so happens that the human body is one of the most receptive, or can be anyway. It really depends on the individual."

"Receptive to what?" Kim said.

"Everything," Rishi continued, "The whole spectrum of this universe's energy. The aliens are going to experience it through a human body and clone it back into theirs."

Kim's eyes narrowed as she looked around, warily. Something didn't feel right. There was more to this picture that she couldn't quite see yet.

I suggest a starting point, a small group, limited to time exposed and then a period of evaluation, Chief proposed.

"You're welcome to start here. Your first meal on the planet is on me," David offered.

A moment of silence followed as the group looked at him, some surprised, some scrutinizing but all considering it.

Very generous of you. We accept, Chief said, *That is, if everyone approves.*

There was a quick glancing around from everyone with no obvious objections, but it looked like Kim was biting her tongue.

It was decided for the time being that the visitors would come to the diner first, check in and plan their course for experiences on the planet.

"These are exciting times," Alice said optimistically.

"Why do you say that?" David asked.

"There are new elements coming into this world that are completely unpredictable, and I find that captivating."

"Yes! Me, too," Aunt Margie chimed in. "And one in particular will be fascinating to watch growing up," she said pleasantly as everyone looked at Kim.

Chapter 61

18 Months Later

David slipped the spatula under the sizzling burger and swung it over to a toasted bun next to a pile of crispy fries. He plucked parsley from a bowl, garnished the plate and set it under the hot lamps for pickup. He took a moment to glance out at the diner and smiled, glad to see so many people in the restaurant. He saw Rishi sitting in the corner booth with his back to the window talking to a stranger whom he assumed was one of the special *visitors*.

They were getting harder and harder to spot, apparently benefiting from Aunt Margie's pamphlet on how to orient to their new bodies. As suspected, the Fabricator's perfectly normal bodies weren't enough and some aliens had to be rescued out of asylums for the mentally incompetent. Not exactly the experience they were hoping for.

"Hey, Chief," Roberto said, coming up next to him, "We're all out of Sophie's batter."

David turned and stared at him.

"Oh, sorry, I mean, Boss, we're out of Sophie's batter."

"Look in the fridge next to the eggs."

"So, who's this Chief anyway?"

"It's not a big deal. I just want to eliminate any confusion when she shows up."

"What kind of girl has the name Chief? What does she look like?"

"Good question," he said, palming the pickup bell, "I'm sure we will find out pretty soon."

Pam came up to the counter. "David, the *group* is requesting your presence," she said sarcastically and walked off with the burger.

He looked at the corner booth and evidently had just missed Aunt Margie and Alice's entrance. They had a stranger with them, a tall, slender woman, and were waving him over.

"Go ahead, Boss, I've got ya covered," Roberto said, and moved to the center of the grill.

Out of habit, David grabbed the coffee, topping off cups as he zigzagged his way to them. He inconspicuously checked out the stranger as he poured, then glanced at the clock. It was just before noon and he wasn't expecting Chief until late in the afternoon.

Usually when a visitor was sitting with them it was an alien from a specific school of thought; biology, philosophy and lately quite a few from the psychology field. The aliens were experiencing some inner turmoil of their own from a small rebellious group. It is human nature to fight change and apparently it had been the same for the aliens over thousands of years. He could only imagine.

"David, an old friend is here to see you," Aunt Margie said, gesturing toward the woman.

David did a double take and finally saw it. "Chief, you're early. I didn't recognize you with hair," he chuckled.

"Gentlemen don't say such things to a woman," Rishi chastised.

"Oh, sorry. My apologies," David said, "Then, thank you for finally gracing my humble restaurant with your presence."

"Hello, David, nice to see you," Chief said, ignoring his remark while sliding her coffee cup toward him.

"Ahhh, so you're ready for the coffee experience," David said as he poured.

"Yes, I have been getting mixed reviews on this consumable of yours and have decided to explore it myself."

"What have you heard?" he said, suddenly concerned.

Chief didn't respond, but with a slight smile, picked up the coffee and sipped while staring at him.

David looked the group over and remarked, "I hear Europe has made some incredible advances in the technology for rapid healing."

"Yes, it's wonderful and will be all over the world soon," Aunt Margie said.

Chief put her cup down. "What do you think?" David asked.

"Not bad but I suspect it's an acquired taste," she said diplomatically.

"No, I mean your visits. How are they working out for you and your citizens?"

"Oh, that. Well, like your coffee, some like it and some don't," she said, eyeing her cup. "And so far, I'm liking it."

"Really?" David said pondering, "How many now have visited?"

"Over two thousand," Chief said.

"What are some of their impressions as humans on Earth?" David asked.

Chief thought for a moment, then said, "So far, nobody can stand liars, but everyone on our planet loves Spock."

"A baby doctor? What is it about Dr. Spock that you like so much?"

"No…not Dr. Spock…Spock from the Starship Enterprise."

"You know he isn't real, right?" David said, studying her straight face and honestly couldn't tell if she was joking or not. The group laughed and Chief finally smiled ever so slightly.

"Ohh…you're getting too good at this, too fast," David said shaking his head.

He glanced outside just as a black SUV turned off the highway into the parking lot. He saw it had government plates as it pulled up to the restaurant and parked outside his window. He squinted and looked at the driver staring at him. Colonel Roberts.

"Great," David muttered. "I was wondering when I was going to hear from these guys again."

Rishi saw the look on David's face and looked outside. "Ahhh, it's a reunion."

Stepping out of the SUV, Roberts shifted his glare through mirrored sunglasses over the restaurant then headed for the front door. David left the group to meet him.

Roberts swung the door open and glared at David as the door bell tinkled over his head.

"Well, hello, Cooper," Roberts said, squaring off in front of him while putting his hands on his hips to avoid a handshake.

"What do you want," David said, not offering his hand anyway. "I know you're not here for the food."

A sudden outburst of ooh's and ah's filled the diner, as Kim displayed a baby in her arms for a booth full of customers.

"Heard you two had a kid. Guess congrats are in order," Roberts said, his tone lacking sincerity.

"Yeah, don't bother," David said, looking him over. "I figured you'd be tied up for a while. How'd you get out so early?"

Roberts smiled slyly, "Apparently you didn't hear about my case for self defense. I had some witnesses come forward."

David scoffed, "I bet you did...what do you want?"

"I need you to come to the base with me," Roberts said.

"You can't be serious. Am I being arrested? You going to kidnap me again?" David snapped.

"No, no, we don't do that anymore. It's more like a request for you to do your duty for your country. We've located the ship and want you to help us bring it in. Think of it. You can fly it again. I know you enjoyed that."

David looked at Roberts in disbelief. "You crack me up. You wasted a trip out here," he said, and turned away.

"I'll pay you a hell of a lot more than you're making here," Roberts said.

David slowly turned back. "I would have to be out of my mind to go anywhere with you, let alone back to where you guys *tortured* me. Remember that?" he said glaring through Roberts's mirrored glasses. Roberts took them off and they looked eye-to-eye.

They heard the sound of cooing as Kim approached, and they watched each other to see who would look away first.

"What's he want?" Kim broke in.

"He was just leaving," David said.

"What are you two doing?" Roberts said, shaking his head in disappointment, looking back and forth at them. "You both have so much talent. What are you going to do with your lives? Stay out here and flip burgers and pop out kids in the middle of the desert?"

David looked troubled, turned to Kim and stared at her and his son for a moment. "I'm ok with that…"

"Doesn't sound too bad to me," Kim agreed as they both turned back, smiling at the Colonel.

The bell on the door dinged and a guy poked his head in, squeamishly looked around, then tentatively stepped into the restaurant.

"Oh, come on, Nichols," Roberts appealed, "You know what we do at the base is a lot more exciting than this. Start a day care center," he suggested.

"Forget it, Roberts," Kim said firmly, "and it's Mrs. Cooper."

The timid customer, obviously a *visitor,* looked their way and approached when he saw David give him a welcoming smile.

Roberts put his glasses back on and studied them, stone faced for a moment, not noticing the docile person coming up next to him.

"Hi, I'm Sam," the meek voice squeaked and Roberts slowly looked down at the frail, wimpy hand stretched out.

Roberts turned back to David and Kim in disgust. "Really?" he said and coldly walked away.

"Hi, Sam, I'm David," he said, shaking hands, "Welcome."

"Hi…uh, thank you," he muttered, looking away from the human walking out the door, "Did I do something wrong?"

"Don't worry about him, Sam. You will find that there are some people that are just naturally grumpy. I'm Kim," she said. Gesturing toward the counter, she added, "Would you like to have a seat?"

"Sure, I guess," he said, bewildered as he and the baby exchanged stares. "Who's this?"

"This is Odin, our son," Kim said proudly.

"Hello, Odin," Sam said feebly, offering his hand and trying to touch the baby. Odin burst out laughing, stuffed half of his hand into his mouth and playfully pulled away.

"Kim!" A familiar voice from behind caught her attention and she swung her baby away from the alien to the man behind her.

"Hi, Red!" she said, offering Odin to his outstretched arms.

"You are so much like your daddy," Red said gleefully, playing with the happy baby.

"Come on, Sam, let's get you settled," David said, and led him to the counter.

"Get him a piece of pie on me," Red bellowed, without taking his eyes off Odin.

David nodded and showed Sam to the counter. "Here, have a seat," he said, and circled around to the other side.

Sam swung a leg over the stool and looked around at the other customers. David had set him apart from everyone so he could be easily oriented.

"I heard you have pancakes here," Sam said, his eyes curiously studying the items in front of him.

"Oh sure, Sophie's pancakes. You'll love them, and while you're waiting," he said, reaching under the counter to a stack of thin, soft covered booklets, "here's something that might be of interest."

"Thank you," Sam said, as he looked down and read the cover:

HUMAN BY DESIGN

by Aunt Margie

The Official Manual

He opened the book and on the first page, it read in bold letters,

WARNING

NOT FOR EARTHLINGS

STOP READING IMMEDIATELY IF YOU ARE NOT PART OF THE

HUMAN BY DESIGN PROGRAM.

IF YOU SUSPECT YOU ARE DESIGNED AND NOT AWARE OF IT,

YOU MUST TAKE THE TEST AT THE BACK OF THE BOOK

WARNING***WARNING***WARNING

HUMANS OF NATURAL BIRTH THAT READ THE CONTENTS OF THIS MANUAL WILL BE EXPOSED TO HUMPHREY'S DISEASE, ALSO KNOWN AS

HYPER-REFLECTION OR CENTIPEDE SYNDROME.

SIDE EFFECTS INCLUDE INSANITY, EYE PROBLEMS,

RECLUSIVE IMPULSES, HALLUCINATIONS, DEPRESSION,

IRREGULAR HEARTBEAT, EXTREME SOCIAL AWKWARDNESS,

IBS, COPD, ED, VD, RA, OIC, OPEN SORES

AND NOT NECESSARILY IN THAT ORDER.

ASK YOUR DOCTORS IF THIS INFORMATION IS RIGHT FOR YOU

AND THEY WON'T HAVE A CLUE WHAT YOU'RE TALKING ABOUT.

***

David chuckled on his way to order Sam's pancakes. This one was fresh off the boat, he thought, sliding his hand along the pickup counter, looking for Roberto.

"Roberto, I need a stack," he hollered at him, as he came out of the cooler.

"You got it, Boss," Roberto replied.

Kim came up, her arms needing a break. "Come here, buddy," he said reaching for his son.

She took a relaxing breath. "What'd you think about Roberts?" she asked.

"What's to think?"

"About him showing up here and finding the ship?"

He looked at her. "I'll bet these guys have him chasing his tail," he said gritting his teeth, "He's lucky I didn't punch him in the nose," and then went back to playing with Odin.

"You held it together really well," Kim said, enjoying watching them together.

David looked up, "Oh, I tell ya, he's lucky I didn't bring a world of hurt down on him."

Kim smiled at the sound of her man's macho talk as their son's tiny hand patted his cheek, grabbed the corner of his mouth and yanked it down. David suddenly looked surprised.

"He's smiling at me! Look, he's laughing!"

"He's laughing *with* you, honey." Kim said.

They stood silently together, watching their son for a moment, becoming mesmerized by the mystery of life and the individual they had brought into the world. The pickup bell rang. "There's your stack, Boss," Roberto announced.

"Is that for our new friend?" Kim asked.

"Yup, for Sam," David said, poking his finger into Odin's belly button."

"I'll take it," she said, and slid it off the counter.

Kim carried the stack, amused to see Sam staring at the palm of his left hand and looking quickly back and forth to his right index finger pressing into the pamphlet.

"One stack of Sophie's pancakes for Sam," Kim announced, setting the plate down in front of him.

"Thank you," he said, startled as if he had never seen such a thing before. He looked up and saw her curiously peeking at the pamphlet. "Have you read this?" he asked.

"It's for you guys. I've glanced at it a couple of times. It's just the mechanics—stuff Earthlings already know intuitively."

He looked serious, his gaze shifting to staring through her, muttering, "That's fascinating. You are so bonded with your body that you don't remember."

"Remember what?" she asked, pushing the syrup and jam toppings toward him.

He suddenly became uncomfortable and looked away.

"Everything OK?" she asked, leaning her head to the side, to look in his face.

"This will take some getting used to," he said appearing confused.

"Is this your first time?" Kim asked.

He looked back at her, startled. "Am I being uncommon? Am I going to draw attention?" he inquired with a quick, worried look.

Kim chuckled. "No, no, no, you're doing just fine. Look, you're among friends and safe here. Besides, being uncommon is actually encouraged around here."

He relaxed and turned to look at the stack of pancakes in front of him.

"You mind if I ask you a question?" Kim said, as he lowered his face to the steaming breakfast.

"This is amazing! The odor is wonderful!" he exclaimed, deeply drawing the aroma into his nostrils and then reaching for a fork. He paused to study the utensil for a moment, then looked at her. "Oh, I'm sorry. You asked me a question?"

"Oh, it's nothing. Not a big deal," she said, waving it off, not wanting to interrupt his experience. Besides, she wasn't really sure how to ask what she was thinking.

Sam turned back to the food, pointing at the toppings. "What are these?"

"Some people like to add them on their pancakes."

"Which one do you use?" he asked curiously.

"I like this one," Kim said, pointing to the strawberry. "Do you mind if I ask you something personal?"

"Not a problem," he responded, scooping the jelly.

"What was it like to go from you to human?"

"Oh that…" he said, plopping preserves on the pancakes. He thought for a moment while he spread the jam and then said, "You know how you never know the exact moment you fall asleep? How it catches you by surprise and then you are dreaming without realizing it? It's like that. But the dream is your next reality." He glanced at a customer, seeing how he was using the edge of his fork to cut his food and clumsily copied him.

"But how do you know how to act and know the language?" Kim asked.

"It's a package that comes with the body, like a starter kit," he said, pausing with the fork, about to take a bite. "As you can tell, we still have a lot to learn." He stuffed the large portion into his mouth. His eyes widened then rolled. "Wow…this is…" he tried to say, mouth full, but the flavors were overwhelming and he mumbled something inaudible.

Kim caught herself wanting to school him on talking with food in his mouth. She realized she must be talking with an innocent, fresh, and most likely young alien in human form for the first time.

"What was it like for you?" Sam abruptly asked while maneuvering the flapjacks for another bite.

"What do you mean?"

"To go from you to human?"

"I never thought of that. I don't remember anything like that," she said thoughtfully, her eyes wandering upward.

"That's why you're confused," Sam said nonchalantly and stuffed his mouth again.

"Funny, hearing that coming from you," Kim said.

He stopped chewing and looked at her. "I'm funny…joking?" he awkwardly said through the food in his mouth.

"No, it's—never mind. What makes you say I'm confused?"

He thought for a moment, looking at her and wondering if he should continue.

"What is it?" she said smiling. "You're among friends. You have nothing to worry about here."

"There's this thing we do on our planet. It's weird to be telling you this as a human in your language, but I think it could be a good thing for you." He took a drink of water, set it down carefully, then held his hand out. "Here"

"What?" she said startled, looking at it.

"Give me your hand."

She tentatively put her right hand into his and they clasped as if shaking.

He closed his eyes and was quiet for a moment. "I'm not sure if it's going to work, but if it does you will see yourself at the beginning. Just pay attention to who you were before jumping into this body—the one you are in now." He then adjusted his grip and closed his eyes.

"Wait!" Kim said "First tell me. Why do you do this on your planet?"

"I'm not sure. They say it's necessary to remember so we don't repeat."

"Who says?"

"The elders—the ancient ones," he said, his eyes taking a quick glimpse at the corner booth.

Kim nodded, then looked down at her hand. "Okay, what do I do?"

"Nothing, or rather don't try to do anything but be open. You'll also find it works better when you close your human eyes."

The moment Kim closed her eyes she was inside a vast darkness that was drawing her toward a wormhole floating in front of her. It was filled with images of her in different stages of her life. With incredible clarity, she saw herself as a young adult, her first kiss and first sex. She regressed, becoming a child, things she had long forgotten, her first words, her first steps, hearing voices and music through the shell of flesh surrounding her in prenatal sanctuary.

"Death," she thought. This must be what it's like to see one's life flashing in front of them before they die. She became the observer, seeing her mother for the first time, her father, too. The three of them were together but not in bodies. They were together in a different way. They were agreeing on something. She felt them as if she had known them all her life. They embraced and she felt their love and understood things happened the way they were agreed upon. Someone else approached and she saw it was Sam.

Kim opened her eyes and saw Sam staring at her. She caught a tiny glimpse of a strange look on his face that she would think about for a long time. Her instincts told her to withdraw and she pulled her hand away.

"That was incredible. I saw my parents."

"I was there. Did you see me?" he asked.

"Yes, was that supposed to happen?" she asked.

"That's part of it. I see your world and you can see mine. Did you notice?"

Kim thought for a moment and images of another world flashed in her head. "Whoa…" she murmured.

"Think of me and this experience and you can explore it all you want," he said, while cutting into his pancakes.

Kim watched him, still reverberating from her own experience. "Thank you, Sam. Thank you for sharing that with me," she said.

"You're welcome," he answered, eyeing the piece of pancake all the way into his mouth.

Kim walked back to David in a daze and found herself pondering immortality. Strange, she thought, and realized it was Sam's world.

She heard her son cooing loudly and saw David jostling him, playfully blowing raspberries on his stomach.

"Get him all squared away?" David asked, as Odin leaned over, reaching for her.

"There's my guy," she said, taking him into her arms, running her hand lightly over his head. She felt him melt into her, bonding while cradling him.

"Everything ok?" David asked.

She looked at her son and shook her head. "Have you ever thought of what it would be like to live forever?" she asked, stroking Odin's cheek.

"I'll bet everybody thinks of that at one time or another, especially when they start getting old," David said.

"But if we did or could actually do that, how would any of this fit in?" she said, her eyes searching his. They stared at each other for a moment, consumed by their own thoughts. They glanced at Odin. He, too, seemed to be deep in thought as he stared at his mother.

"I think Odin wants to know, too," David said softly. "I suppose we could live forever like the aliens, but it doesn't sound like much fun."

She nodded, smiling at him in agreement.

Sam was getting up, apparently finished with his breakfast. They exchanged waves before he headed for the door.

David put his arm around Kim, drawing her close while he watched Sam walk out. He looked down at his son and was relieved that he could grow up without worrying about the Aliens jacking with him. He stroked his son's head and said, "I suppose that since this doesn't last forever, we should probably enjoy it while we have it."

Kim looked at him, smiling. "I agree," she said, and they adored their son while he chewed on his hand.

There was activity toward the front of the restaurant and they saw the group was preparing to leave.

"You want to say goodbye to Chief?" David asked.

"No, you go ahead. Me and snickelfritz are going to take a nap," Kim said.

"Okay…see you guys later," he said, and ruffled Odin's hair as they walked off.

David headed toward the front door to intercept the group and noticed Sam staring at him through the glass. He had been watching them from outside. Strange and curious learning curve these aliens have, David thought.

David caught up to the group at the front door. "Chief, great to see you," he said, shaking her hand and checking her out. "It's a good look for you."

"Thank you, David. You are complimenting, right? Sarcasm is very difficult for us to detect and interact with correctly."

David chuckled, "Kinda, sorta, but I mean it. You look good."

Chief pushed the door open and flashed a decent smirk at him on her way out.

Aunt Margie noticed it. "I think she's got it," she said, smiling. It was David's turn to smirk.

"Oh, David," Alice said. "Release your inner feminist."

"I'm a feminist most the time when I'm not getting ganged up on," he said, watching the two of them chuckling out the door.

"Don't worry about it, David. We men must stick together," Rishi said, patting his shoulder.

"Right, thanks Rishi," David said, and hollered after him as he walked out the door, "See you tomorrow?"

Rishi answered with a wave over his head while walking away.

David saw the group migrate toward Chief who had stopped to talk to Sam. They huddled together, exchanged conversation, a regular group of people just hanging out talking. He glanced around at his regulars inside the diner. *If they only knew.*

Another regular approached the diner, walked past the group without batting an eye and stepped inside, "Hello, David," the middle-aged man said.

"Hi, Kelly, come on in. Your usual today or trying something new?" David asked, turning his back to the group outside and walking along with his customer.

Sam was busy fielding questions with the three entities about his new experience in a human body when a car pulled up next to them. The group looked and everyone recognized Carl behind the wheel. "Can I give anyone a lift?" Chief asked.

"Yes! That'd be great!" Sam said, enthusiastically.

Rishi shook his head, "Thank you, but we have plans."

Aunt Margie reached out and shook Sam's hand. "Good luck to you in your upcoming experiences," she said pleasantly.

"Thank you," Sam said.

"Sam," Alice said, taking his hand in hers and covering it with her left, "I believe we have met. You have been on this planet before?"

"Oh, sure," he grinned bashfully, "We all have, but not in a body like this. It's so strange."

Alice's eyes narrowed. "Yes, that familiarity again. I can't quite place it," she muttered.

Sam looked at her, cocked his head, and she gave up. "Well, good luck to you," she said, patting his hand.

The two aliens watched the trio walk off until out of earshot. Chief turned to Sam, "Do you think they know?"

Sam was watching Alice carefully while she chatted with the others and was slow to look at Chief. "I think she suspects something but she can't know who I am."

"Did you get what you came for?" Chief asked.

Sam looked down at the pamphlet, fanning through it with his thumb. "More than I was expecting. This will be useful."

Chief watched Sam for a moment, staring at the booklet and finally said, "Charade...It's the word this body keeps coming up with. Will we be stopping this soon?"

Sam looked up at him, "Not yet. You will still be considered the leader so I may obtain more candid observations."

'Yes, sir," Chief said frowning. "You did verify them as being the target couple?"

"Yes, and the child seems to be as expected. Unfortunately, I was unable to retrieve its genetics."

"Why not just take the child," Chief asked, impatiently.

"Couple of reasons," Sam said, eyeing Chief. "Even though we are interacting with humans without them knowing, the Entities are watching. We can't just start kidnapping them again."

Chief nodded. "And the other reason?"

"The child is responding to their attention in a unique way. I believe it will be worth watching for a while. When it is time, we'll take the child," Sam stated, and abruptly grabbed his chest and bent over in pain.

"Sir! Are you alright?"

Sam was slow to stand erect, panting for air and muttering, "Persistent thing, insisting on being involved all the time."

"Your body is defective?"

"No," Sam said, easing his grasp on his scrunched-up shirt. He looked around while massaging his left arm, then glanced at Chief. "Do we have any interface chairs left that haven't been converted for this program?"

"Yes, many of them are still waiting for reconfiguring. Why?" Chief asked curiously.

"I want to see how they're doing it."

"Doing what, sir?" Chief asked, even more curious now.

Sam slowly headed to the car. Chief watched him closely as they walked. "What's going on? Who do you want to fuse with?" he asked again, opening the door for his leader.

Sam hesitated before getting in, leaning on the door. He took another breath, still showing signs of the fleeting pain. After a moment of looking around the alien planet, he turned to Chief and asked, "What was it like when the male, David, fused with you? You said something like…solitary? No, *lack* of solitary."

"It was a rude comingling of existence that lacked order. I couldn't think for myself anymore and my own needs were clouded with the needs of others. For the first time in my life I felt fear. It was horrifying."

"Fear, that's what it is," Sam said, putting his hand over his heart and feeling for its beating. "This circulating organ does not harmonize well with the brain. Somehow there are leaders of this world able to keep this organ from interfering," he said, tapping the rolled-up pamphlet on the door a few times and getting in the car. Chief closed the door behind him and got up front where Carl was waiting.

The car jostled out of the parking lot onto the smooth highway and accelerated under the hot overhead sun. Soon they were speeding along the terrestrial landscape to a destination known only to them, making their unearthly plans.

Printed in Great Britain
by Amazon

74733359R00180